A Broken Gears Tale

Raven's Cry

Dana Fraedrich

Dana Fraedrich

Other titles by Dana Fraedrich:

SKATEBOARDS, MAGIC, AND SHAMROCKS
Skateboards, Magic, and Shamrocks
Heroes, Legends, and Villains

BROKEN GEARS
Out of the Shadows
Into the Fire
Raven's Cry

This book is a work of fiction. Any references to historical events, real people, or real locales are used fictitiously. Other names, characters, places, and incidents are the product of the author's imagination, and any resemblance to actual events or locales or persons, living or dead, is entirely coincidental.

Maps by Hannah Pickering and Heather Boyajian. Chapter heading design by Heather Boyajian.

Cover digital scrapbook pieces courtesy Doudou's Design

ISBN: 0692068082
ISBN-13: 978-0692068083

Invarnis
Duskwood
Prism/
Springhaven
Cobalt
Bay
Dogwood Lane
Bone
Port
Bone
Bay

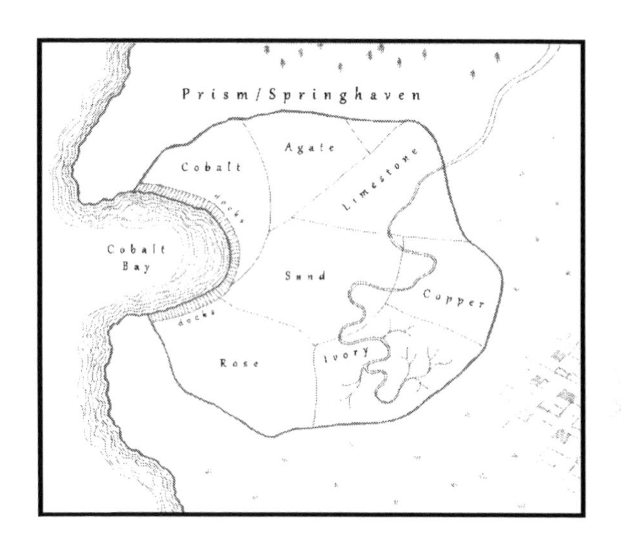
Prism / Springhaven
Agate
Cobalt
Limestone
docks
Cobalt
Bay
Sand
Copper
docks
Rose
Ivory

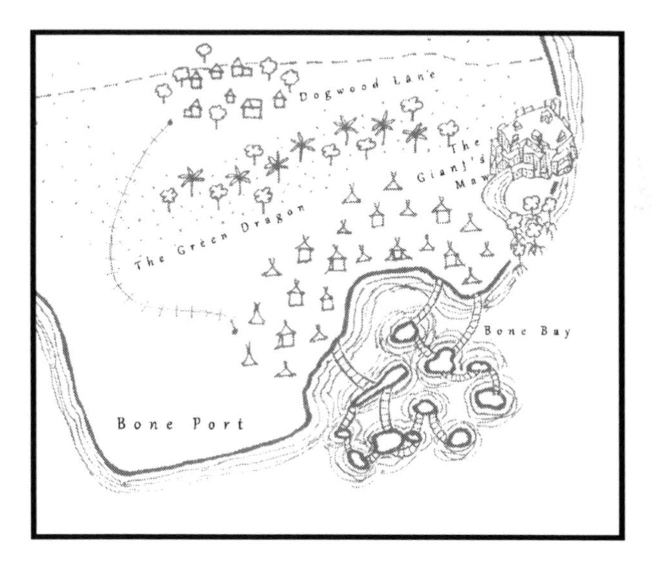
Dogwood Lane
The
Giant's
Maw
The Green Dragon
Bone Bay
Bone Port

Raven's Cry

Contents

Part 1

Fourth Age: The Wolf

~*The Prayer*~

"Oh stars, not again. Please, not again."

The words came to my lips as automatically as the air I breathed, but as desperately as if death snapped at my heels. I faced the horizon. Above that stark, cold line, the first pink rays of sunlight were beginning to break through the velvety indigo. As soon as that glowing orange orb crested the horizon, I felt the magic begin to pulse through my veins like a terrible and perfect symphony. It begins in my heart, my very core, and spreads with each beat, circulating poison.

"Please, just once. Just for one day, let me have peace."

The melody running through my veins soon surrounds me like a warm, gentle wind, but it holds no comfort. It's filled with grief and sorrow. Soft, unnatural light joins the wind. I can see it as my vision changes, a graceful cyclone of disturbance around me. Then comes the darkness. The sensation of soft feathers whispers against my skin until sight returns to me.

The world has not changed, yet all is different now.

~Chapter 1~

Excitement rippled through the nobility that evening as reports of a newcomer to our small court spread. His name was Nicodemus, Duke Gregory's friend, esteemed guest, and mysterious *magus*. Dinners at the Ivory Palace were meant for the court only, but who in their right mind would refuse such a rare opportunity? Not our cunning regents, that was for certain.

Magi lived in secluded communities outside of our cities and towns. They communed with nature and went out of their way to avoid contact with the outside world, or so the most common accounts went. The tales I heard whispered that evening seemed ill-fitting and farfetched. He was wealthy, though no one knew how he had acquired his money. He was also reclusive—at least that part was in keeping with the rest of his kind—but he had built himself a dwelling more akin to what one would find in the city. Duke Gregory had only met him because his hunting party had stumbled upon the man's house when a storm forced them to seek refuge.

"It's set deep in the woods, surrounded by orchards and gardens," Countess Melody of the Bladed Mountains and Valley said. "He has a menagerie of animals and a grand estate half the size of the palace."

"I bet he's a smuggler, dark and lonely and misunderstood."

"You've been reading too many adventure stories."

"Do you think he's looking for a wife?"

I took a deep breath as I strolled through the crowd, holding back the wave of fear rising from my chest. I'd just had a revelation of my own. If I sought to slake my curiosity, I would have to… *mingle*.

I was just as curious about the newcomer, to be sure. Curiosity is in my nature, but it's so much easier to learn from books than from people. Books don't judge you or ask prying questions.

Perhaps I should leave, I thought. *I can ask around about him tomorrow. Maybe I can feign sickness.*

With such a relatively small court—Queen Gertrude and King Ansel Pendragon, three duchies, six counties, eighteen baronies, and an associated spouse for most—I knew most everyone fairly well. So I shouldn't have been nervous. You'd think so anyway. I had grown up around all of these people. I knew the names and faces, the quirks and proclivities, and the associated perks and favors owed to serve my people. The categorization of these onto lists and their subsequent utilization were my forte, but the banal face-to-face interactions in between always turned my stomach. Whoever decided small talk was a useful pastime should be shot.

At least most of the rest of the Southern Assembly was not here tonight, as the weather back home was currently turning marvelous. I envied them. I only came to Prism, the capital, because my family was visiting on business. Many northerners were here, however. They didn't love the harsh winters that blew down from the Bladed Mountains. A mixture of the Midlands Assembly—those in charge of the city of Prism and the regions around it—was here too, plus everyone's children who were of age.

Yes, I think I'll catch up tomorrow, I decided.

I had just turned towards the closest exit when an arm wrapped around my shoulders and gave them a friendly squeeze.

"Going somewhere, Cali?" From the corner of my eye, I saw a warm, teasing smile spread across a face I knew as well as my own.

"Uncle Ducky, I think I'm going to be ill," I whispered.

"Nonsense!" he guffawed. "It's just nerves. Here, some wine should sort you out."

He snapped a waiter over to us and handed me a crystal goblet of crimson courage. I sipped politely, knowing I was going nowhere.

"Have you seen him yet?" Ducky asked, his eyes scanning the room like a Gryphon on the hunt.

"No. I think I'll—"

"There he is!" Ducky thundered so suddenly I jumped, nearly spilling my wine. "Gregory, my good man!"

Ducky then whisked me towards the Duke of the North. Trailing him was obviously the man called Nicodemus.

The magus dressed in the same fashion as every other man in the room, but he glowed with power. It rested on the surface of his skin, a halo of light so faint I questioned my eyes. It remained, and so I realized somewhere in the back of my mind he truly was luminous, if only slightly. To be honest, I was so caught up in keeping my composure, I almost failed to notice this marvel.

"Richard!" replied Duke Gregory. "Didn't think I'd see you here tonight. You're missing some prime hunting days."

"Pah, business had to come first, I'm afraid. But isn't our timing fortunate?" Ducky reached a meaty, enthusiastic hand out to the newcomer. "The man of the hour. You must be Nicodemus. Duke Richard Jones, Lord and Servant-Protector of the Southern Reaches. And this beauty of heart and spirit is my niece and potential heir, Lady Calandra Allen. Currently unattached, if you can believe it. And you?"

I felt my face warm with an unwelcome blush. The villainous plot had reared its ugly head again! My older brother, Carlos, was destined to be the Count of Bone Port and the surrounding Bone Bay territory, thank the heavens. I think everyone in my family was pleased with our birth order, as I had shown little interest in marriage. Ducky, however, had his own aspirations for me and liked to dangle a much larger inheritance like a carrot.

I was nineteen then. Most ladies my age were already married. My parents, shrewd but kind people, weren't what you would call nurturing, but they also weren't monsters. They wouldn't force me into a life sure to make me miserable. Secretly, I think the way every court event exhausted me worried my family. Ducky believed having someone to help shoulder responsibility would fix everything.

To be quite honest, the idea of marriage terrified me. Or rather, I wasn't interested in anyone we knew, and the idea of getting to know new people was enough to make me run for the hills. People are so very tiresome, you know. Where my parents had begrudgingly accepted this, Ducky had redoubled his efforts and practically threw me at every new and eligible young man we came across. He never gave a copper crown about decorum.

As Ducky ushered me forward, I resisted the urge to point out that he was also unattached. It was possible the magus, like Ducky, preferred men, and I wanted to remove the attention from myself. I wanted even more to stay out of Ducky's game entirely, though it was a bit late for that.

The cloaked magus chuckled softly and smiled, reaching for my hand. I offered it to him smoothly. That, at least, was something I had done often enough to execute without thinking. When Nicodemus took my hand and bowed, I felt warmth emanate from his skin. That subtle glow limning his figure combined with the sensation of a late spring breeze washing over me, he might well have been a small star. I smiled and, for once, it was not by rote.

"Pleased to make your acquaintance," he said. His voice thrummed warmly in the low din of the grand dining room, a sound I both wanted and needed to draw closer to hear. "No titles, I'm afraid."

"Not even a surname?" I asked. In my periphery, I saw Ducky's eyes flicker towards me.

I could practically hear the wiry hairs of his beard bristle with excitement. I had broached something like actual conversation with the most intimidating stranger we had ever met! Wonders never cease.

"Not even a surname," Nicodemus replied. "My people have no need of such."

"Your people?" I asked.

Nicodemus looked around, and I followed his gaze. Nausea returned as I realized every eye in the room had swiveled onto to us, and I wished to disappear into my bejeweled shoes.

"Lady and gents, would you all mind if we moved this conversation outside? I'm feeling a bit warm," Nicodemus said.

Stars, yes! Thank goodness, I thought.

We made our way out to a veranda overlooking the royal gardens in the distance. Along the way, Ducky suspiciously managed to entangle himself and Duke Gregory in a conversation with Baroness Leliana, who had half a dozen or so eligible daughters.

I felt people watching us as we made our escape, but no one moved to join us just yet. They wouldn't risk appearing too eager. Save for Baroness Leliana, that is, but with so many daughters, who could blame her? They'd have to crowd the doorway to spy on us, and that wouldn't reflect very well on them at all. They may have been a swarm of ogling, goose-necking gossips, but heaven forbid they actually let it show!

I gulped the cool outside air, lightly scented with recently bloomed honeysuckle. My heart immediately slowed without all those faces peering over glasses and whispering behind hands.

"Your… uncle, was it? He seems quite friendly," Nicodemus began.

I could tell he was taking care not to offend me, but he clearly had questions too. Ducky was fair with neat ginger hair, and I was nearly as dark as my father with wild ebony locks that barely capitulated to the strokes of a brush.

"He's not really my uncle," I explained. "Not by blood, but in every other sense. Apologies. I'm not being clea—." I blinked at him. "Your glow is gone."

Nicodemus rubbed the back of his neck and replied, "Ah, yes. That's a little party trick Duke Gregory requested."

He gifted me another smile. It sat sheepish and crooked on his face, as if it wasn't brought out terribly often and therefore unpracticed.

What a shame, I thought, surprising myself with the sentiment.

"I understand," I said with an answering smile, soft and encouraging. There was a pause, and I sipped my wine.

"I had no idea the court was so numerous."

I was grateful for the new thread of conversation and picked it up perhaps a bit too enthusiastically.

"There are even more than this," I told him before explaining about the Southern Assembly. "We're small compared to the Arnavi, though. Those are our neighbors from across the sea. Their Nish, erm, government, is like a spider's web."

"Ah."

I seemed to have led Nicodemus into another conversational dead end. A tiny cry suddenly peeped from the edge of the veranda. Without thinking, I turned away and walked towards the sound. The sides of the veranda were latticed and overgrown with thick foliage. Carefully hunting through the leaves and vines along the stone floor, I found my prize. A baby bird, half feathered and still blind, sat caught in the exuberant plant life.

"You poor thing!" I cooed. I scooped underneath him, catching up a few leaves as I did. "Come here, darling. I'll take care of you."

"It's probably going to die anyway, you know," Ducky's voice grumbled from behind me.

He and Duke Gregory had apparently rejoined us when my back was turned. I suspected Ducky could smell the conversation dying and had come to rescue it.

"Well, perhaps not now," I replied, almost whispering. "Look at him. He *needs* me."

Ducky came into view at my side. A comforting whiff of pipe smoke and whiskey floated towards me as he drew close to my cupped hands.

"Definitely going to die," he asserted.

"Uncle Ducky, you're horrible." Nevertheless, I was smiling.

He always did this to me. I looked around for the nest and spotted a scraggly collection of twigs and straw above.

"Give me a boost," I said.

Without further protest, Ducky got on one knee and offered himself as a step stool. He held one of my hands for support as I carefully lifted the baby bird, which was cheeping plaintively in my palm, towards the nest. As gently as I could, I deposited the little dear back into it.

Brushing my hands together with satisfaction, I said, "There now. All better."

"That was very kind."

I turned, surprised at hearing Nicodemus speak. I had altogether forgotten about him and was thankful for the way the darkness hid my blush.

"I, er, I just hope he'll be alright. Or she. It couldn't have been an easy fall."

"Might I check?" Nicodemus offered, and that uncertain smile reappeared.

"Can you?" I asked. "I mean, um, by all means, please."

"I have a gift with birds," was all he offered by way of explanation.

The power rolling off of Nicodemus was palpable as he strode forward. His glow returned, brighter than before, as he reached his hands towards the nest. His dark eyes glinted through a broken wall of dark, messy tresses. This was the most alive I had ever seen anyone. You know the sparks that form in dry, cold weather? Nicodemus seemed made of those. I was honestly concerned he might set something on fire. Nothing nearly so spectacular transpired, however. He merely glowed for a few moments and then stopped. It was there and gone so quickly I wondered if I had imagined it.

"Well, that was certainly… something," Ducky said.

I burst into laughter. Never, in all the years I had known him, had I heard Ducky at a loss for words.

"If you think that's impressive, you should have seen some of the wonders he spun for us at his home," Duke Gregory said.

Nicodemus began to object when Ducky demanded, "Show us one."

"Ducky!" I scolded. "He is not a trick pony. Nicodemus, I apologize. My uncle forgets himself when he is excited." I shot Ducky a glare.

Nicodemus shook his head. "It's quite alright—"

"Then let's see something!" Ducky pressed. "Just one miracle, eh?"

Nicodemus glanced at Duke Gregory, who nodded once. The magus sighed and gave in. With a graceful twirl of his hand, he conjured the image of a perfect sunset colored rose. Dipping his head, he handed the rose to me.

"It's real!" I gasped as my fingers grasped the cool stem.

"It's not," Nicodemus assured me. "It's easier to see through once you know it's an illusion."

I concentrated, telling myself I held nothing but air. Eventually, I could no longer feel the stem between my fingers, and the rose grew translucent, but it still moved with my hand. As I mused on this phenomenon, a wretched, torn sound suddenly ripped through the uneasy peace we had found on the quiet veranda.

The scream silenced the murmuring court within first. I hurried back towards the doors and looked in, though Ducky blocked most of my view as he took a defensive stance before me. Everyone looked at one another, waiting, hoping we had perhaps imagined it. The scream came again, louder and angrier, closely followed by glass shattering above us. We shrieked as shards rained down from the crystalline dome which had, until a few moments ago, topped the royal dining room. What had caused the damage was far more terrifying, however.

A Rukk, one of the enormous, predatory birds against which we had no defense. The creature's talons were the size of a man, its beak large enough to swallow an elk whole. Looking back, I realize it was a lucky thing its wings were so large. Only that saved us from certain death. The Rukk's outstretched wings could not fit through the shattered dome. Despite the glass jabbing into its flesh, the Rukk jerked and bobbed, trying to snatch up some delicious human morsels by any means possible.

People ran in every direction, yelping in panic. Carlos and his family were, thankfully, back in Bone Port, but I needed to locate my parents. I had to ensure they were safe. Before I could spot them in the scrambling mass, a voice deeper and louder than humanly possible thundered through the room.

"STOP!"

To this day, I don't know if he was addressing us or the Rukk. The people, however, obeyed and froze in their tracks. Every head turned, and we saw Nicodemus staring up at the Rukk. His body sizzled with blue and silver light as his eyes shifted between indescribable colors. He made a sweeping gesture for us to get back. We did so without question, pressing ourselves against the walls, unable to tear our eyes from the incandescent magus. The Rukk ignored his commands, and alarmingly deep cracks began to pattern the ceiling around where the dome had been. Bits of it were already falling down around us. Thank the stars no one had been struck by falling debris.

Nicodemus raised his hands skyward and glowed brighter yet. The clouds rumbled above, and a great crack shredded the air as the sky ripped open. Sweat beaded on his brow. We all recognized what he was doing, but I don't think any of us believed it. Tales circulated about magi calling nature itself to their aid, harnessing the power of the elements, but those were the most fantastical stories of all. Before that night, I didn't know anyone who actually believed it was possible.

The heavens grew angrier, as did the Rukk. Boulder-sized chunks of stone and plaster dropped from the ceiling. The Rukk had nearly broken through, the combination of its weight and efforts severely compromising the strength of the roof above us. Nicodemus thrust his fists into the air and, with a pained heave, dragged a bolt of lightning from the tumultuous clouds, striking the Rukk with it. The Rukk shrieked so loudly it shook the windows, cracking most of them. Nicodemus grabbed more bolts, quickly pulling smaller ones, spearing them into the Rukk. It was one well-placed—or perhaps just lucky—jolt to the Rukk's skull which finally bested the horrible beast. As it slumped over dead, the bird's head slid through the shattered dome, its golden eyes staring blankly at us all.

During the next moments that passed, the stillness crackled with the question of whether or not the danger had truly passed. Nicodemus hunched with exhaustion, looked around him and took in our gaping faces. Queen Gertrude and King Ansel appeared from the crowd and tentatively crossed beneath the hanging head. Nicodemus straightened halfway up before folding over again into a weak bow.

"Your majesties…" he puffed. "I… I apologize…"

Queen Gertrude silenced him with a single raised finger.

"Speak no more except to answer this: is it truly dead?"

"Yes, my Queen. It is."

And thus was Nicodemus' introduction to the royal court of Invarnis.

~Chapter 2~

From that moment on, the palace buzzed about Nicodemus day and night. What followed surprised no one.

The King and Queen employed him into their service and bestowed upon him the newly created title Grand Magus of the Royal Court. Rumor had it he had humbly refused at first, claiming he had simply been doing his duty as a fellow human being, but their majesties impressed upon him their desire to strengthen and protect the kingdom. How could he refuse such an honor? And so Nicodemus became a prominent member of the court overnight. He received invitations to soirées and galas, mothers practically threw their unmarried daughters at him—Baroness Liliana more aggressively than anyone else—and every hunter wanted him in their party. Despite his popularity, Nicodemus often broke away from his admirers and hid.

"I need a place to… catch my breath," he told me one day not long after that harrowing evening.

I had, unsurprisingly, tucked myself away in a corner of the royal library. Whether he had tracked my movements or truly stumbled upon me by chance, I don't know. Either way, I smiled in return.

"I understand. Please, have a seat."

Stars, how I wish I had turned him away.

He accepted my invitation. This was the first of many such occurrences. We split our time between talking and long stretches of companionable silence. I told him about my life, and he told me of his.

"I've always been curious by nature," he confessed. "It has long set me apart from my people. Magi are… very traditional, but they have never judged me for it. Rather, they permitted me to indulge my inquisitive mind." He chuckled. "I'm afraid my discoveries have occasionally proven painful."

"How so?" I asked, leaning forward in my chair, my book forgotten.

"I was quite badly burned as a child during a Phenix cycle ceremony. I understand your people are unfamiliar with the truth around their fire, correct?"

"I don't know. We've heard tales, of course, but I don't know of anyone who has actually seen a Phenix alight. You'll have to enlighten me." I allowed the barest hint of a smile to tug at my lips.

Nicodemus chuckled at my pluck. "You know people who have hunted them, yes?"

I nodded. Uncle Ducky fell into this category, though that particular success occurred when I was young. It was the only Phenix he'd ever shot in his life.

"Please understand, I do not condemn hunters. I simply believe the creatures are more spectacular alive than stuffed. For instance, Phenixes only ignite when they die of natural causes. When the time is nigh, they begin to drop their tail feathers in quick succession. We build pyre-nests for them, contained within a ring of stones so the fire won't spread. When the time comes, we all gather and celebrate the marvel of the bird's death and rebirth. It is a beautiful sight. Unfortunately, my curiosity got the better of me. I got too close, and the bird's final death-flares caught me. Nothing our healers couldn't fix, of course, but it was enough to make me question myself for a while."

"Oh my goodness! Bless you. Truly, your parents didn't pull you away?"

"No. We don't have family units as you do. Our circle, all of those we live with, is our family. And once we reach a certain age, we're expected to remember what we've been taught and take responsibility for our actions. That may seem harsh, but I certainly learned from my mistakes."

I sat stunned. So much to digest. One question after another flew through my head, and I decided to leave off the issue of family dynamics for now.

"How do you convince a wild Phenix to roost in a man-made nest?"

Nicodemus smiled again. "I admit we entice the creatures with food, but the Phenixes trust us. We live alongside them, sharing our space and our food with them."

"They are domesticated then?"

"Not in the least, but we and they know we are no threat to one another. I wish the same could be said for all creatures. Some of my kinsfolk have attempted to make peace with the odd Gryphon. It is a noble but… ill-conceived venture."

This was the way of our conversations most of the time, and we quietly grew close. Away from prying eyes and gossiping lips, I grew comfortable speaking to Nicodemus about all subjects. He asked about my family, especially curious about how Ducky had become my adoptive uncle, and my upbringing in a place like Bone Port. He showed as much curiosity about my alien way of life as I did about his. As one might expect, I often asked about his magic.

"Magi have different specialties just as everyone has different talents for art or singing or mathematics," he explained in his usual soft-spoken way.

I scooted forward in my chair. "What are your specialties? I mean, how do your abilities compare to those of other magi? For instance, can they all summon lightning the way you can?"

"I do not mean to boast, but I am better with elemental magic than most of my peers. I am… perfectly adequate in other areas such as healing and ward spells."

"I'm sure you're just being modest," I said with a smile. "Is it very strict, the… process of magic?"

"Once again, everyone feels their power differently. Some access it better after completing a series of rigid steps. I have always been a bit more relaxed in my methods. I enjoy pushing the boundaries of my power, experimenting with different ways I can use it."

Given how close we became over time, I suppose I should have had an inkling of what Nicodemus was about when he asked my father and Ducky round for drinks one day. I was utterly clueless, however. They returned in the highest spirits I had ever seen, bursting into my mother's formerly quiet sitting room like a pair of drunken water buffaloes.

"Didn't I tell you, Felipe?!" Ducky roared, slapping my

father on the back. "Didn't I tell you she'd surprise us all? I always said so!"

My father threw back his head and guffawed. "I gladly eat my words, old man."

I stared at the two like they'd gone mad. My mother, meanwhile, broke in more sensibly.

"I take it my suspicions were correct?" she smirked.

"Indeed, my dear, Isabella. Indeed they were. I shouldn't have doubted you for a moment," my father replied with twinkling eyes.

"Wonderful news, but let us not forget there's still a piece missing," my mother added. Her smile remained, but her eyes sparked sharply in contrast to her husband's.

My father and Ducky stopped and blinked at her, their arms still wrapped around one another's shoulders. Though my father was of the Arnavi people from across the sea and therefore much darker—not to mention far less round—than Uncle Ducky, the two resembled each other uncannily as they stared at my mother. She gestured towards me.

"Our daughter has yet to agree to the match."

My father and Ducky turned towards me, and I blinked back at them for several moments.

"Match?" I finally said stupidly.

My father appeared to gather his senses again as he stood up straighter, breaking away from Ducky. He tried to give me his stern business face, but a grin kept peeking through.

"Calandra, my darling. Nicodemus has made you an offer of marriage."

"When?" I replied automatically. "I don't recall being present for one."

My mother mumbled something under her breath as she sipped her tea, arching an eyebrow at the two men. She turned her gaze onto me and glowed with the same pride she'd had when I'd negotiated my first business deal.

"See?" Ducky said. "I said the lass'd have something to say about it." He turned to me and playfully narrowed his eyes. "Everyone thinks you're a wee meek mousie, but you're a sleeping bear. One wrong poke and *YEEARGH*!"

Ducky then mimed an enraged bear attacking with teeth and

claws. My mother pinched the bridge of her nose between thumb and forefinger.

"Circumstances surrounding it aside," my father said, almost having to shout over Ducky's growls, "what do you think of the idea?"

I looked away and considered it, separating feelings from information. Yes, I was furious. Nicodemus, bartering with my father and Ducky as he would for a prize cow. I was peeved with the latter two as well, but I knew their hearts better. I would address that issue later, and I expected it to be a rather easy conversation. Ducky's apology would likely involve food. Regarding the match itself, the idea shocked me. Nicodemus had become a comfortable friend, someone in whom I could confide. As a husband… I had never considered the possibility. I knew I didn't love him, but I liked him immensely. I looked to my mother.

She, Isabella Allen, had married for love. My father was a successful trader, having joined a ship's crew as a lad and worked his way up. He'd met my mother after striking a rather lucrative and mutually beneficial deal with her father, who had been Count before her. Not long after, he gave up his name for hers—as was common in our day to keep family names consistent—moved his business' home base to Bone Port, and left the rest of his family to start his own.

I knew I wasn't likely to receive such a grand offer again. I had to play in order to win, as they say. More than that, however, the possibility of marrying anyone at all shrank with each passing year. Not that I much cared about that for myself, but I knew my family worried about me and, given Nicodemus' new position, the match could be beneficial. And after all, I believed Nicodemus and I would be happy together. Not in the same way my parents were, but content. I shifted my gaze to Ducky.

"Have you offered him a title if we marry?" I asked.

Ducky gave me a knowing half smile. "I told him that was your decision. If you do not want the position, I understand."

I relaxed in my chair. Politics was something which didn't concern me in this case, as Nicodemus already seemed overwhelmed by one title. He may yet be disappointed, however. I had often considered what good I could do for the Southern Reaches as Duchess, but I'd never been willing to take on the role alone. Given what I knew of Nicodemus, if I wished to be married, he seemed a fairly safe option. And who knew? Perhaps our fondness would one day transform into love.

My expression deflated into a grimace as I considered the social responsibilities which might be required of *me* as wife of the Grand Magus, nevermind if I accepted the title of Duchess. I knew Ducky wanted me to take it, and I suspected he believed I could handle anything that came with marrying the Grand Magus too. He'd always spoken highly of my potential, citing talents from my father and mother and my own inborn shrewdness. I would be required to attend court functions as was already the case, but perhaps the higher rank would also afford me a certain leeway for what some might describe as my "eccentricities." That was the word I had heard used to describe Uncle Ducky's proclivities anyway. The upper classes do have a way with words, don't they? Especially when they're judging others. It was those proclivities which had kept other men from seeing Ducky as a threat and also prevented him from having any blood heirs. My gaze drifted back to my father as all these thoughts coalesced into an ordered set of pathways.

"Firstly, Papa, I beg you to remember your own words: circumstances always matter."

He twisted his lips around in an expression of chagrined pride. I wondered if he was trying to keep from laughing. Ducky apparently had no qualms about it and shook my father's shoulder.

"Secondly, I have some terms," I continued. "If he agrees to those, then I accept."

)(

It should surprise no one that direct conflict is not my forte. In business dealings, I can use facts as my shield. I gather information and mold it into the correct hooks. When it came to Nicodemus, however, I debated with myself about how to proceed. My communications with him would require delicacy. We were both members of the court now, after all, and therefore forever doomed to travel in the same circles whether or not we married. And I didn't know if he held secret romantic feelings for me or if he, like me, saw this as a safe bet. I suspected the latter, as he had eligible young ladies clamoring after him at every turn. Marrying me, marrying anyone really, would solve that problem to some extent.

On the surface, my terms were simple. I wouldn't accept anything less than the sort of marriage my parents had. They had always been equal partners, but how to succinctly explain what that meant to someone I had only briefly known? Again, possible help lay within information I didn't have: what my acceptance meant to Nicodemus. My father and Ducky were infuriatingly unhelpful on the subject.

"What did he say when you met?" I asked, pacing the floor of our shared office.

It hadn't been but a few hours since the news came, and I had already written, crossed out, and rewritten several responses to Nicodemus. A small mound of scrunched up paper sat in the corner of my desk as my father perused some accounts with Ducky.

"He said he desired your hand in marriage," my father replied, not looking up from his work.

"But *why*?" I pressed. "For what *specific* reason does he want to marry me?"

"Expecting a sonnet, are you?" Ducky gibed.

I rolled my eyes.

I wished I felt comfortable enough to address Nicodemus as I had my family, but he and I had never seriously debated an issue. Most of our interactions had been educational with some light banter in between. We'd shared our feelings with one another, often commiserating about our shared dislike of small talk, but we'd never outright argued. That was something else entirely and carried a different set of fears and consequences. I considered writing a strongly worded letter to express my umbrage at the way he had handled the situation. I preferred this solution, to be perfectly honest, but I knew from personal experience how much a simple statement could be misconstrued when presented on paper. Blast it all! I'd have to address the issue in person.

After several more drafts, input from my family, and a night to sleep on the words, I penned a request to discuss the proposal. Nicodemus and I agreed to meet in his rooms two days after the initial offer had been made. In my note, I pointedly avoided giving him any indication as to which way I was leaning and dressed just so for the occasion. And by that I mean I wore not a formal gown, but a pair of wide, swishy trousers traditional in Bone Port, topped by a waistcoat and short-sleeved business jacket, all in bright jewel tones. It wasn't in keeping with the current fashion of Prism—midlanders liked dresses and cloaks and slippers, none of which were practical in Bone Port—but it made me feel confident. Nicodemus seemed taken aback by my attire. He had dressed formally for the occasion and pulled uncomfortably at his high collar.

"Good afternoon," he greeted, giving me a low bow.

I curtseyed in response, the lightweight material of my trousers billowing on the air like Fae wings. "Thank you for agreeing to see me."

I knew I wasn't being fair, retaliating to how Nicodemus had conducted himself without addressing it, but I found I couldn't help myself. My insides simmered with indignation and anxiety in equal parts.

Motioning towards a table piled high with refreshments, he asked, "Shall we sit?"

By the lavish spread before us, I saw Nicodemus had been listening that time I'd told him the way to my heart was through my stomach. No matter how badly this conversation went, at least there were sweet rolls to be had. I bobbed my head approvingly and took a seat.

We sat for several uncomfortable minutes in silence, Nicodemus pulling at his collar again while I sampled the treats before us. He opened his mouth several times and, apparently thinking better of it, closed it again without saying a word. With each passing minute, I grew more uncomfortable even with the food to occupy me.

Think of it like a negotiation, I told myself. *It's only business.*

"I'm… I am here in regards to the marriage proposal you made." I bit off each syllable as I forced out the words and then internally winced at how harsh it sounded. This wasn't how I liked to conduct myself with potential business partners, so I capped my statement with a softer and rather awkward, "Please."

"Yes, I, ah… I suspected as much." I didn't respond at first, so Nicodemus continued. "I confess, Lady Calandra, I don't understand… this… whatever is happening at the moment. Your demeanor puzzles me."

I took a deep breath to steel myself. "I am offended, your lordship, that you proposed this potential engagement to my father and uncle instead of to *me*."

"I-I understood in your society parents give approval for such… con-tracts." From the way he hesitated on the last word, Nicodemus clearly wasn't certain it was the best one to use.

I wanted to present several arguments, starting with the fact that my mother had not been invited. I considered each one, envisioning the potential ramifications and rabbit trails they could lead down and already felt exhausted by them.

"For future reference, customs vary between families and circumstances. It would behoove you to discover those beforehand…"

Heavens, I sound like my parents, I realized.

I shook the thought out of my head. "In any case, I am my own person. This choice is mine, no one else's, to make."

Nicodemus' eyes grew wide. I assumed he now saw the size of the offense he had committed.

"I am deeply s-sorry, Lady Calandra," he stuttered. "Truly, I was trying to be courteous. In no way did I mean to… to insult you. I have nothing but the deepest respect for you."

I softened and sighed inwardly as Nicodemus continued on, complimenting my intelligence and independence and so on. Respect was all I had been after, and I moved us along as soon as Nicodemus finished with his current, faltering stream.

"Thank you. I accept your apology and your proposal."

"I hope… wait. Sorry, what?" He looked positively flummoxed.

I giggled. "I accept your proposal of marriage."

Nicodemus' face split into a glowing smile—literally, he began to glow—and he fumbled around in his pockets for something.

Producing a bit of folded cloth, he said, "I understand rings are also traditional, yes?"

Within the fabric laid a ring of expertly crafted silver, fashioned into the shape of intertwined vines with minute leaves.

"It's lovely," I told him and held out my hand. "Thank you."

He slipped it onto the correct finger, looking at me once as he did. Things were even more awkward after that, if you can believe it. We stood, and he looked as if he wanted to embrace me, but I made no move to close the space between us. That put kissing out of the question. Instead, he bowed and asked if I would accompany him to inform the King and Queen. I nearly backed out of the room right then but swallowed hard and nodded.

)(

King Ansel and Queen Gertrude agreed to our union after only a few questions, and we held our nuptials on the shores of my beloved Bone Port a month later. The long waiting period allowed for my father's relatives to be informed and arrive for the ceremony. Since magi did not observe marriage as we do, Nicodemus' circle was not invited. Several weeks later, after many discussions with Ducky and Nicodemus, the former named the latter and I co-heirs of the Southern Reaches dukedom. We had leaned on one another for strength before their royal highnesses and during the wedding planning and come out stronger for it. Therefore, I concluded we would rule southern Invarnis well as a team. Nicodemus agreed more easily than I expected, and I assumed this came from a place of wanting to make me happy.

On the day we made this decision official, I couldn't help but laugh as Ducky proclaimed our inheritance from his vast receiving hall.

I use the words "receiving hall" generously here. Hunting trophies of every type and size, from wee golden hind antlers to a stuffed bear poised forever in mid-attack, bedecked the walls. The chandelier in that room… good heavens, the chandelier. It was made of common deer antlers. Ducky had the rack of anything below ten points added to this monstrosity. Over the years it had mutated into a gargantuan abomination of style. And yet, as ghastly as the thing was, every time I visited the Duke's manor, I looked up to see how much it had grown. I had grown with it—though far less hideously, if I may say so—as I spent many a happy holiday there.

And the ravens! Ducky was especially fond of ravens for both their intelligence and usefulness. He had his own rookery and had given a few favorites free range of the house. An especially large one called Diamond was ever on his shoulder or nearby when he was home.

After the inheritance ceremony, Ducky threw a grand party, which neither Nicodemus nor I were particularly happy about. Everyone had come to celebrate *us*.

Imagine our horror.

We only just managed to survive without outright abandoning the guests.

~Chapter 3~

Transitioning into so many new roles all at once was not easy for Nicodemus. Ducky immediately began grooming him for his position as Duke of the Southern Reaches. Nicodemus' upbringing complicated the matter. Our laws made little sense to him, as the magi lived by democratic, community rule. They were free to leave and join other clans as they wished, though strong attachments often prevented this. I often considered how trapped he must feel in this new life, but he always smiled and assured me he'd known what he was getting into when he'd offered to become my husband.

"These are minor challenges in the pursuit of a greater goal," he would tell me.

Our marriage was surprisingly happy, given how uncertain it had begun and the ensuing difficulties. One day during a particularly frustrating portion of the wedding preparations—choosing the invitations—he'd taken out his anger on a nearby houseplant.

It sat smoldering as Nicodemus demanded, "Why does it even matter? Who will care?"

"Everyone," I'd replied whilst trying to hold onto my fraying patience. "It's yet another detail that shows we care and are capable of handling even the smallest of tasks with the utmost attention."

"This is asinine," he insisted. "People, so obsessed with superficial, meaningless… convinced of their own superiority, empty and… *ARGH*!" He claimed another victim, this time a small potted fern on the table.

The fern turned brown and withered within seconds, just as its cousin had. I took a breath and scowled for a moment at the smoking leaves as they curled in on themselves.

"Nicodemus, please. If this is so taxing for you, why are you even going through with it?" I was mostly successful in keeping my voice even. "Why even offer me your hand in the first place?"

He sighed, stopped pacing, and sat down in the chair beside me. Cautiously taking my hands in his, he raised his eyes to mine. Both his eyes and his voice were soft as he spoke.

"I know I am not an effusive man." I wanted to argue the scorched houseplants probably had something to say about that but remained quiet to hear him out. "I cannot make great declarations like others, but I wish you to know how I feel. From the depths of my soul, Calandra, I am entranced by you. I don't know from whence this feeling… no, not feeling. That is too feeble a description. This writing on my heart has been etched as if into stone. From that first night on the balcony, I could not stop wondering about you. Thinking about spending the rest of my days with you fills me with the greatest joy. *That* is why."

I stared back at him, stunned and silent. I could not understand how such a thing had happened, but I found myself delighted by the sentiments. I believe these words, and more like them which followed, caused me to fall for Nicodemus.

)(

We split our time between Bone Port and Ducky's estate. Travel during the Fourth Age was as harrowing as you might imagine. We did not have the great steam engines of today, nor had zeppelins been invented yet. The threat of attack by enormous creatures like Rukks or dragon-kin, which usually avoided large cities, loomed constantly in the vast countryside and wild forests. Vampyres roamed the land and could easily pick off members of small communities. It fell to the nobility to fund and maintain safe paths for travelers. Even the inns dotted along the road were partially funded by the area's reigning dukes and duchesses, which in turn helped the innkeepers pay for armed guards and weapons. Even so, any magical creature determined to do a traveling party harm had a fairly easy job of it. This was especially true within the depths of the Green Dragon, the dense jungle which borders Bone Port to this day.

The moment you enter, you begin to miss the relatively cooler breezes of the seaside. Because the Green Dragon sits in a valley, the air sinks heavily in on itself and collects heat from the sun and all the life within. Through sheer human stubbornness, a path for carts and coaches existed, but I preferred to go on horseback. It was quicker, more comfortable, and allowed for easier communication with our entire party. Plus, Otter was the best horse I had and still have ever known. We slathered ourselves in lemongrass oil to keep the insects at bay, which only made them somewhat bearable.

Particularly early in my marriage, a great and curious preponderance of birds appeared during one of our journeys.

Birds are the jewels of the jungle, painted in every color imaginable, from vicious pinks to rich blues and yellows so bright it's hard to believe such a color is natural. They dance and sing like they know how beautiful they are, swishing their long tails back and forth, puffing up feathery collars as large as the rest of their bodies. It's magnificent, and they were all around us! None of us native Bone Portis had ever seen such a sight. I looked to Nicodemus.

"This is your doing, isn't it?" I said, awestruck.

He smiled back. "It is. A gift for my precious gem."

"A gift with birds indeed," I replied, remembering what he told me the first night we met.

"How?" Basira, one of our caravan guards and a friend of mine, asked. She looked around us as if trying to decide whether there was any chance this was a bad idea.

"They know I am a friend," was the only response Nicodemus gave.

I brought Otter around to him, and he kissed me. In the short time we had been married, my wish had come true. Our friendship had blossomed into romance. Though we in the south have never been as restrained as the rest of Invarnis in our displays of affection, and despite how close we had grown, I still blushed. My face grew hotter as I heard Basira coo behind us. Eduardo, another guard and close friend, made obnoxious kissy noises.

We stayed for several minutes to admire the birds, which sang as if giving us our own private concert. As we listened, a different voice joined the chorus. It was a terrible, grating roar, like the sound of a ship being ripped apart by a storm. The spell shattered, and every bird fled in a rainbow explosion.

"Dragon!" Basira cried. "Go, my lady! Go now!"

"No!" I returned, pulling a spear from where it had been attached to my horse's barding.

"Calandra, you must," Nicodemus said, his jaw set and eyes searing in the direction of the noise.

"Separated, some of us will fall," I replied. "We stand a better chance together."

Our guards, four in total including Basira and Eduardo, said nothing more, but Nicodemus was not finished.

"You cannot risk your life! I won't let you!"

"I will not leave my people," I growled.

His skin had begun to glow with power, and I opened my mouth to tell him to direct his protections to our party as a whole. Before I could, however, the encroaching beast crashed through the trees. It rose before us, the size of an aurochs with horns to match. Venom green, it shaded into the canopy as we stared up at it.

Eduardo struck first. He rushed the beast and stabbed it in the side. It rounded on him and raised its lethal claws to return a strike when another attack rocked its opposite side. That was Basira. I charged on my horse while it was distracted and aimed my spear at its throat. It turned back before I could make my move. With barely a touch, Otter swerved us out of harm's way. When I brought him round again, I saw the triangular head drawing back.

"He's going to fire!" I shouted.

My guards scattered, but Nicodemus remained still, glaring hate at the dragon as his light grew brighter. I screamed at him to get out of the way, but it was too late. The dragon roared, spewing liquid flames from its mouth. Nicodemus roared back and threw his hands towards the beast.

Ice.

Solid, unmelting ice met the fiery blast. The two powers hissed and steamed as they met. The dragon could only hold out as long as its breath did. Nicodemus went longer and slammed the magical ice down the dragon's gullet. It choked and retreated and shook its head to break free of the stream. Nicodemus did not relent even as it vomited chunks of ice, and my guards attacked again. The ice, now smaller, razor-sharp shards, pelted against the dragon's scaly hide. They did not penetrate, but the beast rasped its displeasure and turned. Basira, Eduardo, and the others jumped back. It decided we were more trouble than we were worth and, with a few more petulant snaps of its jaws, begrudgingly left.

We looked at one another, unable to believe we had all come out of the fight unscathed. I looked to Nicodemus, and he looked back at me. His shocked expression mirrored mine.

"You can fight," he said to me.

"Of course I can," I replied without thinking.

He shook his head as if considering something. "I never knew."

"Surprise!" Eduardo grinned.

I laughed, and the mood instantly lifted. We camped that evening in a well-used clearing.

At night is when the Green Dragon truly comes alive. Screams and howls waft over the trees. The insects whine and buzz with an entirely new ferocity. And there are the growls. These are what had us all on high alert. Darkness emboldens panthers. Even with a party as big as ours, a large one might be tempted to leap out from the cover of night and drag an unlucky victim back into the shadows.

"I believe I can assist," Nicodemus offered.

"You don't need to do that," I said gently. "We are used to this, and you must be tired from your exertions earlier today."

He smiled and kissed my forehead. I knew him well enough by now to know this was a sign he was going to go ahead and do whatever he had planned anyway. I didn't protest. Even with Nicodemus there, I still worried for the safety of my people.

We all leaned in as he began to cast his magic. Not even I was used to the phenomenon yet, even though he exhibited it often when he and I were alone. He used those private moments to experiment, as he had referred to it, with his abilities, and I never failed to encourage him. He circled our little encampment, one hand held out towards the surrounding jungle and the other against his heart. He whispered to himself, though I don't think any of us could understand what he said. Magic, bright against the darkness, trailed from his outstretched fingertips. It resembled grains of white sand, glimmering in the firelight and falling to the ground around us. The ring he had created continued to shimmer after he finished.

"There," Nicodemus explained. "I have encircled us with protective energy. It will make anything seeking to attack us think twice, and it will hold for long enough to wake us if that is not enough of a deterrent."

"Thank you, Master Nicodemus," Basira said with a bow. "Even so, we will assign a watch tonight as usual."

We slept soundly through the night and visited a small waterfall the next day.

The site was fondly named the Nursery, as dragonlings hatched there and remained until they grew big enough to defend themselves. These, like the swamp dragon we had battled the day before, never developed wings like some of their cousins and so had trouble escaping predators. Most were eaten before adolescence. I enjoyed watching them, however, as the dragonlings shone such a bright opalescent white, you could see them swimming all the way down to the bottom of the waterfall's pool. That, and they weren't yet big enough to even consider eating us.

"This is my favorite place in the entire jungle," I told Nicodemus as he joined me. "I cannot pass through without visiting it."

He smiled and sat beside me.

"You're stronger than I realized," he said.

"Thank you."

He looked at me for a long moment. His eyes were sad, and I assumed fear of losing me gnawed at his heart. I leaned my head on his shoulder, but his face didn't change.

)(

We arrived at Ducky's estate, the seat of the southern duchy, without further incident. We had come to receive yet more lessons. Well, that was why Nicodemus was here anyway. By then, I needed little in the way of *formal* education. I say formal because Ducky had arranged something rather unconventional for me. He'd hired a cavalcade of tutors to help me overcome my crippling shyness, as he liked to put it.

"Nic can get away with it. I'm sure the Grand Magus can get away with any number of gaffes. You, though, they won't make excuses for you," Ducky had told me.

"They make them for you," I retorted.

"I don't scare them like you do," he gibed. "I don't care how you do the job, just so long as you *can*."

My heart shivered inside of my chest. "You think I might fail?"

"Of course I don't, petal," Ducky said, wrapping an arm around me and squeezing me against him. "I wouldn't have pushed for it if I did. I just meant they see your potential, and it terrifies them. Vipers, the lot of them."

I made a face at him.

He smirked back. "Practice will make it easier. You'll thank me one day!"

So much for my plan.

I couldn't deny his logic, but that didn't mean I had to enjoy it. Seeing as small talk was my weakness, my instructors did no more than introduce themselves. They left it up to me to engage them, to entertain and occupy them. Every session served as a miniature version of court events. Some members of the "socializing team," as Ducky termed it, were pleasant, some were sour, and one was downright abrasive. None of it was an act as far as I could tell.

By the end of each day, I was exhausted, as was Nicodemus, though what he learned from his lessons made the wheels in his inquisitive mind turn. He had no patience for some of our customs, especially those which limited personal freedoms, but he adapted via his curiosity. As we wound down each night, he postulated how different society might be if this law was changed or if that more didn't exist. I knew from personal experience Ducky was an excellent teacher, and I was pleased for Nicodemus' progress, even if I did have trouble showing it after a day of meaningless chatter.

After a fortnight of lessons, Nicodemus approached me with a surprise.

"You should take the day to get out with Basira tomorrow," he said. "Sunshine always does you good, and I've already arranged it with Ducky. Maybe you should travel into Dogwood Lane for dinner. You never know, you might have to stay overnight and cancel the next day's lessons too." He tapped my nose affectionately as he suggested this mischief.

I giggled and kissed him. "Thank you. I can't guarantee I'll be a much better student when I return, but I am very grateful."

"I think you should take as much time as you like," he said, looking at me earnestly. "You work so hard. Promise me you'll take a nice long day for yourself tomorrow?"

"I promise."

)(

The next day, Basira and I rode out together, me on Otter and her on Grim, her personal steed. Grim was a beautiful sable stallion who had a bad habit of running after mares. The dreary sky hung heavy with clouds. It was the kind of weather that made me want to curl up with a book and a cup of tea. I wore heavier clothes than usual that day—a practical pair of trousers covered by a long skirt, along with a cloak, just in case—as the Southern Plains get much cooler than my native Bone Port. We roamed over the rolling Southern Plains, saying little and stopping for lunch by a river. As much as I enjoyed being with Basira—she was one of the few people who understood how nice quiet time with a friend could be—I couldn't help wanting to head back and enjoy that book.

"I won't be offended," she said, as if reading my mind. "Eduardo was talking about organizing some games today. And I need a new pair of boots." She smiled impishly.

"Are you sure?" I asked. "We haven't spent much time together of late."

"You could come with me," she offered.

I grimaced at the idea of yet another day full of people. She laughed and flapped her hand at me. "You're more than welcome, but I understand if you don't want to."

I finally returned her smile. "It would be kinder to not make you compete against me as well."

"Very kind," she smirked.

I laughed, and we headed back to the manse after finishing lunch. Basira offered to take Otter for me, and I headed inside. I spotted Frederick, Ducky's Head of House.

"Please let my uncle and husband know I'm back," I said. "I'll be in the library if they need me. And please have some tea brought up."

"I'm afraid Master Jones and Master Nicodemus are not to be disturbed, my lady," Frederick replied with an apologetic bow.

"They won't mind if it's about me," I assured him.

I turned to walk away when Frederick's voice stopped me again.

"No, ma'am. Master Nicodemus said no one under any circumstances. He said he can't have his lessons interrupted today."

I knit my brows together, pondering this curious directive. "How strange. Very well then. I shall let them know myself. Please delay that tea for half an hour."

"Yes, my lady," Frederick said as he bowed again.

My mind bubbled with questions and possible explanations. What was Nicodemus so serious about learning? I hurried into the lower levels of the estate. Ducky had his private office here because it was close to the wine cellar and generally cooler than the rest of the manse. I puzzled at finding the outer door locked and, without thinking, pulled my key from my belt pouch. Ducky had long trusted me with access to every room within his house. His main office lay beyond the receiving room, and I strode straight into it. It too was locked, but I was ready with my key and so entered in one smooth motion. The sight which met me next stopped me in my tracks.

Ducky sat slumped over in his favorite chair, his head drooped onto his chest. Diamond sat placidly on her stand nearby. I hurried towards Ducky and shook him. No response. The click of the door closing again caught my attention, and I looked up to see Nicodemus standing against it. His face was grave, as if etched from stone, his eyes hooded.

"What's happened?" I demanded, trying to rouse Ducky again.

I noticed something shift underneath Ducky's broad chin. I worried whatever it was might be strangling him. It was a strange talisman or charm made of several fire colored feathers, small bones, and a soft, withered lump that looked unsettlingly like an eyeball. It was loose around Ducky's neck, thankfully, and his chest continued to rise and fall. Only then did I notice the shattered glass on the floor, its contents spilled across the plush rug and hardwood.

"Why haven't you called for help?" I asked, looking back to Nicodemus. "I think he's had some sort of fit."

I moved towards the door. Nicodemus blocked my way, and I raised my eyes to his, wide and afraid.

"You should not have been here for this," he said. His voice was low and cold, a tone I had never heard from him before.

"Nicodemus," I breathed. "Move out of the way. I'm going to fetch help."

"No," was his only reply.

I glanced back to Ducky. My voice came stronger this time. "Nicodemus, move, or I will—"

My words stopped as Nicodemus gripped his hands around my throat. I fought, reaching for the closest soft bits, his eyes. His arms were longer than mine, however, so I drew out the small dagger I kept on my belt. Time was running out, and I stabbed and sliced indiscriminately. He released me as spots began to dance over my vision. I stumbled back, catching myself on the wall, and heaved in cooling gulps of air. Nicodemus scowled at me as he healed himself and glanced at a clock sitting near Ducky. I launched myself back at him, taking advantage of this opening. He caught me before I could plunge the dagger into him again. I kicked instead and caught him between the legs. With a strangled groan, he threw me away from him, summoning a gust of wind to assist. I hurtled backwards over the desk and landed hard on the floor behind. Pain reverberated up through my elbows and into my shoulders. It was a lucky fall, as a blast of icy wind howled overtop the desk in the next moment.

A new kind of fear twisted itself around my mind. I took shelter underneath the desk and heard chips of ice buffet against the wood around me. Frigid tendrils snaked their way between the cracks, making me shiver. It lasted no more than a few moments, but my terrified brain stretched those into an age.

Nicodemus stopped his attack and rasped, "Stay there!"

I did, listening to the pounding of my own heart thudding in my ears. I was too shocked for tears. My mind struggled to grasp what was happening. I had to save my uncle, but I sat frozen by the fear of what else Nicodemus would do, *could* do.

A new thought broke through the wall of horror in my brain. During these moments I had hidden here, he hadn't come after me. Something else was a higher priority than killing me. I swallowed hard and said a prayer to the stars before creeping out. Peeking around the edge of the desk, I saw Nicodemus holding Ducky's wrist over a small silver bowl etched with unfamiliar symbols. Blood ran from a slash across Ducky's wrist, and I choked back a gasp. Was Nicodemus somehow secretly a Vampyre?

Fear gripped me again. I forgot all the things that made this impossible as the new idea wrapped its tentacles around my mind. I watched in horror as Nicodemus healed Ducky's wrist and wiped the blood away, blotting out any evidence it had ever been there. He spoke words I didn't understand and stirred the blood in the bowl with a talisman matching the one around Ducky's neck. Lifting the bowl to his lips, Nicodemus chugged the contents, making my stomach turn. The twin charms began to glow, the bloody one in Nicodemus' hand giving off a sickly red light and the other shining bright and white. Nicodemus reached for my uncle and placed his hands on both sides of Ducky's drooping head.

"No!" I heard myself cry.

I didn't understand what was happening, but Nicodemus was going to hurt Ducky, maybe even kill him. I don't understand how I saw everything so distinctly just then, but the memory is burned into me more clearly than any other moment of my life. I ran towards Nicodemus with my dagger drawn. He looked to Diamond and gestured towards me with his head, still reciting his alien words. Diamond took off and cawed angrily, aiming her talons at my face. We met as I neared Nicodemus. While I reached for him, I tried batting Diamond away. That hideous light from the charms grew bright during my short journey. It exploded as I touched Nicodemus, my hand still on Diamond, and all went dark.

~Chapter 4~

When I awoke, the world appeared strange. I remained still for a long time trying to collect my thoughts. I vaguely remembered a fight for my life, deep terror, and that I should be concerned about… something. Even so, my thoughts kept returning to one question: why are there bars here? I tried to reach for them, but my arms only flopped heavily and felt strange. Memories trickled back to me. I told myself it must have all been a bad dream. Surely what I remembered couldn't be real. I wanted to get up, to go find Ducky and Nicodemus and ensure all was well, but I felt so weak and wrong. I could barely move. Sounds reached me, and I looked in their direction. I recognized a door, but it looked strange. Every color was brighter, more intense. Some even glowed, and I grew even more suspicious of a brain fever as I perceived new colors I had never before seen. The door opened, and Ducky came through.

Thank the stars, I thought, still too weak to form words.

I reached for him, stretching out digits that felt alien, though I couldn't reason how exactly. His eyes landed on me, and I warmed inside. It had all been a nightmare after all.

"Awake at last I see," he said. "I'm pleased you're not dead."

I laughed feebly, but the sound rasped raw and twisted. I tried to speak, to question why I sounded so terrible. A croaking, gurgling cry was all that came out. I tried again and heard the same. With rising panic, I demanded answers. Nothing but more of that horrible cawing issued from my throat. With too-heavy limbs, I scrabbled to stand. Why wasn't anything working right?!

"Oh, hush, little one," Ducky cooed. "Hush, hush. Come here."

Too-large hands took hold of my body, pinning my arms to my sides, and the floor rose up to meet me. I suddenly realized something else hideously wrong: Ducky was huge! His broad face took up my entire field of vision as he attempted to soothe me, stroking my head and back. With a desperate effort, I flung myself away and saw two sweeping, ebony wings. I screamed and heard another of those terrible cackling noises emit from my throat. I thrashed, and the wings flapped clumsily around me. Ducky, meanwhile, drew back and watched me.

Help me! Uncle Ducky! I screamed in my mind, which flew from my mouth as a desperate croak.

I flailed towards him. Surely, whatever was happening, my dear uncle could see I needed him. He did, and I settled into his hands as I had in his arms as a child. I looked around in an attempt to calm myself and spotted a window. That must mean we were no longer in his office… if I had ever been there in the first place. I still doubted my memories. Through the lead-lined windowpanes, I watched as the last bright sliver of the sun dipped down behind the horizon.

Something like music began to stir. I swiveled my head, trying to identify the source. Only when it grew so loud that I could hear nothing else did I realize it sang within me. The notes melded with the rapid beating of my heart, wrapping around me and ruffling against my skin. Ducky put me down, and I looked up to see his eyes ablaze with curiosity. My arms lightened, the colors around me dulled, and things returned to their usual size.

"I…" I began, and stopped as I realized I could speak properly again.

I lifted my hands, inspecting them. My caramel skin had returned! My body felt like mine again. I couldn't decide whether I wanted to laugh or cry and instead let out a hysterical kind of sob.

"I think we're both glad I took you out of that cage when I did," Ducky said.

I looked to him, my brow twisting in confusion. "Cage? What cage? Ducky, what is going on?"

A cold, insidious smile crawled across my uncle's face. I had never seen Ducky smile like that, and it frightened me. I looked into his eyes. What met me there was not my beloved uncle. Something else stared back at me, but I recognized it. His face suddenly changed, and the foreigner inside disappeared. I doubted my senses again, but I couldn't shake what I had seen.

"What do you remember?" he asked me. "Today has been… rather harrowing."

I hesitated. Ducky's tone was all wrong. I recalled the horrific memories from his study. The blood, Nicodemus' attack…

"Where's Nicodemus?" I grasped, hoping to appear concerned about my husband.

"Nicodemus is dead, Calandra."

I sat and waited. I watched Ducky for any sign of familiarity. I knew how he, the real Ducky, would have comforted me, the words he would use. He didn't reach for me, didn't soften, didn't call me Cali.

"You!" I screeched, leaping for the imposter's throat.

He caught my wrists in one broad hand and muffled my screams with the other. I reached my fingers toward his eyes, wishing to rake them out of their sockets. I kicked, but the angle was all wrong. Guards burst through the door, and Ducky ripped his hand from over my mouth.

"She's overcome with grief!" the imposter cried. "Quickly! We must restrain and sedate her for her own safety."

"No!" I protested! "He killed Ducky!"

The guards, whom I knew had long and faithfully served my uncle, came forward to do his bidding.

"Stop!" The voice cut through the air like a sword. Basira stood in the doorway, flanked by Eduardo. She added, "Lady Calandra is our charge."

"I am her uncle and she my heir," the imposter shot back.

"You're a fake!" I cried, still struggling. "You killed him!"

He changed tack, molding his voice and gaze into an entreaty. "Please, I only want to keep her safe."

Basira jerked back. She said nothing, and I saw her considering her options.

"I'm sorry," I gasped, seeing my opportunity as cold realization cut through me. "I'm so sorry. The shock…" I released tears that had been waiting behind my anger. "I need to rest. Basira, please, escort me to my chambers."

"I really think it would be better if—" began the imposter.

"No, I'm fine now. I'm sorry for my outburst. Nicodemus…" I cried a little more.

The imposter nodded and released my hands. "Very well. I will accompany you."

I rose as steadily as I could, keeping my eyes on Basira. I squeezed her arm against me, and she led me to my room, to the space I had shared with Nicodemus. We said nothing as we walked, and I heard the imposter tromping behind us. It was as if he wore an ill-fitting Ducky suit and hadn't yet learned how to walk in it. I could tell from Basira's bearing she knew something wasn't right. When we arrived, she led me through the door and turned, blocking it.

"I must help my lady change," she said with a bow. It looked as if the imposter was going to object, but Basira continued. "I appreciate your concern, my lord, but propriety. It will not be long."

That stalled him long enough for Basira to close the door without being pursued. I felt her eyes on me as she turned. I sifted through memories and information. I tried seeing what I had just done through the eyes of another. The view from that perspective was grim.

"I'm not mad," I said, turning at last back to my friend. "Please, believe me."

"What's happened, Calandra?" Basira asked.

I whimpered, forcing back the tears I had relied on not minutes earlier. "It seems insane even to me."

"Just tell me. We don't have much time."

I nodded. She was right, so I started with what I thought was the simplest part. "That is not Ducky."

I may have misjudged, but my dear friend nodded. "He's certainly not himself."

"Something has happened," I said, shaking my head wildly. "Nicodemus, I… I think he did… *something*. I think he's taken on Ducky's form."

Basira said nothing, and her silence crushed me. Every cross word I had ever heard muttered behind my back came rushing back to me.

People had always called me odd. How could a noble child be so timid and shy? It wasn't natural for someone with my breeding to be so anxious. I must have a fragile mind.

"I'm not mad," I repeated. "Please, I know how it sounds. At least believe me when I say we are not safe here. We must get aw—"

A heavy pounding against the door stopped me. I trembled as Basira looked between me and it.

"Don't open it," I begged.

The pounding persisted. "Basira, I demand to see my niece!" boomed from the other side of the door. "I order you to open this door."

"Don't!" I whispered, knowing the imposter outranked me.

"It's going to be alright," Basira assured me.

"No! No, no, no, no!" I said, grasping at her.

She looked at me again and nodded.

"Right now!" thundered the imposter.

"Apologies, sir," Basira called back. "There are personal issues to which we must attend. If you like, I will fetch you wh—"

The door burst open, flying back and crashing against the wall on the other side.

"I will not tolerate being lied to, wretch!"

"My lord, if you please," Basira began.

She moved in front of me, taking a defensive position. The imposter barreled forward and shoved Basira back. She attempted to catch herself but tripped over my foot. I grappled to catch her as she fell, but the imposter had already yanked me away. Basira's hands grasped at empty air, and her head smacked against the stone flags with a sickening crack. A moment later, a pool of blood began to spread from under her skull.

"NO!" I screamed.

I tried to rip myself away from the imposter, but he was too strong. I heard him calling for guards, heard him tell them I had "killed her in a fit of passion" and that I should be locked away with access to no one.

"See that she's secure. I couldn't bear to lose her too."

)(

I was tied to a chair in Ducky's study for lack of a better place to put me. Sobbing, I pleaded my case to the guards, but even I could tell how insane I sounded. They left me alone after securing me. I looked around, wondering what had happened here after I blacked out. No sign of the evil that had transpired remained. The imposter appeared hours later with food and water.

"Calandra, dearest," he said within earshot of the guards. "I hope you're feeling better."

The door closed, and that familiar yet strange face changed again.

"Thank you for making my task so much easier," he hissed.

I forced myself to be calm. The hours of solitude had given me some perspective. I had to proceed carefully after all that had happened.

"What did you do to Ducky?" I asked softly.

"He's still here, in a sense." The imposter tapped his temple. "Not up here, mind you. Just his body."

"You killed him," I accused.

He smiled like a throat being slit. "I had to make room for me."

"Nicodemus."

"Precisely."

A long pause passed between us. We stared at one another, Nicodemus studying me as I seethed.

"What did you do to me?" I demanded.

He chuckled. It was hollow, everything Ducky's laugh had never been. "To be honest, I'm not entirely certain. You have to understand, the ritual is a cobbled-together mess to begin with. *I'm* not even sure how it works."

"What. Happened?"

"The Vampyres certainly know a thing or two about sustaining life. Blood must bestow some power which mere food cannot. Don't mistake me, I have no desire to become one of them. Too many disadvantages. Instead, I've taken the best bits of several creatures—Phenixes, Vampyres, Fae, and a few others—and mashed together my own method for achieving immortality. Grand, isn't it?"

I furrowed my brow. "How did you hide your true nature for so long?"

“To be fair, I take on personality traits from my current host. That last one, he was never going to last long. As meek and weak as a newt, but rather good with elemental magic. I, as I have said, have always had a gift with birds. They listen when I call. I have to say, though, I rather like this new body. He may have been an irritating lout, but he’s very robust.”

I growled but checked myself. I couldn’t have anyone thinking me any crazier than they already did. “And what about me? You haven’t answered that part of the question yet.”

He smiled his terrible smile again. “I’m still finding out, but I have a theory. Did you know dawn is approaching?”

“Just tell me.”

He said nothing, and blood boiled in my veins. Basira and Ducky were both gone. I wanted to scream again, but I swallowed it. We sat like that in silence for I don’t know how long. Eventually, music began playing in me again.

The melody sang like wind off the sea, but it howled as if caught on cliffs. It grew louder with every beat of my heart. Something soft brushed over my skin, but when I looked, nothing was there. My vision grew bright, and the world began to grow. My arms grew heavy again, and I heard my voice crackle with that terrible sound. The experience disoriented me, and so I did nothing as Nicodemus’ hands grasped me. He tucked me under his cloak and held my mouth, which felt all wrong, closed with finger and thumb. Nicodemus locked the door behind him as he smuggled me out of the office. I heard him issue instructions to the nearby guards. Due to my delicate state, I was not to be disturbed under any circumstances. The guards confirmed their understanding, and Nicodemus walked back up into the manse’s main level. Once we were away, he pulled me from within his cloak.

Softly, he said to me, “Come on, Diamond. I think it’s time you found a new home.”

~Chapter 5~

From within various cages, I watched everything I loved fall apart. Nicodemus kept me close. By night I was a prisoner within his private rooms, concealed behind false walls and illusions. I could see out, but no one could see or hear me within.

My eventual, permanent prison consisted of three solid walls and a grid of floor-to ceiling bars. It lay tucked within a hidden alcove in Ducky's old chambers. I hadn't known about this secret of my uncle's home. The manor had been built long before Ducky ever came along, though, so it was entirely possible he also hadn't been aware of its existence. Or, if he had been, he likely didn't know the original purpose of the concealed room. Whatever its mysterious origins, at some point it had clearly become a storage room for odds and ends.

Nicodemus brought me straight there and threw me into a cage normally used for transporting large animals. Before my permanent prison was erected, other cages of various sizes surrounded me, along with forgotten furniture and even a few grotesquely deteriorated hunting trophies, all covered in a thick layer of dust. Not long after he'd assumed his new identity, Nicodemus hired some unsavory looking characters to clear out the room and assemble the larger cell. He killed them in front of me after the fact and used their bodies for research.

This hideaway became where he conducted experiments and practiced his magic. He couldn't risk anyone catching him in the act. Thank the stars it wasn't larger. Even with the limited space available to him, the horrors performed in that room "to further his knowledge" were beyond count. He didn't spin his evil machinations only within those enchanted walls, however.

)(

I perched on a stand that had belonged to Diamond before she'd been consumed by the magic of that vile ritual. As I was tethered securely to it, I couldn't do much more than look around the room.

Through the center stretched a large table where Ducky had often entertained guests. Around it, my entire family sat, joined by several close friends, including Eduardo. From an open window, sunlight spilled into the room, far too cheerful for the dismal scene.

I forced myself to remain calm and still, searching for an angle, waiting for a fortunate moment. Having observed how quickly Nicodemus adapted to Ducky's body and personality, picking up my uncle's old habits and quirks within days, I knew I had to be craftier than ever. With so many people who loved me gathered here, though, surely I could make them see I was not Diamond, that sitting with them was not the man they had known so well.

Nicodemus sat with his hands clasped before him. He took a deep breath and looked around at those gathered. The way his eyes glistened with false remorse made me want to vomit.

"As I know you've all heard," he began, his voice low and hoarse, "Nicodemus is dead. I tracked his trail as far as the river gorge. As far as I can tell, he took a walk that afternoon after our lessons and lost his footing along the edge. His body was… unrecognizable. It's been cremated. If you all…" He gestured towards my parents, letting them fill in the blanks.

My mother and father exchanged pained expressions. They looked back to Ducky, and I saw their throats bob with emotion.

"Richard," my mother said, "where is Calandra?"

The snake's face crumpled, and he raised a fist to his mouth, pretending to collect himself.

"Isabella, my dear…" Nicodemus whispered. "Felipe, I'm so sorry."

Nicodemus explained through fake tears how I, driven mad by grief, had killed Basira by accident in a fit and later escaped before throwing myself off a cliff. I hissed as he recounted the tale of dispatching every guard to search for me before it was too late.

Wild animals, he claimed, found my body before the search party did. As proof, he produced a bloody and tattered piece of my outfit. When he'd reached into my cage—I was still confined to the first, smaller animal cage then—and ripped that bit away from the rest of my skirt, I hadn't known what he intended to do with it. Seeing it again as he used it to twist everyone's mind against me, I cawed and flapped against my bonds. The sight of my parents crumbling silenced me momentarily. My brother, Carlos, wept as he held his children and wife. Eduardo buried his face in his hands and sobbed, keening for both Basira and me. Nicodemus shared all this while sunlight bathed them all in its joyous rays.

No... I said, hearing that wretched voice cry from my throat. *No! No! No! It's me! I'm here! I'm not dead! He's lying to you! Why can't you see it?!*

I came as close as birds can to screaming, frantically pulling at my tether whilst flapping my wings as fast as possible. My voice rang out hideously amongst the wails and tears of my loved ones.

Nicodemus wiped his eyes and approached me. "Apologies." He stroked my head, and I snapped my beak at him. With his back to the rest of the room, he smiled cruelly at me but adjusted his tone to appear even more broken than before. "The old girl hasn't been the same since… since everything."

)(

I am indescribably grateful to every power in the universe for one particular mercy. Not once in the ten plus years Nicodemus wore Ducky's form or any time after did he reach for me with lecherous hands or force himself on me. We'd shared ourselves with one another before I discovered his true nature, but he showed no sexual interest in me once my captivity had begun. The experiments he performed on both my forms, however, were no less violating. It was in me Nicodemus found his perfect test subject.

My true hell began after we simultaneously discovered yet another surprise about my condition. As Ducky had loved his drink, so did Nicodemus in his body. After imbibing too many one night, I watched and waited for my opportunity. He stumbled too close to the wall made of bars. I snatched his keys and, when his back was turned, silently unlocked the door. I worked quickly, for the small, windowless space limited my options, and I knew not how long I had before Nicodemus noticed me. Out of my cage, I grabbed a hunting knife from his belt and drew back to strike a killing blow. He turned as I did, drunkenly unsheathing his sword.

I felt the steel slice through my midsection with sickening clarity. Every fiber of flesh separating screamed agony in my mind. I gagged on my own breath and then on blood. Nicodemus' mouth hung slack. His eyes goggled at me stupidly. I gripped the blade piercing my body and pulled myself off it. I don't know where the strength to complete the task came from, but I freed myself, slicing my hands open as I did. More blood choked up my throat and dribbled out of my mouth. I stared at him, gurgling and fighting for air, waiting for my legs to buckle beneath me. They never had the opportunity.

The scene sobered Nicodemus. He suddenly moved as quickly as I had, taking advantage of my shock and shoving me back into my cell. I stumbled and cried out as deeper torment ripped through me. I'd squandered my chance. From outside the bars, he watched as I sunk to the ground and stared idiotically at my own blood on my hands. As the shock wore off, pain rolled over me. I was soft back then, and I wailed as the wound continued to bleed. I sank down further, overcome with hurt and confusion. I begged Nicodemus to help me, told him I was dying, but he remained still and observed me. I feebly tried to staunch the bleeding, but it was fruitless between the size of the wound and the sharp agony tearing through me. Blood loss was my friend that night, as I eventually fainted.

Seeing the way I had remained alive ignited Nicodemus' malicious curiosity. *This* was what he wanted for himself. The wound didn't even have a chance to become infected, for it stitched itself back together while I was in my raven form the next day.

Nicodemus began with my blood. A feverish desire to examine it in closer detail, to gain a deeper understanding of it, drove him to develop new technologies for that purpose. I know he unraveled many mysteries about blood via his research on mine and his own, for he dictated his notes with enchanted implements. As witness to his process, I also learned he anonymously disseminated any knowledge which didn't serve his purposes to the wider world. How I wish he had been content with these advances.

Unsatisfied with his lack of progress in unlocking the secret of my healing ability, Nicodemus eventually began testing my limits. He started small, slicing off a finger pad here or carving away a fillet of flesh there. Then he clipped off fingers and toes at the first knuckle. After that came cleavers for hands and feet and wings, followed by saws for entire limbs. With precision, he sliced and removed organs. My insides served as a model for his carefully sketched diagrams of the human body. Through his experiments on me, he gained understanding of how we work internally. I'll never know how I didn't go mad during this time. So much pain and blood, my night-long screams echoing off those enchanted walls. He never beheaded me, though I wished he would. I thought that would end me, and I think he suspected it too.

With every bit of me Nicodemus cut away, with it went a piece of my will. I know I said I was soft back then, and I was. At least, compared to now. Even so, I want to believe the way I crumbled over time is defensible, but I can't help wonder what might have happened had I fought harder against the first cracks in my spirit. These small fissures became rifts, and then yawning gorges that split and shredded my inner being. He didn't even have the decency to praise how my pains benefitted the world. Instead, Nicodemus poured poison into my ears as he worked.

"If only you had been obedient that day. You have only yourself to blame for where you are."

"You imagined yourself strong. If you were, you would not be here. You are *weak*."

"This is what you get for trying to escape."

Every word gnawed at my mind and injected lasting venom into my soul.

In another set of tests, Nicodemus denied me food and then water and then both to see how lack of nourishment affected my body.

"Let the love you had for me feed you, idiot girl," he sneered as I begged for mercy.

I grew skeletally thin, which showed in my raven form. "Diamond" finally passed away during this time, only for me to later fill the same spot again—once his starvation experiments had ended—under a new name. Hunger pains wracked me for weeks, but my internal systems never shut down, and Nicodemus meticulously documented all these developments and discoveries.

A flaw in my prison presented itself not long after these atrocities began. If Nicodemus came to collect me while I was a raven, I would simply fly to the top of the cage. Unfortunately, he had no qualms about shooting me down with his magic each time instead of simply securing me to the wall or floor. Uncle Ducky had always enjoyed a challenge. Even though I knew it was probably down to Nicodemus' own inherent malevolence, the idea of that trait carrying through from Ducky to its perverse form in Nicodemus shattered me further.

On top of everything else, that wretch had the unmitigated gall to query me, to request answers to cruel questions for his vile research. As the years passed, I did not age, nor did I change. Thank the stars nothing new presented itself, and Nicodemus eventually grew either bored or content with what he knew of me. By then, however, I was a ruined shell of the person I had once been.

)(

Nicodemus eventually needed to select a new heir. As much as my own pain tormented me, I feared for his next victim. I pleaded with him every night to stop all his designs. I cried and knelt and begged, promising everything if only he would stop.

"But I have such glorious designs," he smirked at me.

Over the decade or so that passed, Ducky's body grew old and slouched, his hair grey and thinning. The spirit squatting within was still strong and sharp, however, and I knew he must do something soon. What he did was far worse than anything I could have imagined. And I, dressed in my glossy black feathers and suffused in a haze of misery, was forced, as I always was, to play audience to his machinations.

I was not alone on this day, however. A great crowd had gathered in the vast courtyard of Ducky's estate. I knew well the look of effort in Nicodemus' eyes as he tamped down on his power. I had seen it often throughout the years as he kept his abilities hidden. I could tell he would have glowed, as his previous body did, with joy as he surveyed the eager assembly. I also recognized many faces within the crowd, fellow courtiers from my past and their offspring, now years older. My family, all with fractures in their eyes even still, stood near the front. King Ansel and Queen Gertrude sat in attendance on thrones I recognized from other events they had overseen. Nicodemus addressed the crowd from atop a temporary podium. Next to him loomed a huge shape covered by an enormous sheet of cloth. It was at least fifteen feet tall and pointed at the top with a much wider base. He gave the appropriate greetings and thank-yous before dropping the axe.

"Many years ago, we suffered a great loss. Not only were young people, full of life and potential, my beloved niece and heir included, ripped from us far too soon, but we lost Invarnis' first and only Grand Magus as well. Life is a battle for survival. We cripple ourselves when we disregard tools available to us. Magic is one of these tools. Therefore, I have spent the last several years searching for magi. In cooperation with local circles, and with the blessing of our esteemed regents—"

At this, their majesties nodded their approval.

"—I have found a new Grand Magus. Allow me to present Uriel."

Applause and cries of joy rose up. A young man, appropriately handsome, mysterious, and humble in equal parts, climbed the podium. I started on the stand to which I was tethered. *I recognized him!* Far too well, I'm afraid. He had shared Nicodemus' bed more than once.

"Hello," he said to the gathered crowd, dipping his head courteously. "I am honored."

Oh stars, he's the one, I thought.

"That is not all," continued Nicodemus. "I have also made the difficult decision to bequeath my entire estate to our new Grand Magus. Not to worry, my relatives have been given titles and land to more than make up for it." A chuckle went round the audience. "Additionally, in an effort to improve security, I have sent envoys to every corner of Invarnis. I am extending an invitation to all magi who are interested to come here. Today, I dedicate the Eldritch Synod, a sanctuary of magical learning and service."

With a flourish, Nicodemus whipped the sheet off the object beneath it, revealing a statue of himself! Rather, what he looked like before he took on his Ducky-skin. The statue's arm was thrown up in a pose of power, an invisible wind fluttering his cape. I vomited. I actually threw up my breakfast right there. Nicodemus turned cold eyes onto me and chuckled.

"It seems my dear pet, Coal, isn't a fan. Well, there's no accounting for taste."

)(

Nicodemus didn't tarry after dropping me some food through the bars that evening. Minutes later, through the enchanted walls of the hidden room, I saw Uriel enter Nicodemus' chambers. Nicodemus crossed the stone floor and kissed him deeply. I watched with questions whirling about in my head, lifting me from my melancholy daze. The possibility that Uriel was in on Nicodemus' schemes had occurred to me. Heavens forgive me, I hoped he was for his own sake.

"You were splendid today, my love," Nicodemus purred into the lad's hair.

"I still don't think I can do this," Uriel confessed. "I'm not strong like Nicodemus was. He singlehandedly killed a Rukk."

"And a swamp dragon," chuckled Nicodemus. He kissed Uriel again and added, "Now, don't let me hear you speak such nonsense again. You are everything this kingdom needs."

"I just want to do well. I don't want to fail their majesties," Uriel replied, kissing Nicodemus back.

"Precisely."

"RUN!" I screamed from inside my prison. "HE'S GOING TO KILL YOU!"

My hopes dashed, I shouted at the top of my voice until my lungs burned. My hands split and bled as I pounded on the walls and bars. Even after my voice gave out, I fought to be heard.

Nothing. Uriel heard none of my shrieks.

)(

It happened not long after. Once Uriel had been established as the new Grand Magus, Nicodemus drugged him, dragged Uriel's limp body into the secret room, and performed his heinous ritual again. And I could do nothing but watch as he stole yet another life.

I stared in silent horror as Nicodemus simply… vanished. My uncle's visage hovered like a ghost over Uriel's prone form before sinking into it and disappearing. How many times had Nicodemus done this? How many souls had he blotted out in order to possess their bodies? Moments after the deed was done, Nicodemus, dressed in his newest disguise, opened his eyes, blinked, and turned towards me. An abominable grin slashed across his face.

Seeing the loss of yet another life rekindled some of my old fire. It was no bigger than a match flame and, in the same way, it flared bright within me for a moment.

"I will kill you," I hissed. "I don't know how or when, but I will watch as the light dies from your eyes."

"Powerless and pathetic as you are?" he drawled. "Not likely. Speak to me like that again, and I'll cut out your tongue."

His words blew an icy gust through me and extinguished the light again.

During the next few days, I saw Nicodemus weave a new tale. He produced a body made up to look like Ducky's had there at the end. Posing as Uriel, he claimed the old Duke had died peacefully in his sleep. During the service, I cried from my perch, cawing mournfully for poor, deceived Uriel.

)(

Magi both young and old came to the estate and sought what this strange new place could offer them. And Nicodemus shared generously. All his collected knowledge was available, save for two pieces: the secret of his immortality and me.

Part 2

The Fifth Age: The Rule of Magic

~Chapter 6~

Over the next few decades, as Nicodemus' Eldritch Synod grew, so did Invarnis' understanding of the world. Judge me if you must, but I was glad for this time even as it birthed horrors for our people. You see, Nicodemus' new project kept him so busy he had little time for any remaining curiosity in me and my condition.

Everything has degrees, and deep evils seem lighter if you are broken enough.

He still often took me out with him by day, but he never lost his caution with this practice. I believe he enjoyed having me serve as witness to his maneuvering when he could manage it. The Fourth Age closed with the dedication of the Eldritch Synod. As Nicodemus paraded me about on his Uriel-masked hand, he preened as those around us predicted the new Fifth Age to be a time of enlightenment, and they praised him (or rather, his various forms) as the architect behind it.

It wasn't long before people began to see ravens as the mascot of the Eldritch Synod, and so Nicodemus soon always had one by his side as an accessory. He didn't bring me out as often after that. I imagine it was less fuss to keep a real raven at hand, though he never failed to have me with him during an especially aggrandizing daytime event.

The irony of my situation did not escape me. The shy, little courtier who wanted nothing more than to be left alone was now well and truly so. Even when I was around other people, I was no longer required to make small talk or participate in any of the activities that used to twist my stomach into knots. Perspective really is everything, isn't it? Being left to myself so often now with nothing to do, I called up long-ago lessons from my parents and my childhood and was infinitely grateful for the way they insisted we learn to entertain ourselves.

Given the way beauty and danger go hand in hand in nature, children from my gorgeous Bone Port are taught from birth how to both appreciate and survive it. With these necessary skills comes freedom as one proves themselves capable—Bone Porti parents are not nearly as fretful as some of our more northern countrymen. As we grew, Carlos, Basira, Eduardo, and I spent countless hours exercising our imaginations as we ventured further and further from home.

From within my dark cell, grasping onto the light of my memories, I did the same during these long years. I found patterns in the bars of my cell to match the constellations I knew and missed from the world outside. I created my own too and dreamt up stories of how they had come to be included in the tapestry of this false sky. With these memories came strength. Not much, mind you, but enough to know I must preserve my sanity and whatever humanity I could. I realized during my time alone, as I recalled my home and family, what time away from Nicodemus gave me, and I thanked the heavens for all that kept him away. I plucked feathers from myself during the day and hid them away to amuse myself with at night. I made ebony fans, carefully tied with a few strands of hair, and arranged the feathers along the floor into shapes and words.

I considered using bits of my clothes in my activities as well. While I was desperate for anything to divert myself, my outfit did not benefit from whatever strange magic kept everything attached to my body intact. Over the years, it had become tattered and dull, though it had only experienced half the wear and tear it should have. Besides begging for food and mercy, both for myself and others, I had never asked Nicodemus for anything. I wasn't going to start with new clothes and so decided against it in the end.

I saw the world through a small frame indeed during that time. Everything I observed when Nicodemus brought me out revolved around magi and his schemes to bring them into a greater position in our world. By their power I saw creatures that had once been impossible to subdue chained and cowed. They captured Gryphons alive, inconceivable as that may seem. At first it was to study them—everything began with studying—and then to keep them as pets and force them to serve as steeds. Nicodemus undertook a project to do the same with dragon-kin, but they would not be broken and so became victims of sport, baited and set against others of their kind or groups of criminals for entertainment. Fae were caught and kept in terrariums and lamps and then on enchanted strings as amusements. Vampyres were captured and kept as the most curious and dangerous of all pets and experimental subjects. Nicodemus kept prize Phenixes in his chambers, enclosed by obsidian. These, I thought, were the most beautiful of all and my companions for years, in as much as a creature who can neither see nor hear you can be your companion. Nevertheless, I spoke to them for hours on end and watched with fascination as they grew.

I saw the world change. The magi who came to learn under Nicodemus transformed with each generation. He molded minds to his purpose, convinced them they were above the world. What began as pure curiosity and want to learn and discover twisted into entitlement and conceit. The magi began to draw lines between themselves and non-magical people. They devised new punishments for criminals and forced debtors to take oath-bonds of servitude, which enslaved them to their new masters. Magic became the new currency of power. To father or give birth to a magus brought instant honor to the parents.

I observed all of this through a few hours here and there outside of my cell and as Nicodemus' chambers changed over time. He took on the guises of each successive Grand Magus. No matter how many times I saw him perform his monstrous ritual, it never failed to shake me to my core. Each time, my heart broke for the victim. Even the most odious ones—every generation of magi I saw over the years was progressively more terrible than the last—didn't deserve to have their entire life stolen by Nicodemus. I begged for mercy for them and didn't care that he seemed to enjoy the sound of my pleas. The bit of my soul still illuminated by memories of my old life shouted into the tar-stained blackness around it that I could not stand by and accept this deepest of evil. I had surrendered to so much, but not this. At least I knew better than to be surprised when Nicodemus laughed at my requests.

)(

I did not fail to notice when the number of Phenixes in Nicodemus' room began to decline. At one point, he'd had eight. My ears had pricked up when I'd overheard him discussing with a colleague their failure to cycle. This man ended up being Nicodemus' next possession victim. By the time Nicodemus was down to three Phenixes, the magi had determined the main difference between magical and nonmagical creatures: magical ones did not breed in captivity. Thinking back, I realized I hadn't attended as many dragon-baiting events or Gryphon races of late. I hadn't thought much of it beyond gladness at having been left alone more often than usual and an assumption that Nicodemus couldn't be bothered with me and my timetables. Time passed like a river for me by that point, though; I had little care for the minutiae of single days by then.

When I learned magical creatures were becoming harder to find, I immediately thought of the Nursery deep within the Green Dragon. Me. I had exposed that precious place to Nicodemus' foul influence. I wondered if it was bereft of the vulnerable dragonlings now. Was there anything I hadn't spoiled?

Given the reports I overheard regarding the dwindling magical creature populations, imagine my surprise when Nicodemus had a Vampyre covertly delivered to his chambers. He forever silenced those who had executed the task and shoved the creature into my cage with me, bonds and all.

To me, Nicodemus said, "I want to see what happens." He turned back to the Vampyre and added. "Now, blood drinker, what can you sense about her?"

The Vampyre hissed and attacked the bars.

"Do as I say or suffer again," Nicodemus drawled. His current host had been a cruel snake of a man, and I imagined I could see his tongue flick behind his teeth.

He brandished a strange weapon towards the bars. It was a metal rod, dull at the tapered end, with an iridescent stone set into the pommel. The Vampyre ignored him, and Nicodemus pointed the tip of the weapon towards his new prisoner. A strip of lightning shot towards its victim, lighting up the bars and making the Vampyre grip them and judder before crumpling to the ground.

"I won't ask you again," Nicodemus said. "What do you sense about this girl?"

The Vampyre scowled as his endless black eyes searched me. I met his gaze steadily. I had little to fear from his kind, nothing that compared to the torments I had endured under Nicodemus anyway.

"You're human," my cellmate said, addressing me.

I nodded. "Yes. At the moment."

"Something… doesn't fit," he added.

"I know. When the sun rises, I turn into a raven. With its setting, I change back."

The Vampyre turned back to Nicodemus and curled his lip, revealing long fangs. "I take it this is your doing, worm?"

"In a way," Nicodemus chuckled. "It was not on purpose. I've tried to replicate it without success."

"What?" I asked, my eyes wide. "What happened? Why would anyone agree to such a thing?"

Nicodemus turned his steely smile onto me. "I'm so glad you asked. You see, it's not so difficult when the subjects are condemned criminals. Everyone wants immortality. It's just a matter of minimizing the sacrifice." His face darkened. "They all perished."

My mouth opened and closed like a fish's.

"It would seem you are nothing but a fluke. A mistake. I shall continue to try to find a use for you, but I don't hold out much hope."

Nicodemus' words sliced across my heart like a knife. A clock within his apartments chimed, and he left the Vampyre and me together. Neither of us said anything for a long time. He gnawed at the bonds around his wrists as I chewed over Nicodemus' words. I was worse off than those criminals. Condemned yet never able to find release. I didn't even know when the change would come, having only moments of warning when the curse began to sing in my veins each day. This sparked a new thought in my mind, and words flew from my mouth, abruptly shattering the silence.

"I've heard your kind can feel the approach of the sunrise."

The Vampyre looked up at me. He had his hands wrapped around the bars again. I suspected he might have been testing their strength. He made no response and looked away again.

"Please," I said, coming nearer. "I haven't had any sense of time in… since… only the change."

I knelt down beside and reached towards him. He growled, a low warning rumble from deep in his chest. I drew my hands back.

"How do you know?" I pressed.

"Why would I help you?" he asked at last.

"Because we are prisoners together. What do you have to gain from *not* helping me?"

"I have nothing to gain for it," he sneered, turning away again.

"You used to be human! I… I don't know what to call myself, but we are not so very different."

He laughed. The sound of it was like pouring dark, thick oil. "I have transcended petty concepts like humanity. For hundreds of years, I have lived above you cattle."

"That seems to be changing. The magi have taken over everything, even nature. If I must bargain for such a kindness, then take my blood. You'll only waste away and grow weak in here otherwise."

"I don't need your charity," he snarled. "And you reek of magic. That wretch won't hold me here like he has you, weakling. Now get away from me before I snap your neck and play with your corpse."

I stood and sighed. I had no wish to endure unnecessary pain. A few steps away, however, I spoke again.

"What's your name, Vampyre?"

He didn't answer me.

)(

As I predicted, my cellmate grew gaunt and grey without sustenance. Nicodemus brought me food as usual and asked questions of us.

"Has it fed from you yet?"

"No," I replied flatly.

"Why not?" He directed this query at both of us.

The Vampyre refused to speak even as Nicodemus shot him with the curious lightning rod.

It wasn't long before I stepped in to try and spare my fellow prisoner. "Stop! He says it's because I reek of magic."

Nicodemus' eyes lit up as his interest piqued.

"Is that so?" he said more to himself than to me. "So he can sense the enchantment."

"Can you sense enchantments then?" I asked. I didn't need to feign interest; it was genuine.

"No," Nicodemus said absently, thinking to himself. "It is a rare gift and difficult to discern in any case. This is good to know." He looked back to the Vampyre and asked, "Can you still tell even when she's a raven?"

I suspected Nicodemus was considering the possibility that, even in my bird form, the enchantment was perceivable. Again, the Vampyre refused to answer, and Nicodemus raised his weapon again.

Another bolt of lightning shot from it. Two more. I noticed the gem in the pommel grew dull with each attack even as I cried for Nicodemus to stop. After the third strike, he finally seemed to hear me.

"He sleeps with the sunrise," I explained. "When he wakes, I am already human again."

"He never wakes? Have you tried to rouse him?" Nicodemus asked. I shook my head, and he added, "Of course you haven't. Idiot girl."

"It would not be in her best interests to try," the Vampyre said, finally speaking.

"What do I care what you do to the worthless creature?" Nicodemus said coldly. "Do with her as you please. She's not done anything for me in over a century."

He had apparently finished with us, as he left without another word.

Afterwards, the Vampyre asked, "Why do you answer him?"

I jumped. He hadn't spoken to me since our first night together. I blinked at him as if the answer should be obvious.

"I am small and have but a speck of power. Still, what kind of a person am I if I don't exercise it to try and stop his cruelty?"

"You take that cruelty upon yourself by caring," he replied.

"I am already in hell. It is worse to see more pain."

The Vampyre's eyes roamed over me curiously. "Tell me about yourself."

The command brought to mind my family, my friends, Ducky, my beautiful Bone Port, everything of the life I unwittingly threw away. The pain of a thousand cuts nicked my insides as I envisioned confessing this loss, my mistakes, to him. I shook my head and turned away. After a long time, the Vampyre spoke again.

"Dawn will be here soon. My name is Thomas."

)(

The next night, as soon as Thomas awoke, I asked him something I had wondered for a long time.

"Are you going to die? Without blood, I mean. What's going to happen to you?"

"Worried for when you'll be alone again?" he mocked. "Pathetic."

"You don't actually think you make good company, do you?" I replied. My tone was entirely serious.

Thomas laughed. The dark, oily sound transformed to warm honey. I remained silent, waiting for a response.

"Fair point," he said at last. He grew serious too. "I'll go mad first. When faced with starvation, we turn into slavering beasts. I suspect I will tear your head from your shoulders and gorge myself."

My entire face lit up. "Would you?! Why wait?"

Thomas looked both baffled and maybe even frightened. I knew he must think me mad, so I hurried to explain.

"I can't die! Nicodemus has removed every piece of me to figure out how to obtain true immortality."

"Yet you are whole," Thomas finished, understanding dawning on him. "You heal."

"Yes, but he's never removed my head. I suspect he worries that will destroy me before he figures it out."

"I see."

"So will you do it?"

"No." Thomas' answer shot like an arrow through my heart, striking hard and quick.

"Why ever not?!" I wailed. "You just said you'll likely do it eventually."

"Yes, when I am driven by animal instincts to survive," he sneered at me. "As I am, I have not the strength to even rend your arms from your body. And besides, to feed from you would give that filth what he wants. I won't give him the satisfaction."

"What difference does it make?" I demanded. "By your own admission, it's going to happen in time. As soon as you do, you will come to your senses, and he'll have gotten what he wants anyway."

"While I have the power of choice, I will not bow to him!" Thomas snarled. "What do I care for your mercy? You are but an ant! An ant that doesn't even know if losing your head will kill you. Perhaps you'll only add to your agony."

"That's a risk I'm willing to take!" I grated back. "You have no concept of what I have endured. Nicodemus will do with you whatever he pleases. Take it from me, he is very patient. I have offered you sustenance, let you sleep in peace. You could restore your strength for whatever purpose you like, but you prefer to waste away like a rat in a trap for your pride. Enjoy your fall into madness. At least one of us might find peace at the end of it. And then *you* will be alone to face him and his questions."

Thomas stared at me with fire smoldering in his eyes. We did not speak again for several nights. Despite my angry words, I let him sleep. The next time we talked, he opened with his usual brusque manner.

"You were proud once." I said nothing in reply, and he asked, "What is your name?"

I hesitated. Would it hurt for him to know at least that? I didn't see how.

"Calandra."

He paused as if uncertain of his next words. "Calandra, would you still be willing to share your blood?"

"Why?" I snapped.

"Because it will hurt if I take it by force," he snarled.

"We share a cage. Do you really want to start a war with me?"

Without realizing it, I had drawn myself up and addressed Thomas like a contentious courtier. He laughed. I wouldn't admit it, but I had come to like the sound. I hadn't heard anything like it in so long.

"I'd like to strike a deal with you, Calandra," he crooned. "Feed me, and I will endeavor to be good company."

"Endeavor?" I replied. "That's the emptiest offer I've ever heard."

He laughed again. "The choice is yours."

"I believe we've established I have the upper hand in this situation."

"Very well." Thomas prowled towards me, every word slow and smooth. As he drew close, his nostrils flared, and he ran his tongue along his upper teeth. "Is there something else I can offer you? Humans have certain needs, don't they?"

He reached out and ran his fingertips down my arm. I perceived the passage of every hair and stiffened. It had been so long since I'd had contact with another person. Contact that didn't come with the promise of excruciating pain, that is. Thomas' touch was warm, much warmer than I expected. It felt as if flowers might grow in the wake of the sunlight it left behind. I had never been overly fond of touching other people in my old life, and most people would never have taken such freedom given my position, but circumstances had altered everything.

Circumstances always matter, my parents had always said. The other half of that advice from them went, *Because there's already too much pain in the world.*

I knew what Thomas had meant. I don't know why he automatically assumed that's what humans needed most, nor did I care. I wasn't interested in it. My needs, as he called them, were much simpler.

"I just want this," I said, my voice barely louder than a breath.

I wrapped my arms around his midsection, resting my head on his chest. A moment later, Thomas wrapped his arms around my shoulders. It felt stilted and awkward, but I didn't care.

Stars, I had missed the companionship of other people.

After I ended our hug, we sat down together in a corner of the cell. He fed from my wrist as I sat leaned up against him, only enough to restore his strength and stave off bestial insanity. To my surprise, he didn't throw me from him as soon as he finished, which I'd fully expected. We hadn't established specific parameters for our agreement, after all. Neither of us moved all night.

"What happened to not giving Nicodemus what he wants?" I asked, examining the fresh pinprick wounds on my wrist.

Thomas was leaning his head back against the wall with his eyes closed. He already had more color in his face. "I don't like it. He's going to be insufferable, but I don't want to lose my senses. And I need my strength to escape."

"Escape?" I blurted. "How—"

"It's going to happen," he interrupted, snapping his gaze to me. "Keep your eyes open."

I didn't believe him, and we didn't speak again until dawn drew close.

"I have something to teach you," he whispered. "Close your eyes and listen."

I obeyed. As Thomas continued, he picked up my hands in his and softly stroked them.

"The dawn sings a song. It grows louder as it draws near. Right now, it's a whisper." Barely making contact, he drew a fingertip across my knuckles. "A feather against the skin. Can you feel the sound move around us?"

I tried to focus, to hear what Thomas spoke of. For a moment I thought I did, but it was gone in the next. It might have been naught but my imagination.

"Don't force it," he said. "Just listen, and it will come to you."

~Chapter 7~

"Your blood tastes like metal and smoke."

Thomas made a face as he licked the latest wound clean. It was a hard-fought battle to get him to mop up after himself, but I'd won in the end after resorting to puerile insults and calling him a sloppy barbarian.

"Then don't eat so soon after I transform," I told him. "Wait until the middle of the night."

"I'm hungry!" Thomas snarled.

"You're always hungry," I said, rolling my eyes.

He hissed at me.

It was pointless to hide the truth from Nicodemus. Thomas' bites left marks, and he looked healthier. Well, he no longer appeared on the brink of starvation anyway. Nicodemus didn't seem to care much, save for what information we could share with him.

"It's foul," had been Thomas' description of my blood when Nicodemus asked. "I shouldn't be surprised. You spoil everything you touch."

"How well I know," Nicodemus leered.

I refused to meet his eyes. I didn't care that he had been the first man I'd bedded. That meant nothing to me, though Nicodemus seemed to think it did. I hated the superiority in his gaze, the unshakable knowledge that he held me entirely at his mercy. And I still feared what new horrors he might decide to inflict on me, even though it meant contending with my cellmate now. He hadn't taken me out since Thomas had been delivered.

Despite my bargain with the churlish Vampyre and the strength it gave him, we'd decided to remain as submissive to

Nicodemus as we could stand—a far easier task for me than for him. Thomas didn't want to endanger himself, and I didn't want to risk losing the only companion I'd had for who knows how long, no matter his arrogance and selfishness. Thomas continued to speak of escape when we were alone.

"We need to lull him into a false sense of security," Thomas said. "Give it enough time. The puffed-up meat sack will eventually convince himself of victory."

While I agreed it would be an effective tactic in other circumstances, it wouldn't work here. Not with Nicodemus.

Despite his original offer, I didn't expect Thomas to be anything like good company. And he often wasn't. He sometimes managed it, however, when slagging off our jailor. He wheedled me again and again into joining him.

"I particularly like the way that one struts around like a peacock invited to a party," was one of Thomas' earliest gibes.

"You don't need to invite peacocks to parties," I chuckled. "They'll show up anywhere there's food."

Thomas laughed his warm honey laugh and replied, "You speak as if you have experience."

I stopped cold and looked away. This was too familiar a scene. This was how Nicodemus had tricked me, by pulling small anecdotes and yarns of information from me, little by little. I was now all too familiar with the power of knowledge—even something as silly as the peacocks our family had been given as gifts—and I refused to give a reply. Thomas looked away from me and continued as if my sudden and obvious retreat hadn't happened.

"That seems an apt description, doesn't it? Parading about and sucking whatever he can from others. The leech."

I couldn't control my expression at his ironic choice of words. He looked back to me as my features scrunched up into the facial representation of a question mark.

"Yes?" he drawled.

"Leeches drink blood," I ventured. As I spoke, a smile crept back onto my face. "That's quite a statement for *you* to make."

Thomas shrugged and said, "I cannot help what I need to survive. He is the true parasite."

I found myself nodding, unable to help agreeing with him.

Another night, one of his less charming ones, Thomas gazed at the walls outside of our cage. In this little hideaway, Nicodemus had framed and hung various proclamations and publications praising his anonymously published work. The gallery also displayed carefully drawn diagrams of my own skeleton and other body parts. I had long ago learned to avoid looking at them, but I could not help noticing the way Thomas' eyes flicked from the walls to me and back again.

"This is all you, isn't it? The thing you said about how he cut pieces of you away," Thomas mused, gesturing towards the collection. He flapped his hand towards the world beyond. "And all that. So much of what they've learned, that's all you as well."

I swallowed hard, my eyes burning, and said nothing. Thomas appeared not to notice and continued.

"He is a gruesome degenerate, isn't he? It's a wonder people like him don't bathe in the filth they're made from." He turned back towards me and asked smoothly, "Don't you agree?"

I couldn't answer him. It was hard enough containing the sobs choking my throat. From the corner of my eyes, I saw his narrow.

"Don't you dare start crying," he growled. "Not over that cretin." He waited, and I felt certain he saw my throat tighten further as his eyes examined me. He didn't soften, yet something shifted in his tone. "Don't misunderstand me, Calandra. I do not mean all of this is your fault. You are not to blame for anyone else's actions." His voice grew rough again. "You are, however, in control of your reactions to them."

I knitted my brows together and turned to face him. "You've killed people, haven't you?"

"Yes." He said it without an ounce of remorse.

"Then how can you say that to me?"

Thomas shrugged. "I do what I must to survive. I admit it's easier to keep a victim alive than kill them off, but should I take a life, I don't blame anyone for seeking vengeance. Not that I'd let them succeed, of course."

"Have you ever considered striking a deal with them like you have me?"

Thomas made a derisive noise in his throat. "Please. Humans are cattle. I made my bargain with you because I had to."

I grimaced and began to turn away again, shaking my head.

"Do you know what I was before I was turned?" Thomas asked. He continued without waiting for an answer. "I was a servant to a minor lord. He had a handful of favorites, all young boys, like me. We lived well as long as we never told our master no. That is, until we had the nerve to grow into young men. He acted as if we did it to spite him. After that, we were whipped for the slightest infraction, or if our master was in a bad mood. I believed down to my core it was my fault. Surely, I had done something to deserve everything that happened to me. And I wasn't good or strong or brave enough to stop it."

I gaped at Thomas. His countenance was cool as he blinked back at me.

"Who?" I demanded, as if the last few centuries had not occurred. "I want his name. Right now!"

A smile split across Thomas' face, and he laughed again. "Long dead and gone. By my own hand, I'm pleased to say. The night I was turned was the best of my entire life. My maker, a Vampyress called Flora, must have possessed some inherent maternal instincts because, when she learned of what had been done to me, she told me what I just told you. And she encouraged me to take revenge."

As Thomas spoke, he grinned. His fangs gleamed in the low magelight, which perpetually glowed from sconces throughout the room.

I barely registered his explanation. In the back of my mind, in a twisted sort of way, I appreciated what she, his maker, had done for Thomas. And a tiny part of my heart, possibly the darkest and most ruined bit, envied the escape he had found, but my focus was still on his old master. Fury so consumed me, I could barely form words. "What a ghastly… inhuman… to abuse someone so… I… how dare he?!"

"To shred and mutilate another's sense of self? To tear down their very soul? How dare anyone, indeed?" he replied, cocking an eyebrow at me.

I hesitated for a few moments, grasping for the right words. There were no right words, however, so I just said, "I'm sorry for what he did to you. Truly, I am."

"As am I," Thomas replied.

)(

"How was he in the bedroom?" Thomas asked after Nicodemus had left us one particular night.

There was a time I would have scrunched up my face and reproved the gall of such a question. After everything I had endured, however, it felt like I spoke of someone else's life.

"Mild," I replied. "Have you ever seen the sea with no waves? That's what it was like."

"Ugh. That sounds terrible," he replied.

I cackled, and he laughed with me. We often cheered one another with talk like this now, badmouthing our captor and even plotting ideas for escape and what to do after. I had picked up on the way Thomas always encouraged it in me, pouring whatever charisma he possessed into the effort. He didn't complain about the taste of my blood as much now either, but his face still showed what he thought of it.

We exchanged information over time. After Thomas' admission, I opened up to him. No more than a crack at first, but it grew over time. Nicodemus had never shared anything so deep with me. Every tale he'd spun had been, at worst, mildly embarrassing. Thomas, however, seemed to let go of any remaining inhibitions after that night. He didn't apologize for his past actions, no matter how brutal, and I was often reminded how differently we saw the world. And yet, I appreciated his honesty, dark as it was.

Thomas told me more about what the world had become before he'd been captured. I told him what I knew about magi spreading their power via their progenies, and he one-upped me. Even the reigning queen was now a magus, as was nearly every other Pendragon.

I told Thomas every detail I knew about Nicodemus' strange ritual. He had never heard of such a thing, which didn't surprise me. Nicodemus had admitted to me he cobbled it together from different places and creatures. Thomas peppered me with follow-up questions. It didn't matter that I didn't know the answers because he soon saw it for himself. Nicodemus continued to take his victims in his private chambers.

"Does anyone know you're here?" he asked his guest. It was very early in the morning, before the sun had even risen.

The middle-aged man was stout with thick, curly, dark hair and fair skin. He ran his eyes over every curtain, tapestry, and stick of furniture appraisingly. There were no Phenixes left, but plenty of skulls, complete skeletons, petrified dragon eggs on plinths, and taxidermied animals decorated Nicodemus' chambers now.

"Of course not," the visitor said at last. "I told my wife I'm heading to Duskwood for business. I'll just be delayed on the road a few days. She's not happy about it. We're trying for a child, you understand. You?"

"Officially, I'm on a hunting trip," Nicodemus replied with a smile. "I'm seeking the last of the Gryphons. We're starting a breeding program, you know. Your Lady Thorne should come see our work."

"Indeed." Thorne pulled a pipe from his jacket and began to stuff it. He said nothing as he lit it and took a few puffs. Closing his eyes, he sighed. "Apologies. I get agitated rather easily without my herbs. It's a shame we can't do this elsewhere. Your wards give me a headache. It feels like the void is screaming at me."

Thomas and I shouted and banged louder.

"Apologies. I've had to increase security, as you're well aware."

"Of course. The rebels have agents everywhere. Stars, it is bad in here, though."

We increased our efforts.

"Allow me to make you some tea," Nicodemus offered.

"Please. The sooner the better."

Even after tea, Thorne wasn't in a stupor like the others had been. He was close, but still had enough of his faculties to know something wasn't right. He tried to stand, but Nicodemus knocked him back into his chair with an effortless gust of wind. He gagged Thorne and bound his hands quickly. The man's limbs may have been enfeebled, but his eyes blazed with rage.

"I really don't like doing it this way," Nicodemus rasped.

Nevertheless, he dragged Thorne's chair into the alcove and secured the concealed door behind him. Thorne's eyes nearly bugged out of his head when he saw Thomas and me. Nicodemus ignored the man's weak but increasingly panicked efforts and progressed with the ritual. Thomas' mouth hung agape as he watched. I had seen this process close to a dozen times now. I still cried out for Nicodemus to stop, but my voice lacked the fervor it used to command. I saw the inevitable coming. The sun rose near the end of the ritual, and Thomas stumbled back into our cell, overcome with exhaustion. He collapsed into a heap on the floor, his eyes on Nicodemus hovering over Thorne's form. After it was done, Nicodemus grinned too broadly at me. As a bird, I flapped and croaked furiously at him.

"Lady Thorne is my first wife since you, Calandra. Let me assure you, she's a vast improvement. I shall enjoy helping her achieve her maternal goals."

For possibly the first time ever, I was glad to be unable to answer him.

~Chapter 8~

"It's in the blood," Thomas told me the night after Nicodemus had possessed Thorne's body. "I can always tell when I'm feeding on someone with magic. The blood is the key to his power. I just don't know how he makes it… transfer like that. And you said he keeps his older powers, yes?"

I nodded. My mind was elsewhere. I had seen this too many times to be shocked anymore.

"What do you know of the Allen clan, the heads of Bone Port and Bone Bay County?" I asked, changing the subject.

"I'm not terribly familiar with them," he replied. "It has been many years since I roamed so far south. It's so bright!"

"Is that the only reason we had less of a Vampyre problem than the other counties?" I asked this more to myself, curious I had never considered the possibility.

"That's where you're from then, Bone Port," Thomas surmised.

I nodded. His eyes narrowed, examining me.

"The Allens are your family, aren't they?"

I nodded again and took a deep, steadying breath.

"I can see the hurt in your eyes," Thomas said, lifting my wrist to his lips. "Will you tell me why?"

I knew this subject would always pain me, but I had discovered sharing with Thomas often lifted an invisible weight from my shoulders. He never judged me, never told me I had been stupid or cowardly. He didn't call me weak or pathetic like he had when we'd first met. In fact, he hadn't insulted me like that since we'd struck our bargain. In addition, talking served as a good way to fill the time while he fed.

“Because they think I went mad and killed my best friend and then myself,” I explained softly. “Nicodemus took on my Uncle Ducky’s appearance and lied to them while I sat tethered to a post in the room. I watched as they crumbled, and I could do nothing.”

I allowed myself to cry as I told my tale, something else I had begun to let go of during my time with Thomas. He scowled at me, but I told him I cried for my family. After he finished, he spoke in shockingly casual tones.

“Well, the taste of your sorrow does a halfway decent job of masking the sourness of the enchantment.”

I slapped him as hard as I could across the face. It barely fazed him.

“How dare you feed off my grief!”

Thomas stared back at me, his face an inscrutable mask. We didn’t speak again that night, or for several nights after. I refused to even touch him. Nicodemus noticed and ordered him to feed on me.

“I paid a pretty price for you, wretch!” he snarled at Thomas. “Do as I say or suffer.”

Nicodemus waved the familiar baton at Thomas.

Thomas narrowed his eyes at Nicodemus. “You didn’t care before. Why now?”

“Do not presume to question me!” Nicodemus shrieked, spittle flying from his mouth.

There shone a mad gleam in Nicodemus’ eye. I’d never seen him like this, not throughout all the years I’d been his prisoner or all the bodies he’d possessed. Despite our argument, I took Thomas by the elbow and tried to pull him back. His eyes flicked to me, and he curled his lips back, exposing his fangs. Before I could blink, Thomas darted behind me and gripped me by the hair. I drove my elbow back before I knew what was happening. It was like hitting a statue. Then he scuttled us to the back of the cage.

“Do it and I tear her head off!” Thomas barked.

I stopped fighting. Had the time finally come? Might I finally receive release?

“You wouldn’t dare,” Nicodemus hissed.

A slick of dark oil sounded through the dim air. Thomas purred, “Wouldn’t I, though? Your only link to actual immortality gone. Wouldn't that be delicious? You are a petty thief. Nothing more."

Nicodemus growled and ripped our cell's key from within his jacket. He wrenched the door open and ran for Thomas. I stood dumbfounded. How could he be so stupid after so many years of caution? Thomas was ready, however. He threw me from him and leapt for Nicodemus. Nicodemus already held the lightning rod before him. As soon as the tip touched Thomas, light exploded, and Thomas screamed.

The door hung open.

I ran for it.

I was through!

Another shriek rang out, and I stopped. Something heavy, a petrified dragon egg, found its way into my hand. My mind screamed at me to turn around, not to go back, but I was already there. I thrust the egg towards the back of Nicodemus' head. It struck a glancing blow, but it was enough. He stumbled to his knees and dropped the rod. I grabbed it.

"You useless wretch!" he shrieked, tackling me.

"GET OFF!" I screeched.

With that thought, the rod attacked again. A bolt of blue-white energy sent Nicodemus flying against the wall. I crawled over to Thomas. He laid still, and Vampyres don't breathe like humans.

"On your feet or rot here!" I rasped in his ear.

Thomas groaned and managed to push himself up. He hung on me heavily as we got to our feet. Nicodemus wasn't moving. I didn't know where the key was—probably somewhere in the cell with us—but I slammed the door shut anyway. Anything to give us time.

)(

Getting out of the Synod turned out to be easier than I expected, though every minute that passed breathed hot on our necks. Vampyres have the ability to meld into the shadows, but Thomas was too weak to execute the trick, and I had no such power. We padded through hallways, stealing into darkened corners at every strange noise. It felt as if an age passed from one turning to the next. The lights were low, which was a blessing, but they were no longer powered by flame as they had been when I'd last walked these halls. Nor were they magelights. The energy within the lamps buzzed low, and I failed to discover how they could be turned down further. Thank the heavens the manor's layout had not changed since Ducky's day. The rooms had been renovated, of course, but her frame remained the same. It took an incredible feat of self-control not to hurtle through the doors and across the grounds once we'd reached them.

My first sight of the rolling hills of the Southern Plains stretching out underneath an inky blanket of darkness and stars almost brought me to my knees, but fear drove me on. We made our way out during the small hours of the night when nearly everyone slept. Nicodemus was either still contained, unconscious, or had decided against raising an alarm. I wondered about the last one. He could easily call for a chase after Thomas, but I was harder to explain, doubly so once dawn came.

The thought of morning light brought tears to my eyes. I would be able to *fly*! I could go anywhere. Bone Port? Across the sea even? I was nearly paralyzed by the possibilities.

"I have to find shelter," Thomas croaked next to me.

He still couldn't walk without assistance. Otherwise, I suspected he would have been long gone. He might have even drained me and left me to my fate. As it was, he seemed to have other priorities.

"I'm leaving as soon as we find some," I told him.

He grunted. I didn't know what it meant, nor did I care. Dawn drew closer. I could feel it, having learned to sense its approaching song from Thomas' lessons. Plains stretched all around us, and I reached back into my memories. Back in my hunting days with Ducky, bears had kept dens in a rocky gully near the river. Just as the sky began to lighten, promising death for Thomas, we spotted a crumbling outcropping that indicated one of the small caves. It wasn't what I remembered. Time and the elements had beaten it down, but we scrabbled our way through the rubble and crawled down into the tunnel. Once Thomas was out of the reach of the encroaching sun, I turned to go. He grabbed my arm.

"Wait. I need to feed."

I ripped my arm away. "I am not your personal wineskin."

He reached to grab me again but hesitated. Drawing back, he said, "Please. I know you're angry. That… damnable weapon."

He gestured angrily at the rod still gripped in my hand. I hadn't let it go for a moment. The pommel gem barely glowed in our dark recess. I sighed. I would need my strength, but so would he.

"It's close to dawn. You won't like it," I sniped.

"I don't care, Calandra. Please."

I growled and thrust my wrist at him. I was already exhausted, so some rest before taking off would do me good. From the tethered flights I'd been granted as Nicodemus' prisoner, I knew how much energy it took.

"We're free from him now," Thomas said before sinking his teeth into my flesh with relish.

Hope bloomed in me. It bubbled up inside my chest and erupted from my throat, a spring of laughter and tears.

"You're right," I agreed.

After he finished eating—I let him take a little extra, knowing I would heal in my raven form—he smiled at me, licking the blood from his lips.

"As you'll be gone by the time I wake, tell me where you plan on going," he said.

"South," I replied. "I ache for my home. Perhaps I'll travel to the land of my father's family, the Arnavi."

"That suits you. The color is already returning to your face." Thomas reached out and poked a playful fingertip into my cheek. He pulled away and said more gently, "I'm sorry for exploiting your pain. Sometimes I forget there are other ways to go about getting what I want."

I smirked at him. "Yes, there are. You could have asked nicely."

He chuckled and nodded, settling down onto the rocky ground. "Sleep tight, Calandra."

"You as well, Thomas."

)(

I awoke to the sound of rocks being pulled away from where we had shored them up against the entrance. The lightning rod sat next to me, about as long as my whole body now. Whispered voices echoed off the walls. With my raven eyes, I saw dim light shining against the stone walls further up the tunnel. Then came the shadows. I cawed and flapped against Thomas. He was senseless, still trapped in his death-sleep. I had never woken him during the day, and I frantically wondered if it wasn't actually possible. Had he just been posturing for Nicodemus? I swore internally and took off. From a lack of practice, I was not terribly good at flying, but thank the heavens I didn't need to be. I darted towards the dim figures, cawing at the top of my lungs with talons outstretched.

"Ach! Bat!" someone yelped, swatting at their head.

I was already gone but having trouble with turning in the narrow space. I cawed again as I landed.

"You idiot," someone else said. "It's just a bloody crow."

I objected loudly and took flight again. I swept low, buzzing the heads I could maneuver around. They batted at me. I managed to nearly avoid a collision. Someone produced a ball of magelight. It flashed orange and bright, temporarily blinding me. In the most ungraceful move in avian history, I hit the wall and tumbled to the floor. The group pressed on. One of them trod on my wing, breaking it. They jumped in surprise but restrained another yelp.

"Come on!" I heard over my squawks of pain. "The sun's nearly down. It'll be awake soon."

My cries of alarm increased. If they dragged Thomas out into the sunlight… I hopped down the tunnel, crying protestations the whole way.

"What is wrong with that bird?" someone asked.

No one else seemed much fussed by my unnatural behavior. When I arrived at our hiding place, the interlopers were hauling Thomas to his feet. I hopped around them, pecking at ankles and croaking my little heart out.

"Grab that blasted bird!" someone snapped.

I tried to retreat, but my broken wing slowed me. Hands grabbed me, and I cried out in pain as they crushed my wing the wrong way. I watched helplessly as they dragged Thomas from the cave.

Hurry up! I urged the setting sun.

Evening hummed through me. She was preparing to sing her symphony of freedom, but we weren't there yet. I nipped at my captor's hands, and they dropped me with an ugly curse. My wing was already mending—I could feel the bones snapping back into place and tendons stitching themselves back together—but fire still shot through me as I made a mad attempt to fly towards one of those dragging Thomas. They kept a hold of him as they stopped to swat at me.

"What did I say about that damn bird?!" came the voice from before. I guessed this was the one in charge.

Don't! I croaked uselessly. *Please! Stop!*

We neared the mouth of the cave. I shot for it, wheeled around in the open air, and zipped back talons first. A magus, the one with the light, led the party from the tunnel. I screeched angrily, and my talons struck a direct hit to her face. She cried out and stumbled, blocking the rest of her group. I landed nearby, no longer able to stand the throbbing in my wing.

"Holly, what's wrong?" came the leader's voice.

I saw him emerge with some difficulty around the magus.

"The crow, it attacked me," Holly replied. "Ed, I think it's protecting the Vampyre."

"Do Vampyres keep familiars?" the one called Ed asked.

"No…" Holly began.

She trailed off as she looked towards me again. She didn't seem to notice the blood trailing down from her forehead, and I regretted not hitting her eyes. Evening finally sang her song. She crooned comfort to me as the waking moon provided low, mellow notes behind her. I felt night's warm caress wrap around me, streaming relief into my arm, but my eyes remained on the cave. In a few moments, Thomas would wake. I rolled my shoulder to ease the residual ache out of my now-healed arm.

"Leave now if you want to live," I said, trying to sound menacing.

A commotion broke out behind Holly and Ed. They both leapt away from the cave mouth. Light flashed from within, and I realized I'd left my only weapon inside the tunnel. Two more people scrabbled out. Someone screamed. The group drew things I didn't recognize but which were undeniably weapons.

“Don’t!” I cried, all bravado gone. “Don’t hurt him!”

Thomas emerged. Blood covered the front of his dirty clothes and dripped from his mouth. I screamed again in his defense, running towards him. I crossed the line the interlopers had quickly formed. A sound like thunder exploded behind me. Something tore through my shoulder. Two more thunder cracks. I reached Thomas as blood burst from his chest. A small hole had been blasted through his flesh. Then another. I grasped his hands as he glared hate at the people around us. His skin cracked like the bark of a pine tree. He turned to burning embers and flakes of ash beneath my fingers and crumbled.

I howled and fell to my knees, raking my hands through the still-warm pile of what had been the only companion I’d had for years. I screamed again, keening to the first stars of night. Physical pain began to break through the emotional. My shoulder pulsed crimson fury at the attack. I stood again and turned, not realizing blood stained my outfit as much as it had Thomas’ shirt. I saw their weapons trained on me now, but I didn’t care. I turned my gaze onto the magus, the one called Holly.

“You people ruin everything you touch,” I snarled. “Every. Single. Thing.”

I advanced on her. She looked frightened but stood her ground. As I closed the last few strides between us, something hard knocked against my head, and blackness overcame me.

~Chapter 9~

When I awoke, I was human. Either I had been out for an entire day or it was still that same night. I kept my eyes closed at first, listening. Dawn wasn't yet singing. Blast! An entire day must have passed. But how? I remembered the previous night, Thomas' death, everything, but I pushed all emotion to the back of my mind. Doing a mental check, I found myself free of bonds. Muffled voices spoke nearby. They were arguing, but I couldn't make out any words. I assumed it was about me.

I opened my eyes and took in my surroundings. No bars. One door. No windows. A bed.

This last item caught my attention, but I brushed it away in the next moment. I needed to be free. I crept towards the door and found the voices were clearer here.

"What do you suggest we do?" The voice sounded like Holly's. "I will not let you lock her away."

"I wasn't suggesting that!" This second voice, if I wasn't mistaken, was Ed's.

"Then what *are* you suggesting?"

"I don't know!"

"Very helpful!"

The argument slowed and deteriorated from there. They were at an impasse. I considered waiting, but I would be vulnerable come dawn. Granted, the room was large and contained furniture for me to perch on but, should my captors desire to catch me, it would be an easy job. Better to face my fate now when I had some modicum of power. I scanned for potential weapons, but only furniture stared back at me. No books, no ornaments, nothing I could conceal behind my back. Taking a deep breath, I turned the doorknob and was surprised to find it unlocked.

The room that greeted me was large, with a long table in the center and several bookshelves lining the walls. Everything within the room looked to be in the midst of transition, with papers, books, pens, and other odds and ends scattered all around. As I suspected, Holly and Ed were there, as well as one of the others from the previous night's party. All three turned towards me. I was glad the table separated us.

"You're awake," Holly said. She managed a half smile. "I'm pleased. I worried we had damaged you." Her eyes shot towards Ed, annoyance flickering in them.

I scowled at her. Filthy magus. I saw the way her eyes returned to me, roving over my shoulder. I felt certain she'd sell her soul to know how I had healed so quickly.

After an awkward silence, Ed spoke. "We have questions for you. It will be easier if you answer them directly."

"Ed," Holly scolded.

They exchanged a heated look, but he did not relent. I logged this away.

"Would you like to have a seat?" Ed asked, motioning towards a chair.

I shook my head.

"Are you hungry?" Holly asked.

Her eyes rolled over me again. I hadn't seen myself in a mirror in more years than I knew and had no idea what I looked like. I knew my hair remained tidy, though it had lost its old bounce. When I'd looked at my hands previously, they'd looked thin, almost skeletal, even when Nicodemus had remembered to feed me regularly. The saving grace with my ragged clothes had been that they were comprised of several layers. Though the fabric appropriately covered me, it was stained all over with blood and grime.

I shook my head again. My stomach twisted angrily at that, but I had learned to ignore such things.

"Very well. You will not sit and you will not eat," Ed said. "I'll take that to mean you'd like to get straight to answering our questions. Let's start with something simple: what is your name?"

I glared at him.

He looked back coolly. "We're not going to get anywhere this way."

"Release me," I said at last. "You have no right to cage me."

"You're right," Holly replied. I looked to her, and she added, "We don't."

"Then let me go," I rasped.

"We need help," Ed said.

I hissed at him, thinking of Thomas. It was a habit I'd picked up from him. "You killed my friend!"

"Your fri—" Ed began, clearly surprised by my choice of words.

"Without a second thought," I continued. "You people are all the same. Arrogant and cruel. I wish the earth would open up and swallow you all."

"When you say 'you people,' who do you mean?" Ed asked.

"Magi!" I spat. I opened my mouth to spew more curses but wasn't fast enough.

"We agree then," he said. "Present company excluded."

I took a step back. This was not the response I'd expected. I looked at them, not understanding. As they watched me, their expressions twinned my own.

"I really do think we should talk," Ed said at last. "Jones, will you order us some tea, please?"

I looked to the third person. I had barely given her a second glance before.

She had a strange look about her. Her hair was cut short, shorter than any woman would have dared in my day. And she was huskily built. As I looked at her, her strangeness made itself clear to me. She looked like Ducky. Not a doppelgänger, no. It was subtle. The line of the nose, the tilt of the eyes. Then she smiled at me. It nearly knocked me back another step. That was Ducky's smile.

)(

They explained to me we were in a private sector of the building. Good. Because what we said to one another wasn't easy. I began by demanding to know more about Jones.

"Captain Agatha Jones of the Lamplighters, rebel scum, at your service," she said, giving me a salute. "Please don't call me by my first name. Seriously."

"Jones!" barked Ed.

"Oops, how terribly irresponsible of me," Jones replied flatly. Turning back to me, she added, "There's another long, boring title in there: Lady something-something of this random scrap of land, but it's a bother to use. You understand."

"Are you… are you related to Richard Jones, former Duke of the Southern Reaches?" I asked.

"I think it's time you answered a few of our questions," Ed broke in.

I curled my lip at him, but he was unimpressed. I wanted, needed, to know more about Jones, but Ed stood firm, demanding answers for answers.

The following conversation was strange, to say the least. Even with what Thomas had told me, I had trouble wrapping my head around this new world. Holly, Ed, and Jones seemed to have an even harder time understanding me.

"It is the two-hundred-and-thirty-second year of the Fifth Age," Ed told me.

Almost four hundred years. That's how long it had been.

"This Nicodemus is alive? Inhabiting Grand Magus Thorne's body?" Holly asked.

"And you've been his prisoner?" Jones added. "Calandra. Of Bone Port."

I nodded as bile rose in my throat. I knew I had been imprisoned for generations, but the number… stars, how had I remained sane? Jones broke in again, steering us in a different direction.

"Richard Jones was my great-great… I don't know how many greats uncle. Lady Catherine was his sister and my many-greats grandmother," Jones told me.

Once the telling began, it was difficult to stop, as each answer bred a dozen more questions. I sifted through what I had already learned and looked around at Holly, Ed, and Jones. A memory niggled at me, insisting I address it.

"Rebel scum," I mused.

Ed shot another look at Jones, who smirked at me.

"What does that mean? Rebels against what exactly?"

Ed sighed and rubbed his face, out of tiredness or frustration I didn't know. "The magi. We mean to dismantle their rule over Invarnis and restore equality."

)(

"Dawn is nearly here," I said.

We'd talked all night. I eventually had to just let the information wash over me, as I simply couldn't process any more. When I made my sudden declaration, the others looked around the windowless room.

"How can you tell?" Holly asked.

I narrowed my eyes at her.

"The transformation," she answered for herself. "We've observed it in you twice now."

I was content to let her believe whatever she liked about that.

"We can help one another," Ed said. "You know our enemy better than anyone. Stay here for another day. See what we're doing. Consider joining us. If by tomorrow evening you still want to leave, we won't hold you."

I glowered at him. They all watched raptly as I changed again.

All six eyes remained glued to me, barely blinking as I shrunk, as my fingers and toes elongated, and my skin sprouted ebony feathers. Even though they had observed the process before, the wonder was not lost on them now. None of them outright gaped, but their eyes grew wide, and their eyebrows lifted and furrowed into different configurations.

"Can you still understand us?" Jones asked.

I bobbed my head in assent.

"We'll have more food brought up," Holly said. I hadn't partaken of the tea Jones had ordered. "And new clothes. It's all yours if you want it, no strings attached."

I ate after Ed and Holly left. Jones stayed behind to watch me. She chatted idly about herself a little, which pleased me, even if I didn't learn anything else of consequence. From what she said, it didn't seem she knew what Ducky had been to me. Then again, I had only shared my first name. The thought pulled my heart into my stomach. It had been such a long time since Ducky had named me his heir, and I had never actually held the role. The idea that Nicodemus might have blotted me out from all history was yet another blow, one I had never considered.

Partway through the day, someone came to relieve Jones of her post. It was the other member of their party from the night before. I remembered five in total, though I assumed Thomas had killed one, given the blood and screams. I had learned from our discussion they had been scouting the area, though none of them would tell me why. Near the end of the day, they'd seen the evidence of someone having moved the rocks around our cave entrance. Holly had sensed magic, both my enchantment and that which made Thomas what he was, and they'd decided to investigate. The newcomer eyed me like he was considering hurling me against the wall.

Joke's on him, I thought darkly.

I watched as Jones pulled him aside.

"Not her fault," I heard her say. "Vampyres… I'm sorry." She turned back to me and said, "Calandra, this is Flynn. He'll be… he'll be here with you until nightfall." She looked around and walked to the table. Plucking a drawing charcoal from it, she said, "If you need anything, write it on the wall. Or paper, whatever's easiest for you."

"Jones, what are you—"

"Relax. If Holly or Ed are angry about graffiti, I'll take the heat."

Flynn's face turned into a series of unhappy lines, arching across his forehead, beneath his nose, and along his mouth, but he said nothing more. I fluttered over and grabbed the charcoal before flitting up to perch on top of a sconce.

Flynn kept throwing me ugly looks throughout the rest of the day, and I stayed as far away from him as I could. During this time, I remembered the lightning rod I had stolen from Nicodemus. I scanned the room for it and flew into the bedroom to search too. No luck. That would be my test. If I asked for it that night and they refused, I would know my captors' true intentions.

)(

"It's a powerful weapon," Ed said. "Being able to replicate it would help our efforts enormously."

"But it isn't ours to keep," Holly argued. Her voice grew soft when she addressed me again. "Of course you may have it back."

Ed looked like he wanted to disagree but said nothing. Holly drew the rod from her robes, and I started back. She slowed and placed it gently on the table next to us before stepping away. I snatched it up, deciding I'd figure out where to store it later.

"Calandra, would you like a tour of our base?" Jones asked. She had returned with Holly and Ed. "Perhaps it would be helpful for you to see everything."

She smiled at me again, and it made me want to cry. I agreed, stuffing my feelings down. I wasn't about to refuse such an opportunity. She led the way out of my rooms, around a few corners, and into a world both alien and familiar. Two steps from the side door we had exited through, I froze.

"We're in Bone Port," I breathed.

I inhaled deeply, savoring the salty air tickling my nose. I pricked up my ears, listening carefully for the dull roar my heart knew so well. When I heard it, it was as if I could soar on wings again. My feet flew beneath me, my arms pumping wildly. Tears blurred my vision as the ocean came into view. Distantly, somewhere back in a place that didn't matter, I heard Jones calling after me, but nothing could stop me now. The constant shush of the waves, masked behind wards and walls before, made my heart ache. I careened into the surf, laughing and crying as the briny mix splashed into my mouth and eyes. I tread water, letting another wave roll over me, and I knew I would never be happier than I was in this moment. I don't know how much time passed as I kicked and swam and twirled like a dolphin, still laughing, but the euphoria eventually began to fade. I looked back and saw Jones standing on the shore. I swam back to her as a new feeling rushed in to replace my joy, threatening to drown me in it and the water. Back on the sand, with the tide lapping at my toes, it was as if an undertow ripped my feet out from under me. I collapsed onto hands and knees and wept.

"I'm sorry," Jones said, crouching next to me. "Calandra, I'm so sorry. I-I thought you'd be happy. I thought you were, at first."

I nodded, tried to explain myself, but it came out confused. Jones remained beside me until I collected myself.

"I am," I croaked at last. "Truly. Thank you."

Jones smiled. "Would you like to see the rest?"

I nodded and took a steadying breath.

)(

The shore, of course, had changed. It changes moment to moment, but the sand beneath my feet welcomed me like an old friend. The water waved exuberantly as if it knew I had returned. I could tell even from this distance the Green Dragon had grown larger since my day. The basalt cliffs had different shapes protruding than I remembered, but they were as tall and proud as ever.

We—me, the Lamplighters, and more—were housed in a long, low building that hadn't existed during my time. A basic shipping business served as the front. Clever considering the amount of trade Bone Port did both domestically and internationally. Jones explained the building had originally been the city infirmary, but that had been moved to a smaller structure given improved healing techniques.

"I'm not a terribly good student of history," Jones explained, "but your medical technology wasn't very advanced, was it?"

I didn't know how to answer given my lack of knowledge about current times. Instead, I explained, "We had apothecaries and physicians. They came to our homes, however. We didn't stuff our sick in a building to die."

"We don't either," Jones said. "Only those in serious need stay there. Shall I show you?"

I wasn't certain I wanted to see ailing people but, feeling rather curious, I agreed. What met us there can, even to this day, only be described as miraculous.

Machines were powered not just by the wind and motion of the surf, as they had been in my day, but by something Jones called electricity, and some of the former created the latter. This electrical energy transferred to more complex instruments, though the snag laid in the fact that only magi could move the energy, pushing it through tubes to where it could be used. At least, that was how

Jones described it after several failed attempts to make me understand in greater detail. In the infirmary, this energy powered devices that provided light like what I had seen whilst escaping Ducky's manor, captured images of patients' innards, and could even restart a stopped heart. Procedures had been developed to remove either partial or whole healthy organs from the living and the dead to replace failing ones within others. Apothecarism had advanced alongside these, and learning was encouraged with open surgery theaters and free education. On top of it all, magi of varying power levels used their powers to heal patients.

Given it was proper night now, things were quiet, and Jones and I could talk openly.

"Perhaps we can find a cure for your… condition," Jones suggested as we strolled through the corridors of the infirmary.

The thought of those magi healers coming anywhere near me made me recoil, but my mind wondered at the possibility.

"Then again, Ed thinks you have an advantage," she added, thinking to herself.

My head whipped around. "What advantage?"

"Not like that," Jones said, her eyes soaking up every detail of my posture. "He just mentioned how you can infiltrate areas we can't. As a bird, I mean. I think he'd like you to work as a spy."

"I won't be used by anyone. Not again. Not ever!"

I turned my feet towards the direction we had come, but Jones stopped me with her next words. "Paid position. Voluntary. Not a prisoner."

"What's to stop him from detaining me?" I shot at her.

"Me and Holly," she said. The softness in her eyes was too familiar, and I looked away as she continued. "We've already told him we won't let him. We won't let ourselves be like *them*."

"I still don't understand," I confessed. "How can you resist the magi and yet work with them? How can you live openly here?"

Jones smirked. "Because they don't know who we are. We operate in broad daylight under various business covers. Prince Godric assists where he can, but he has his own deceptions to maintain. His mother, Irene number two, is as shrewd as her mother."

I recognized the second name. Thomas had told me about the royal family. The Pendragons still reigned, and Irene the First had been fourth in line, no more than a babe, when Thomas had been out in the world. I could imagine something of what had happened.

"There was an uprising about fifty years ago," Jones explained. "It was put down but left behind remnants. Since then, some edicts have been passed. Just enough to make people feel like they're being listened to. It's not as bad here. The… culture's different." She spun her finger in the air to indicate the local populace. "These folks don't put up with being pushed around as much. It's worst in the midlands."

I couldn't help but smile to myself. The Bone Portis, my people, stubborn as ever.

"Shall we head out for a bite? I bet food tastes better this way, huh?" Jones suggested, interrupting my reverie.

I honestly hadn't considered food as anything but a means to stave off hunger pains in longer than I could remember. Even then, as seemingly free as I was, I wasn't sure of the point in enjoying food. I didn't object, though, and let Jones lead me on.

Few places were operating at such a late hour, but more than I expected.

"What's your favorite thing to eat?" Jones asked as we walked.

I didn't respond for a few moments. I remembered the names of my favorite childhood foods, but their taste was a lost memory to me.

"Is shrimp and coconut soup still made?" I asked.

Jones smiled and led me down the beach to a tiny shack. A few mismatched tables stood in front of the shabby counter.

"Have a seat," she chirped. "I'll go order."

She dashed off, and I looked around. I could run. I could free myself instead of trusting Jones and Ed and never look back. An Arnavi ship was docked in the harbor. I had seen it, already begun to formulate a plan for stowing away and hiding during the journey. I took a step.

I think he'd like you to work as a spy. Paid position. Voluntary. Not a prisoner. We won't let ourselves be like them.

Jones' words came back to me.

Freedom.

Freedom to do as I wished. Freedom to *choose*. I had options.

I didn't run. I stayed, sitting down on a stool, and waited for Jones to return.

"I don't know if it's like you remember, but I think it's pretty great in any case." She paused. "I really hope you like it. I can't imagine… everything you've… yeah."

I smiled weakly at Jones and retreated into myself. I focused on the food, taking time to enjoy it. I couldn't tell if it was like what I ate growing up. It had been too long. But it was delicious. Eating used to be a sport in my house, doubly so in Ducky's. We southerners prided ourselves on our hospitality.

"Jones," I began after I'd emptied my bowl, "who oversees the county of Bone Port and Bone Bay?"

"Countess Ciara Allen," she replied. She lowered her voice to a whisper, "We've been trying to get her on our side forever, but she's hedging her bets, staying as neutral as possible."

"Would it be possible to meet her?" I asked.

I still hadn't shared my surname, but if Jones did research, she could put the pieces together. It was possible they had already discussed my lineage. I wouldn't have put it past Ed to look up any and every mention of me still in existence, assuming Nicodemus hadn't completely wiped me from history.

"Meet her? Or *meet* her?"

"I just want to…" I didn't know how to finish the sentence.

"I bet we can arrange something," Jones said with a nod.

She seemed very confident, like getting an audience with a skittish noble was something she did every day.

~Chapter 10~

The next evening, I met with Ed, Holly, and Jones in the messy conference room again. I suspected Jones had filled them in on everything that had happened the previous night, but they behaved as if the hours between sunrise and sunset had not happened, directing questions to me instead of simply filling me in on what they already knew. It was probably a ploy to convince me to trust them, but I had to admit I appreciated the way they included me as an equal despite the daytime interruption in communication. Jones had just relayed my request to meet with the current Allen family.

"The Joneses and the Allens have always been close," Ed said, rubbing his beard as he thought. "There's even been a marriage or two somewhere in the line. It shouldn't be a problem. Jones, can you go stroke your cousins' egos tomorrow?"

"Sure thing, boss," she replied.

The event seemed feasible, almost easy, the more we talked about it. When I'd suggested it, I hadn't imagined the potential implications. As the possibility of meeting my distant family loomed, I realized that meant they might also learn who I really was… and all that entailed. An old feeling began to claw its way up my spine, a sticky darkness that made my heart beat faster and my throat tighten.

"Does this mean you're staying?" Holly asked, distracting me from my worries.

I realized I had yet to see her and Ed apart. It made me wonder, but I said nothing about it.

"I have my own goals," I replied waspishly.

"As do we all," Ed said. "Even so, you're more than welcome to stay here. You'll need to assume an alias and a cover, of course, for both day and night."

I gave him a withering look while Holly and Jones rolled their eyes in unison.

"Suspicious looking raven you've got there," Jones joked. "Let me see its identification papers!"

"Force of habit, covering all our bases," he admitted, waving his hand dismissively. "Speaking of your other form, have you considered looking in on your descendants in secret?"

"You mean spying on them?" I asked.

Ed looked to Jones, who stared back and blinked innocently at him. He turned away from her, making a noise of disgust, and she winked at me. A shadow of a smile curved across Holly's face.

Looking back to me, he pressed, "You must admit you're uniquely qualified for it."

"I shall do as I please." I wasn't about to admit my plans included doing that very thing.

"Indeed. Well, as promised, you are free to go. If you'd like to continue to reside here, Jones and Flynn can sort you out. Enjoy the rest of your evening."

He left without another word, and his sudden exit left me a little flummoxed. Was that it? I had expected him to try harder to ensure I stayed. Primed for a fight that was apparently not going to happen, I stood like a strung bowstring without an arrow. Holly lingered and looked to me, though I had no intention of paying her any mind.

"Is there anything I can do to assist with your transition?" she asked.

"No," I snapped, willing her to leave me alone.

"Truly, Calandra, I am sorry for what has happened to you. I promise, we're not all like him. I—"

I spun and jabbed a finger at her. The tightly coiled energy I'd prepared for Ed unleashed itself on her. "I don't want anything from your kind! The farther you stay from me, the better."

Holly's mouth opened and closed a few times. Finally, she nodded and left.

"She's right," Jones said after Holly had gone. "They're not all bad. Power can corrupt anyone, not just magi. And not all of them are corrupted. Plenty of that sort live down here."

"They're at the greatest risk," I growled. "It takes but a nudge to push them over the edge. You shouldn't trust her, or any of them for that matter."

"I've known Holly most of my life. In fact, I owe her my life, in more ways than one."

"And for several lifetimes, I've watched countless magi strike cruel deals and commit atrocities behind closed doors. Nicodemus would exploit every single magus' weakness if he had the time."

"Let's be glad he doesn't have the time then. Did you need a room and all that?"

I hesitated. I hadn't agreed to anything and didn't want to make commitments. I admitted to myself a chance existed, slim though it may be, that the Lamplighters could reform Invarnis. With this thought, my heart burned white-hot and furious. While I knew I could take care of basic needs such as food and bathing as a raven easily enough, rejecting their offer might mean cutting myself off from other opportunities.

"I assume I'd have to take up some kind of employment here," I said, crossing my arms over my chest.

"Of course," Jones said, flashing me a smile. "We don't tolerate freeloaders in the resistance."

I made a disgusted noise in my throat and decided to prod her, the heat from my heart and readiness to fight spurring me on. "Your resistance isn't doing much as far as I've seen."

"That's because you haven't officially joined," Jones replied. "It wouldn't be wise of us to show you what's *really* going on without a proper commitment."

I couldn't argue her logic, but that didn't mean I had to like it. I decided to try a different angle.

"I know the goal is equality, that you want to repair the broken system, but is anyone actively aiming to take down the Grand Magus himself?"

Jones' face grew grim. "That's one of the things only members get to know."

I looked more closely at Jones. Her expression told me she didn't like whatever the answer to my question was, but her face was inscrutable beyond that. I clenched my fists.

"I certainly hope you're not all under some idyllic illusion that you can just oust him and replace him with someone else. Because I can tell you you'll only end up dead, or worse, alive to see yourself back in the same bloody spot!"

My cheeks burned as I glared at Jones. Her answering look was impassive.

"If you want the full story, you have to join. Those are the rules."

"HE HAS TO DIE!" I yelled, slamming my fists down on the table.

I felt my pinkie bones break, and my knuckles exploded with pain. I swore and grabbed a chair, hurling it against the wall. When I spun back towards Jones, I found her watching me coolly, which increased my fury.

"Why don't you understand?! They are monsters! *No one* should have so much power! And they. Will never. *Stop*! They will always hurt people, people like me and Thomas and Ducky! He'll… he'll use and destroy and…"

My breath came too quickly now. I couldn't breathe. I sank to my knees and pounded my fists against the floor again and again. My flesh split beneath the abuse, and I screamed. No words, just shrieks of deep, soul-wrenching anguish. Jones crouched down in front of me. She did not reach out to grab me. She never tried to touch me except to place her hands beneath my beating fists. I pulled them away, distantly aware I would hurt her and that I didn't want to. Instead, I covered my face and leaned back against the legs of a chair. I didn't have enough air to scream anymore, so I groaned. My groans disintegrated to sobs. I sensed Jones as she sat next to me, though she still didn't touch me. She sat there for a long time.

"I'm sorry," I eventually whispered.

"You have nothing to be sorry for," she replied.

I couldn't find any words after that. We sat there all night. When the sky began to lighten, Jones spoke again.

"Is there anything you want me to take care of for you between now and this evening?"

I shook my head and stood. I headed into my bedroom and locked the door behind me.

)(

Arguing broke out beyond my bedroom door at one point that day. I didn't know who it was, nor did I care, so I went back to sleep. When I emerged again that evening, Jones sat at the table. Before her sat a fresh pot of coffee. I knew it as soon as I smelled it. I had forgotten that heavenly aroma until now. She spoke without even a greeting.

"Ed says you can't stay in this room anymore. It's being converted."

"Converted into what?" I asked. I looked around. The information didn't surprise me given the space's constant disarray, but I wondered about the timing of it.

"Can't tell you that." She paused and sighed. "Join us, Calandra. I think you'll be glad you did."

"Why?"

"I can't—"

"Can't tell me," I finished despondently. "Does it matter if I do or don't?"

"It very well could. You can do things none of the rest of us can."

I remained quiet for a long time. When I spoke again, my voice was stronger. "I've been considering it, but I have a price."

"And that is?"

"I want to kill Nicodemus. In any way I choose."

Jones shrugged. "Seems fair to me, but Ed and Holly have final say."

)(

Other duties kept Ed and Holly busy for the next few hours, so Jones and I went for dinner again. Real food helped to raise my spirits, as did another strong cup of coffee. Though the dark, complex brew brought back painful memories, it also comforted me. Jones had fixed up my first cup as we sat at the messy table. At the little café where we dined, I took it upon myself to do the next one. Pouring in the thick, sweetened milk, tapping the stirring spoon on the side of the cup, wrapping my hands around its warm, smooth surface… as my hands performed each motion of this long-ago ritual, it felt as if I reclaimed a tiny piece of my old self.

"I didn't have coffee until I was an adult," Jones told me. "It always reminds me what a great little ass-kicker I am."

I chuckled. I had never seen Jones fight, not really, and she hadn't worn armor since I came here. Like most sane people in my hot and humid home city, she dressed to keep cool, her clothes loose and flowing, but the definition in her arms led me to believe she could break most people in half.

When we met Holly and Ed again, I saw what they meant about conversion. I'd barely been gone two hours, and most of the furniture had already been removed. The way Jones' eyebrows went up told me she hadn't realized how soon the changes were coming. She recovered quickly, however, and announced my terms.

"He will have to go to trial first," Ed insisted, "as Grand Magus Thorne, not Nicodemus. After punishment for that has been meted out… well, we'll have to see what the punishment is first."

"That isn't justice, Ed," Holly argued. "Not for Calandra. Given his lifetime and crimes, why are we affording him such civilities?"

"Because we must be better than them," he replied. "Even in Nicodemus' case."

"Do you believe what I've told you?" I asked, looking at Ed straight in the eyes.

A beat of heavy silence passed before he said, "We know you are most certainly cursed. The evidence speaks for itself."

"Why would I lie about this?!" I demanded.

"The truth doesn't matter here because it *appears* Grand Magus Thorne is the one in control. We must punish him accordingly. The people need to see—"

"It matters to *me*!" I snarled. "I don't give a damn what the people need! That… that…"

"I believe you, Calandra," Holly said, stepping forward and shooting an ugly glare at Ed.

Somehow, this calmed me. I looked at Holly's hands to see if she was using her magic, but they remained by her side and as ordinary looking as mine, inert, without even a glimmer of power shining. Jones moved to both physically and metaphorically intercede as well.

"As do I," Jones agreed. "Though I think if 'Thorne'—" she made finger quotes in the air "—were to mysteriously go missing during the raid, we could deal with the fallout and speculation that would follow."

"What raid?" I asked, looking around to her and back to Holly and Ed.

"Jones!" Ed growled.

"Whoopsie," Jones replied. "Damn my eyes and all that."

Ed sighed and rubbed his temples.

Holly interceded again, saying, "It seems we can't promise you this. I think we should consider making an exception in this case, but there are many factors to consider." She glanced towards Ed again. "Will you join us anyway?"

I curled my lip at her, hesitating to answer. Not liking any of my other options any better, I grumbled at last, "Fine."

"Yes!" Jones said, pumping her fist. "This is gonna be good."

"Not so fast," Ed said. "She needs to take the oath."

Jones rolled her eyes so hard her head rotated around with them.

"Ed," Holly entreated, placing a hand on his arm. "Can we not? Calandra's been through enough."

"Don't coddle me," I snapped. "What's this oath?"

"An oath-bond," Ed clarified. "To ensure your loyalty. You will swear by your soul and blood and bones."

"Yes, because she's likely to side with the man who imprisoned and tortured her for several centuries," Jones drawled.

"Are you mad?" I asked. "How could you demand such a price? To take away someone's freedom of choice like that?!"

"I've always said we shouldn't do it." For the first time, I saw Jones look at Ed with proper contempt, her eyes narrowing to slits.

"People's freedom is at stake," Ed explained, looking at all three of us.

"And you don't think this is as bad as what the magi do?" I asked.

Holly shifted from one foot to another, her eyes cutting between Ed and me.

"We don't force anyone to join us. Everyone chooses to make this sacrifice." When I growled at him, he added firmly, "No exceptions."

"Ed," Holly insisted. "Please."

"Fine. Let's get on with it," I snapped.

Ed pulled a scrap of paper from his jacket and handed it to me.

"Take my hand when you make your vow," he instructed.

I skimmed the paper. It was an easy enough promise to bind myself to. Honestly, I didn't see how it would ever affect me, but I still fumed at the gall of the demand. I grabbed his hand and spoke, spitting my words like an angry panther.

"I, Calandra Allen, do swear by my blood and bones and soul I will not turn traitor to this resistance. I will lay down my life for it, if necessary… just so long as Nicodemus dies."

Ed snatched his hand back like he had been burned. "Calandra! This is the strongest of the oath-bonds, dammit!"

"And I meant every word," I spat. "I don't care what I have to do. I will have his life!"

"You could always appeal to the Dritch," Jones said idly. "Maybe they'll give you a do-over."

My eyes flicked to her, but I said nothing.

"This is serious," Holly admonished, though it sounded to me like her heart wasn't in it.

"What's done is done," Ed said, throwing me a glare. "It should be good enough, given our plans. Jones, take Calandra, go meet up with Flynn, and brief them both on the situation."

"Yes, sir." Jones motioned for me to follow and strode out of the room.

Once we had turned a corner in the plain, taupe hallway and were out of earshot, I spoke again.

"Jones?"

"Yep?" she chirped. I couldn't tell if she was still angry with Ed or excited about me joining the Lamplighters or something in between, but she kept a brisk pace.

"Do you ever sleep?" I asked.

"During the day, yeah. What we do, it's not really part of the shipping front."

"So that's a real business?"

"Oh, definitely! We've got to pay for weapons somehow."

"More of those things that killed Thomas?"

Jones stopped and turned to me. "Guns. And… yeah. About that, I'm so sorry, Calandra. Truly. I know he was… your friend. He never could have come back here, though. Friend or not, he was a Vampyre."

"But he didn't have to die," I retorted.

"He killed one of our people. Flynn's brother, Hugh. Ripped him apart. That's why Flynn's so angry about you."

I pressed my lips together. I hadn't thought much about the screaming man inside the cave, hadn't allowed myself to wonder. I recalled the way Flynn had looked at me. "I didn't realize. I'm sorry too. I suppose that's one more thing to blame Nicodemus for."

Jones looked like she didn't agree, but she didn't say anything. We walked on, descended a staircase, and continued down a dimly lit corridor. The clammy walls led me to suspect we'd reached the basement level. Entering what appeared to be a neglected storage room, untidy but clear of dust, Jones headed for the far end of it. She pulled and turned a rusty wall sconce. A disguised lever. A panel slid away, tucking into the rest of the wall. It had been invisible before Jones had moved it, disappearing into a mosaic of cracks and stains in the wall. With the false wall out of the way, a heavy metal door, tinged brown by rust, stood before us. A strangely shaped socket sat in the center of the door, flanked by levers on either side.

"Security system," Jones explained. She drew a leather cord from within her loose blouse. At the end hung a solid metal charm in the shape of an octopus. "This is the key. Push it in until it clicks. And then you pull the levers like so."

I repeated the sequence silently back to myself as I watched. Jones pushed the door open, and a cavernous room opened up before us.

Racks of what Jones had called guns lined the walls, while crates which smelled of smoke and rotten eggs sat stacked like soldiers along the bare floor. Boxes of armaments—repeater crossbows, ammunition, flashbangs, tear gas, all foreign to me at that moment—and armor created a maze with small clearings dotted here and there.

"Wakey wakey, Flynn!" Jones sang, turning around a corner of crates into one of these clearings.

"I'm awake, you vicious trollop!" Flynn grated, running a small knife along a whetstone.

Jones ignored the insult and jerked a thumb back towards me. "Calandra's here for outfitting."

"Why the blazes is she getting outfitted?" Flynn demanded, turning burning black eyes onto me.

He chewed a wad of tobacco, yellow-brown teeth grimacing at me. He looked like he was considering sinking his knife into my throat.

"She works for us now, obviously," Jones replied.

The little nook in which Flynn had been camped contained a variety of strange objects and devices: a long rack of clothing, some kind of printing press, a safe, and a table with countless bottles of variously colored powders and liquids inside. Flynn spit a gob of brown phlegm at my feet despite the brass spittoon sitting at his elbow on top of a box. I opened my mouth to fling some choice curses at him.

"We're on the same team now, people, so we are *not* going to do this," Jones commanded, cutting me off. She motioned towards a little table and chairs. "Calandra, would you like to have a seat? We need to figure out where to put you."

Before I could move, Flynn suggested, "We could test her combat skills."

"You feel up for it?" Jones asked me.

I nodded, glaring at Flynn and pulling my lightning rod from my belt. I had fashioned a holster for it from some bits and bobs I'd found.

"Nope," Jones said. "No weapons. And you're going against me. I won't have you two beating one another to a bloody pulp."

"Don't go easy on her, number one," Flynn said, scowling at me.

"I never do."

"You're in charge of all this?" I asked, still not moving.

"I'm in charge of our muscle," Jones explained. "Ed is our strategist. Holly's our head magus."

"I had no idea," I said.

I ignored Flynn's disdainful glare while Jones shrugged.

"I don't like to brag."

I kept my lightning rod with me but promised not to take it out. The gem glowed bright and milky again. Jones and I walked further back into the maze of crates to a large open area.

"Attack me," she said, taking position a few strides away. "Don't hold back."

It didn't matter if I held back or not. My scuffle with Nicodemus a few days ago didn't replace years of practice lost. My muscles seemed to have a vague recollection of what to do, but my strength, agility, and reflexes floundered, weak and dull. Jones had me on my behind within seconds. Flynn guffawed to himself, ignored by both of us. We went a few more rounds with the same result.

"I used to be better at this," I snapped, at myself or Jones or Flynn I wasn't sure.

"We'll work on it. Flynn, create a training regimen for her to do at night."

"Swimming with sharks comes to mind," he said.

"Follow your orders!" Jones barked.

Flynn grumbled and skulked away.

"You need a job too," Jones said, turning to me.

"I'm good with information. I can keep track of inventory," I suggested. "Or something to that effect."

Jones looked me dead in the eyes. She was harder now. The soft lines of her face pulled into tighter, more angular features. This was the face of a soldier.

"We both know you'll be wasted as a clerk. I won't make you take the job, but I agree with Ed: it'd be a big help if you worked as our spy."

I took a deep breath through my nose. "Fine. If it'll bring me closer to killing that filth."

Jones smiled, her thick features softening again. "Thank you, Calandra. To be honest, I think you'll like it."

~Chapter 11~

I settled into a new room that day. This one, unlike the one before, had other people around it. Almost no one else actually lived in the shipping building, but there were always a handful of watchmen and women who liked having a place to wind down between shifts. Having learned of what had happened to Flynn's brother, I worried how the other Lamplighters would feel when they learned I had been involved in his death and what they might do in retaliation.

"They don't know," Jones explained when I mentioned this to her. "The operation was a secret, so all they know is that Hugh died nobly in the line of duty." I think she saw the look in my eyes because, after a moment, she added, "Flynn is hurt, but he's a good soldier. He won't compromise the mission for his personal feelings."

"Or is his tongue held by the oath-bond?" I asked.

Jones' face darkened, and she didn't answer me.

)(

The shipping business ran twenty-four hours a day, which provided good cover for the presence of lights at all times.

Flynn, as he had been told to, created a training plan for me. Much to my chagrin, *he* was my taskmaster. I ran laps around the warehouse and climbed over crates with heavy supplies on my back. And of course we sparred, though only after Jones had threatened to tear off his ears if he didn't do his job right. And she told me to leave my lightning rod in my room. According to Jones, I bore the physical demands better than anyone she had ever seen.

"I reckon everything you've been through has given you a higher pain tolerance than most," she mused one day. "Plus, there's no fear of permanently injuring yourself."

I didn't respond to her, though I smiled later on when Flynn spat at my feet for passing yet another of his tests.

"Time for you to learn a new skill," he said. "Follow me."

He disappeared around another stack of crates, and I obeyed. After a few more turns, we arrived at a line of cages. I suspected this might be all the Lamplighters had in the way of prisoner containment. Every cage stood open and empty. I wasn't certain if that was a good or bad sign, and Flynn was nowhere to be seen.

"Flynn?" I called. "Where'd you—"

Someone pushed me from behind and into a cage. A second later, the door clanged shut. I spun and saw Flynn on the other side. A hideous grin stretched across his face.

"Think you're so good?" he said. He flicked a hairpin at me, which I barely managed to catch. "Get yourself outta there."

Fury and terror bubbled inside me, pushing the air from my lungs. "Flynn, let me out of here right now!"

"Save yourself, bird brain," he growled back, turning to walk away.

"Is this about Hugh?" I snapped. "That wasn't my fault!"

He spun back, eyes nearly bulging out of his head, neck straining. "Don't you say his name! If it hadn't've been for you, we woulda killed the vamp before it woke up!"

"He was the only one I had!" I cried.

"Hugh was my whole family, and he was worth ten thousand of your bloody vamps!"

He stalked off, ignoring my screams. I heard nothing of him after he disappeared. I sank to my knees, my heart pounding painfully in my chest. Tears sprang to my eyes, but I bit my tongue to keep them back. I looked at the hairpin and then to the lock. I hadn't the first clue what I was doing. My hands shook so badly when I raised the pin to the lock, I could barely insert it. I made no progress during the following hours. Time and again, panic overcame me, and I had to beg it back. I vomited as visions of being trapped again in Nicodemus' cell flashed before my eyes. I called for Flynn over and over with no reply. Dawn was still a ways off when I heard the storeroom door open and shut and voices echoing from that direction.

"Hey!" I cried, my voice hoarse and cracked. "Let me out! Please!"

The voices grew closer. I heard running and called more frantically. Jones, Ed, and Holly appeared around the corner.

"What the ever-loving f—" Jones began.

"Lock-picking lessons, sir," Flynn said, flying around the corner after her.

Ed was already to the door, keys pulled. Meanwhile, Holly rounded on Flynn and punched him, knocking him back a few steps.

"WHAT THE BLAZES IS WRONG WITH YOU?!" Her words echoed off every surface.

I shot out of the cage so fast it was as if I still had wings. I headed for Flynn, but Jones caught me by the wrists, keeping one eye on me and one on Holly, who was advancing again.

"Holly," Ed said.

She ignored him and took another swing. Flynn deflected it as he tried to make explanations, which fell on deaf ears.

"Holly!" Ed repeated, louder this time.

"What?!" she snapped, spinning towards him.

"He didn't know," was all he said.

Gritting her teeth, she balled her fists at her side. She turned to Jones, who was still talking me down. Watching Holly provided a distraction, which helped, but Jones was also both a big and strong enough woman to gently restrain me without much effort.

"Handle your people!" Holly barked as she marched out.

Jones' voice was even as she said, "Flynn, I don't want to hear anything else from you except the words, 'yes, sir.' Now get back to your post."

"Yes, sir," Flynn mumbled before scurrying off.

"Come to my office after your shift!" Jones called after him.

I heard Flynn repeat the response from somewhere beyond.

"Come on," Ed coaxed. "Let's get you out of here."

I couldn't speak. The empty void had nearly consumed me again. We went back to my room, and Ed left to make tea. My room wasn't large, but a small table and some chairs had managed to fit into a corner. Jones and I sat there, my head in my hands, elbows propped up on the table. Jones leaned back heavily in her chair.

"I can't… Calandra, I'm so… stars, what a dumb…" Jones tried again and again.

I grasped at anything to pull myself out of that pit of horror. The words, "Why didn't she blast him," tumbled out of my mouth.

"Who?" Jones asked.

"Holly," I replied shakily. "She hit him. I assumed her magic would be strong… for her position."

"Ah, yes. She did do that," Jones said softly. She sat up straighter in her seat. "You're right. Holly's an incredibly strong magus. You might witness it, in time, if we go to battle. Otherwise, you'll be lucky to see her charge a piece of Quarkz."

I shook my head, trying to focus on the memory of Holly and not the bars that had closed in on me. "I don't understand."

"I wasn't just trying to pacify you when I said she's not like them. Holly *hates* using her powers."

"That doesn't make sense," I replied, finally lifting my head from my hands.

"She doesn't like being a magus," Jones explained, "but they have to expel their power. Otherwise it flows out of them. She'd never use it against one of our own people, no matter what they'd done."

The information shocked me. Despite all the time I'd spent with magi, I didn't know this about them. Then I realized why. I had never seen a magus refrain from using their magic.

"Don't tell her I told you this," Jones continued, pulling me from my reverie, "but Holly comes from one of the most powerful magical families. I got caught stealing food as a child and was given to Holly as a gift, made to swear an oath-bond to her. Everyone at her birthday party laughed and commented what a funny playmate I made for their little gem. Years later, we escaped together. After we took up with Ed and the crew he was forming here, they told us how we could appeal to the Dritch to release me from my oath. Holly jumped on the chance, wanted to do it right then and there."

My face contorted into a puzzle of angles. "How does that even happen? Magi love their power. They're at all times drunk on it."

"Oftentimes, yes. But there are some, like Holly, who recognize the danger of corruption and resist it."

I sat back in my chair, allowing my thoughts to swirl around me. "He let the people forget," I murmured after a moment. "Or maybe he made them."

"Forget what?" Jones asked. She didn't ask to whom I referred.

I looked at her and explained, "Growing up, we all knew the severity of an oath-bond. It was a punishment reserved for the most heinous of crimes, when someone had violated another in the most despicable ways, and even then, it was never permanent. Everyone knew about the ceremony of appeal." I paused as a new thought occurred to me. If Nicodemus had made everyone forget about the ceremony of appeal, it was possible he'd deceived people in other, farther-reaching ways. I hadn't seen any evidence of it, but I needed to find out if my suspicion was correct… ideally, without being wildly offensive. Stars, why was it so hard to talk to other human beings sometimes? "The Dritch… you do know they're just the natural forces behind magic, right? Nothing more than what drives the tides. I ask because I… given the…" I finally decided to abandon delicacy and asked, "You don't worship the Dritch, do you?"

"Nope. Some of the magi, mostly those in the midlands and the Eldritch Synod, mind you, have made some passing remarks that maybe we should. Prince Godric has spoken out against it, and I think his mother knows what it would cost to publicly support the idea. I reckon some would push harder if they thought they could get away with it, though."

I shuddered at the implications. If people saw magic as not solely an impressive ability, but some kind of divine gift, what would that make magi? It wouldn't surprise me if Nicodemus' next grand evolution was to make himself into a god.

"Does Holly—" I began.

"Absolutely not," Jones cut in, shaking her head. "She's our strongest voice against such ideas."

I still couldn't wrap my mind around everything I had just learned. Ed soon returned with tea, and I changed the subject, wishing to continue the conversation but not with him there.

)(

I returned to duty after a day of rest. The incident with Flynn tried to haunt me, grating against the back of my mind. My anger flared, and I asked Jones about learning to pick locks.

"Flynn's the best in our ranks," she grimaced.

From what I had gathered, Flynn knew nothing of my history. Even though he had been told that particular teaching method was not appropriate for me, Jones refused to explain to him why. I didn't know whether or not Flynn would continue to run my combat drills, as we hadn't discussed it yet, but I decided I would endure it if I had to.

"Fine," I replied to Jones. "Where is he?"

I followed Jones' instructions and sought out Flynn at the next opportunity. He was sitting at a table, located in a common area near the bedrooms, with several other off-duty guards. I slammed a hairpin onto the table, scowling down at him. Flynn looked slowly from the cards in his hand to me.

"Teach me to pick locks," I snarled.

"After the fuss you made?" he asked, chewing his tobacco like a cow with cud.

I felt the other watchmen and women's eyes on me. My cheeks heated under their gaze, but I kept my eyes on Flynn.

"You caught me off guard," I replied, trying to sound casual.

He chuckled. I could see he didn't believe me. I didn't blame him. I wouldn't have believed me either. I didn't dare glance at the other people at the table. I didn't know what Flynn might have told them, what he was even allowed to tell them, and I certainly didn't want to turn and see their eyes laughing at me.

"Why should I?" he asked, and I suspected he hoped to hear more amusing lies.

I smiled the way I used to when negotiating a business deal. "It's for the good of the Lamplighters. You help me, I help them, I give you credit. Everybody wins."

Flynn's smile disappeared. I watched with satisfaction as his eyes flicked to his compatriots. When he looked back at me, a cold grin curled up his face, one that promised I would pay for this little maneuver.

"When you put it that way, how can I refuse?"

)(

My objective as Lamplighter spy was to observe private meetings—on verandas, in courtyards, within alleys—and report back everything I heard. Along with information on enemy movements—Jones, Holly, and Ed were aware of magus supremacy supporters within Bone Port—the resistance needed to know what agents of the crown and Synod knew about the resistance. My job was almost laughably easy, for no one watched their speech around a raven preening its feathers or gathering with other nearby birds.

My lock-picking training proved a bigger challenge. Flynn did, in fact, continue running my combat and strength training.

"You wanna learn? I get to make your life hell. That's the deal," he spat at me when we met up again in the storage warehouse.

I gave him my best unimpressed courtier look. "Then let's get started."

Flynn made it look easy, popping open lock after lock in under a minute. I earned my lessons after running drills with twice the amount of weight on me or whenever I managed to knock Flynn back when we sparred. Luckily, I could practice without him, and I did as often as possible in both my human and raven forms. I could also ask Jones for tips, which she gladly provided, but there were always some locks beyond my capability, and only Flynn could help me conquer them.

~Chapter 12~

I wasn't back in Bone Port long before I looked in on my descendants, though I kept these trips to myself at first. Disguised in my onyx plumage, I was able to process wonder and loss from a safe distance. I ventured closer with time and began to listen in on their conversations, to learn more about them. The little ones even offered me bits of their lunch, which I was happy to accept after a while. I decided I couldn't face them as a human. The idea filled me with that sticky, black, suffocating feeling, but I felt safe observing them in my raven form.

Like my family, these Allens had built their home over the water, and they opened windows and doors on days with good weather. I learned they had maintained strong ties to the Arnavi and continued a successful trade relationship with them. My father had always joked he wanted to build a dock right next to the house, but my mother refused. It was one step too far for her.

Somewhere down the line, someone had apparently gone with my father's idea, though the little jetty was nowhere near large enough to receive the enormous main trading vessels. It was easy enough to pick out the master and mistresses of the house over the servants. The current family had three children, all girls. They all knew how to fight and fish and sail. They were proud and self-assured. Their parents were firm but kind, though clearly more lenient with the younger two. I saw the straight line of my brother's nose in them, the curve of my mother's smile. They all had the same thick, black, curly hair I did. I looked for signs of magic in them as well, but saw none. Pride swelled in my heart, but it made me even more certain I didn't want to risk them discovering my true identity.

)(

Over a quiet meal at Jones' cottage one evening, I withdrew my request for a meeting between my descendants and me. When she asked why, I told her I didn't see the point and had changed my mind.

"We still need them to join us," she reminded me.

"I don't see how meeting me would help with that," I replied. "They're not hiding anything as far as I can tell. And their current business focus is on closing a trade agreement with someone called Adjatay."

Jones choked on her drink, nearly spewing it out through her nose.

"They're negotiating a deal with Adjatay?" she rasped.

"Ye-es," I replied. "I take it he's someone important?"

"He's the foreign ambassador of the Arnavi Nish," Jones explained. "A prince unto himself. He's also very interested in bringing magic to their shores."

"Has the sickness even spread to them then?" I muttered.

"No. Well, sort of. Magus blood has never passed into Arnavi children, even those of mixed parentage, and there have been plenty of political marriages arranged in an attempt to gain it. Adjatay himself has married three of his children into magical households here. The Grand Magus, erm, Nicodemus has always kept a tight rein on Heredical studies into why there are no Arnavi-descended magi. I've heard the Arnavi have conducted their own investigations, but without satisfactory results. The Synod party line has always been to let nature take its course."

I made a disgusted noise in my throat.

Jones went on. "The whole business—regulation, the marriages, all of it—has hurt relations with the Arnavi, but your family has kept strong ties with them." She looked at me sideways. "How long have you known about the Allens' proposed deal with Adjatay?"

"Not long," I shrugged, and ignored the skeptical arch of her eyebrows. "So permitting those inquiries over here could potentially help the Arnavi, and if the Allens were the ones to offer it…" I trailed off as, in my mind's eye, I saw the different possibilities branch off into the distance. “How many children have resulted from these political marriages?”

“Oh, scads.” Jones’ voice grew soft as she explained, “They’re seen as a disgrace and often end up across the sea for one reason or another.”

I knew little of Hereditry. It wasn’t a science I had been much interested in while growing up, but I knew some diseases exclusively ailed people of certain ancestries. For instance, only members of the Arnavi were afflicted with a painful condition of the blood that caused red corpuscles to harden. Perhaps what caused the Arnavi to suffer from one malady made them immune to another? The idea made me smile. To think my family might be immune to the virus of magic.

“There will be spoils for the victors, you know,” Jones said, and I turned my attention back to her. “We’ve offered the Allens a place in the new world order. The current system cannot stay in place, but every government needs leaders. Unfortunately, it hasn’t been enough to turn their heads, given that victory isn’t assured.”

I leaned forward. “Why not recruit those whose families have rejected them? Call them back from across the sea to join us.”

Jones smiled and took another gulp of her drink. “I do like the way you think.”

)(

Ed surprised me a few days later when I took up a perch on the Allens’ veranda and saw him there having tea with the Countess and Count. I croaked once, and the youngest Allen came running outside a moment later, plate in hand.

“Gwen, darling,” Countess Ciara said. “Go back inside or play elsewhere. Your father and I have business to discuss.” Gwen pouted, and Ciara added, “You can feed your little friend tomorrow.” She then kissed her daughter’s coffee colored cheek and sent her on her way.

“Does it come around often?” Ed asked, motioning towards me with his head.

“Sometimes,” Ciara said with a shrug she made look elegant. “I assume it has us on its list of places for free food.”

Ed laughed. "I suspect you're right." He waved in my direction. "Go on now. No food for you here today."

I squawked at him and stayed put. He fixed me with a look, but I ignored him. Finally, he turned back to his hosts and leaned forward.

Most of their discussion touched lightly on the state of the country. It seemed they had this conversation often. The Allens did not condone the actions of the magi, but they had their position of influence—which they exercised with care to remain friends to both domestic and foreign powers—and three daughters to think about. Ed paused, probably weighing his words, before he spoke again.

"You know about our movement. The Prince continues to stand against his mother, but it will not be enough, not when so many powerful people are threatened."

"You're talking about open rebellion," the Count, Luis, whispered.

"When the people are forbidden from using their voices, what other option is there? Now, I am telling you this at great risk. We have a force ready to move, but we need to know enough of the nobility will stand with us. You both have influence, and I have been authorized to offer you a larger piece of the pie than before."

The Count and Countess exchanged a glance. "We're listening," Ciara said.

Ed took a deep breath. "When the dust settles, the Prince has decided he will abdicate."

"He won't," Luis replied. "Why would he give up the crown?"

"Because he believes in the power of the people," Ed said. "He wants a Parliament for Prism."

"And what of us here?" Ciara asked.

"The southern and northern dukedoms will become independent. We will reserve a seat in Prism's Parliament for one of your daughters, however, should they wish to move there. You two would be able to help shape this new city-state into whatever you like. Trade agreements would be yours to manage. Might I suggest deregulating the Heredical studies into the Arnavi-magic problem?"

I cawed and flapped my wings. Ed, Luis, and Ciara all looked at me. I continued to express my displeasure at the idea, and Ed stood and approached me.

"Thank you for your opinion," he joked, shooing me from my perch. I wheeled above their heads, still croaking. He called up to me, "If you'd like to discuss it further, please make an appointment with my people."

Ciara and Luis laughed with him. I landed on the roof of the house, where Ed couldn't reach me. I watched as the Count and Countess looked at one another, slipping their hands into each other's.

"We will have to consider it," Ciara said, looking back to Ed.

He nodded. "I understand."

)(

"Are you insane?!" I demanded that evening.

I had a daily meeting scheduled with Jones, Holly, and Ed to deliver the day's reports, for which we met in Ed's office each evening. I had just stormed through the door. Jones and Holly looked to me and then to Ed. Jones, being closer, reached over and pushed the door closed behind me.

"Reports first, Calandra," Ed said, not sparing me even a glance as he sipped his tea.

Still looking to Ed, I thrust a sheaf of papers towards Jones, which she took from me without comment. The papers described my observations from the day: suspicious smoke rising from the sea caves behind the Giant's Maw—the opening to an underground river in the towering basalt cliffs—and descriptions of a few magi looking for "troublemakers." Ed finally deigned to look at me.

"Thank you. Now, in response to your query, excellent thinking," he said dryly. "Jones mentioned your recent conversation to me. Deregulating the Arnavi Hereditry studies is the carrot everyone needs."

"Wait a second! That is *not* what I suggested we do!" I insisted. "Why would you try to help the Arnavi get magic?"

Ed held out his hands in a placating gesture. "I understand where you're coming from, but trust me, it's going to be fine."

I twisted up my face at him like he'd just suggested we all go swimming with nervous pufferfish strapped to our limbs. "What… how… what in the world makes you think it's going to be fine? You have no idea how any of this will play out! Sure, maybe something in Arnavi blood is immune to magic, but what if it's not? We don't have enough information to know for certain."

"It really will—" Ed began.

"Past performance is no guarantee of future success, sir! I-I-I sound exactly like my parents." The thought knocked the wind out of me, and I leaned back against the door.

I looked to the others in the room, uncertain what to do with the emotions surging up from some locked-up place within me. Jones' face was inscrutable for some reason, and I could tell Holly was trying to hide a smile. Ed just looked annoyed and waited for whatever was happening with my face to pass. I shook my head, determined to finish the argument.

"Look. It's a *terrible* idea. You are gambling with countless lives."

"We don't make these decisions lightly, Calandra," Ed said. "You should know that by now. What's done is done, so let's move on."

I gritted my teeth, flinging a new question at him like a dart. "Is Prince Godric truly going to abdicate?"

"Yes," Ed parried. "I wouldn't lie to them about that."

"And how large is your force?"

"Large enough to scare the powers that be, but not large enough to guarantee victory."

"When will you strike?"

"Soon. We're waiting for a few more pieces to fall into place."

He looked to Holly, as did Jones, and silence fell between us when I followed suit. Holly did not look up from a binder of notes as she spoke.

"I'm still working on it."

"Working on what," I asked.

I think the evenness of my tone surprised her because she lifted her eyes to mine. She bit her lip before answering. "Assuming I can get it working, it'll be the clincher to our success."

"What is it?"

)(

Given my unique situation, I explored areas inaccessible to the other Lamplighter spies. The cave system within the Giant's Maw was a network of potential hiding places, as were the sea caves behind it. I knew of others in my same line of work, as we often crossed paths while on our way to deliver reports or receive orders, but I remained separate from them. How could I discuss assignments or tactics with the other spies? Thank the stars our tasks and results thereof were a secret, even from each other. I was cordial, of course, during these brief encounters, but many of the old defense mechanisms from my courtier days came back into play.

Despite my success as a spy, transcribing everything at the end of the day proved troublesome. I spoke to Jones about it, but there really wasn't a good solution. Yes, I could and did abscond with the odd incriminating sheet of paper, but flying is extremely difficult when weighed down by anything heavier than that.

I got to know Bone Port in a way I never had before. With the power of flight, a beautiful vista was never far. Nearly getting snatched out of the air by a sea eagle now and again, however, did take the shine off.

As beautiful as my home city is, and as much as I enjoyed discovering new nooks and crannies within it—locating undesirables and their hideaways was an added bonus—I found watching human targets the most fulfilling. There seemed a clearer goal in mind with these assignments. One family, the Winchesters, Synod supporters and magi all, was one such example.

They were the type of couple who said and did all the right things in public, rubbed elbows with the right people, but behind closed doors, the masks came off. Both wife and husband had affairs going, and they slung venom at one another daily.

"When our guests arrive next month, tell me you'll limit yourself to four drinks a day," Blake Winchester spat at his wife one day. "I don't want you sloppy by two like usual."

"Well, someone's going to have to provide entertainment while you're out with Seashell or Pearl or whatever this one is called," Lissa Winchester shot back.

I perched on the Winchester's balcony and watched Lissa encase her husband's favorite pieces of furniture in ice. Their son, a tyke called Ryan, sat on the balcony with me, eating chocolate biscuits and offering me some. I finally took one after much persistence on his part.

Homes with pets posed a whole other problem. Given a little time, I could cow most animals without a problem. I haven't the foggiest how much a spaniel or tabby or even a goat comprehends, but I think most creatures sensed there was something off about me. Occasionally, however, I encountered one with a chip on its shoulder… usually its tiny, tiny shoulder. The smallest ones were often the dumbest, or perhaps the most insecure. More often than not, my failed spying missions were interrupted by a yapping, disgruntled rat with the audacity to call itself a dog, oversized ears flopping with indignation. Their owners were more absurd.

"Vermin! Vulture! Omen of death! Away from my precious darling!" were usually the sorts of things they shouted at me. You think I'm exaggerating. I promise I'm not.

Even with my goals in mind, I made sure to keep some distance between my marks and me, lest any of them get funny ideas about catching me and keeping me as a pet. That would have been embarrassing for everyone involved.

While I jest, those were some of the proudest days of my life. I helped foil sabotage plots and shielded my comrades from discovery. Some of the plans I overheard and reported back would have hurt a lot of people if enacted and, despite everything that happened later, I'm glad to have been a part of the effort.

)(

Less than a year after I joined the Lamplighters, the war began. Overnight, in fact.

Jones and I were visiting the little soup hut she had brought me to on my first night here, which had become a favorite haunt of ours. The weather had turned lovely as winter neared. True, that also meant the storm season was almost upon us, but there's a small window beforehand when the nights are cool and still. The stall was busy, as this time of year was always popular for bonfires and eating out. Children ran about with sparklers, miniature pyroprismatics on sticks that sparked different colors as the fuse burned down their thin, metal stalks. We chatted idly, and I spied a familiar family approach from around the bend in the boardwalk. It was Blake and Lissa Winchester, the degenerate magi I'd been keeping tabs on, but my eyes landed on a third figure in their midst.

RUN! my mind shrieked.

But my body froze. I dropped my spoon, unable to tear my eyes from the wretchedly familiar figure walking closer. Nicodemus' stolen eyes landed on me. His face split into a broad, maniacal grin, and he raised his hands.

"Get down!" I heard distantly.

My body took off and flew through the air. I hit the sand as our table, soup bowls, and chairs exploded in a hail of cinders and splinters. People screamed and ran. Somewhere in there, Jones pulled a small handheld gun and dagger combination from its holster and fired back. It blew scattershot, which exploded on contact, back at our enemy. I wasn't watching—or perhaps I wasn't comprehending—but she managed to haul me to my feet and drag me away. My legs responded first, finally listening to my panicked brain. More blasts followed, but Jones shot back again and again, tossing flashbangs and tear gas from her belt between volleys, and led us down hidden side streets and twisting back alleys. The Lamplighters had been preparing. Jones knew every contingency plan. We shook off Nicodemus and took shelter in a fish shed pungent with salt and smoke.

"Can he track you?" Jones whispered to me.

I shook my head.

"Okay. Okay…" she panted. "Stay here. I need to—"

"No! Please!" I squeaked, grabbing Jones' arm in a death grip. "Don't leave me! I don't want… he can't find me. Jones, I can't go back. *Please.*"

"Shhhh, Cali," she soothed. "He won't. I promise we won't let him, but I have to get back right now. I have to alert Holly and Ed. I can't stay here with you."

"I'll come with you," I said, clutching at her.

"I can't be slowed down. You understand? This is bigger than either of us."

I nodded, concentrating on slowing my breathing

The end, I thought. *He has to die. I have to kill him. I* will *kill him.*

"I can do it," I said.

"Keep up," was Jones' only reply before running back out of the shed.

~Chapter 13~

"Jones! Report!" barked Ed as soon as we came within sight of him.

He was in the storage warehouse shouting orders left, right, and center. Holly stood nearby, handing out her own directives.

"It's Thorne," Jones replied. "Nicodemus, that is. He's here. Spotted Calandra and went berserk."

Ed swore and turned away.

"This might be the push we need," Holly said. She turned to Jones and me. "Our informants within the Synod have reported the Grand Magus growing increasingly erratic over the last few weeks. Even his most loyal supporters have begun to grumble."

"I wanted the change to be on our terms," muttered Ed.

"Well, it's not," Jones said. "I'm sure he'll cite some BS reason about safety and necessity, but he just blew part of the Shore Shack to smithereens without warning. We have to move. Now."

Ed growled. "Very well. Send one of our rooks to Prince Godric. Tell him it's begun."

)(

Within hours, half the warehouse was emptied. Machines aerial, terrestrial, and aquatic were unpacked and readied. Workers running different pieces of the shipping business donned armbands to denote the force they served. Their emblem, a white flame against a black background. Magic-energized Quarkz were loaded into the machines, all ready to fly, march, and dive towards our common goal.

Flynn and a small company of the Allens' guards arrested the Winchesters soon after the attack. They confessed to having invited the Grand Magus to their home as a friend, but denied all other accusations. Their son, Ryan, was taken in by a few of the Lamplighters until further notice.

As for Nicodemus, he disappeared from Bone Port immediately after the attack and had not been seen since. There was no telling if or when he would take on a new body, but I suspected he would not give up the role of Grand Magus easily. Politically, we all suspected it could go either way. Grand Magus Thorne had turned a good portion of the country against him. The Queen might call for his resignation. Then again, now wasn't a good time for the Synod to cripple themselves with sweeping leadership changes. We could only watch and wait, as our moles within the Synod went almost completely silent after the first week, and we feared for those brave men and women.

We took Bone Port first. That was the easy part. After Nicodemus' attack, the Count and Countess condemned his gross abuse of power and publicly supported our efforts.

"The Grand Magus has betrayed his duty of service," Ciara Allen declared in a statement several days after. "He claims this attack was against an enemy of the state, yet he has refused to provide proof or even any information about this individual. Innocent lives were threatened by this violent assault, and Grand Magus Thorne has no response except to tell us he is not to blame for the damage, but he is due the credit for this mystery person's death."

That last bit had been added at Ed's request, and he actually smiled at me as we watched the speech together under the shade of a coconut palm. I don't know if the Allens' decision had anything to do with the recent trade deal they had struck with Adjatay of the Arnavi, but it was certainly a boon to us, as support from our friends from across the sea came in the form of arms and even troops. It was not a lot of troops, and the group was mostly comprised of angry, rejected offspring born to magi families here in Invarnis, but we were grateful for whatever support we could get.

The barons and baronesses under Count and Countess Allen also sided with the Lamplighters. The Count of the Southern Plains and his underlings did not, being closely allied with the Synod and Grand Magus.

)(

By day, I flew north and observed our enemy's movements. The civilian death toll rose sharply after the nobles picked their sides. Those living in the rural areas between Bone Port and Dogwood Lane and beyond the Eldritch Synod—a town unto itself by now—suffered the worst. The Queen's soldiers and magi occupied and stole whatever they claimed as necessary to defend the security of the country. Besides the trampling and slaughter of livelihoods, atrocities were committed against the people, abuses carried out for no other reason than base depravity. The Lamplighters could not strike at our enemies without also hurting innocents, but we also could not give them time to advance or grow in power. Thus, the strikes from our aircraft claimed the lives of both.

Every war produces orphans and refugees. The Lamplighters knew this and tried to prepare ahead of time. We provided what aid we could, but it never seemed enough. There were always more hungry, more hurt, more homeless and missing and lost. In my spare moments, I found myself providing childcare. We all did, whether it was because the children no longer had anyone to care for them or their parents just needed a break. Holding and bathing and feeding the little ones brought back memories of doing the same for my brother's children. Elian had been five and Lucy two the last time I saw them before the curse.

When I didn't wipe my tears away fast enough, a little girl called Kayla asked, "Miss Cali, why are you crying?"

"It's because I'm missing someone, darling," I replied.

"Who are you missing?" Kayla asked, wrapping one of my sable curls around her finger.

I didn't want to lead her to believe I had suffered the same loss she had, nor could I tell her the truth, so I simply said, "I'm missing my family."

Kayla looked up at me with big, dark eyes. "I miss my family too."

Tears fell from those innocent eyes, and I hugged her close. "I know, darling. I know."

)(

The rebellion had a sister movement in the North, though they had not gained the strength we had. The city of Duskwood broke out in civil war barely a day after our battle began. The nobles there were split almost evenly in their loyalties. The tide turned in our favor when reinforcements arrived by submarine, but not before countless lives were lost in the crossfire.

I wanted to rail against Ed and Jones about these casualties, determined on several occasions to speak out, but I never did in the end.

Circumstances always matter, because there's already too much pain in the world.

My parents' words came back to me again, and they tore at my already shredded heart. Part of me wanted to believe another way existed, that we didn't need to inflict pain to end it, but when I searched, wrung out my brain for any alternative solution, I came up empty. So I didn't throw my objections at Ed and Jones. What good would it do to increase their burden? I saw pain etched into the lines of their faces every day, the creases of regret as they called each new attack.

I wept instead. I wept and pleaded with the heavens for mercy for those who wanted nothing more than to live their lives but were instead caught between two warring powers. A tiny nook with windows facing the sea—it could barely be called an office, though it had been at one point—became my sanctuary, where I hid and poured out my heart. I stopped dead in my tracks one night when I walked in to find Holly there, sitting in my usual spot by the window.

We stared at one another. Tears streamed from Holly's red, puffy eyes. Her hair hung disheveled around her messy face. She had her hands tucked underneath her arms, which she held tightly folded across her chest. Hands capable of terrible power. I knew I looked as rough as she did. I clenched my teeth against the onslaught of tears straining for release. I had practically run down the corridor to get here so no one would see me cry.

"Sorry," I mumbled. "I'll—"

"Please, don't," Holly whispered. She kept her hands restrained, and I realized she had them wrapped around nearly to her back, as far from sight as possible. "Your tears aren't wasted on those we've lost."

Her voice broke, and she hunched over, sobbing freely. Still, she kept her hands tucked away. Her shoulders shook, and I took a step closer. Another step, and I sat down on a cluttered, little desk. Seeing Holly's pain laid out before me ripped away the last of my resistance, and I began to cry too. We sat together for a long time, each weeping without words.

)(

Every night blazed with fire and magelight. We pressed deeper into the Southern Plains. The Lamplighters in Duskwood had ranged down towards Prism like a bitter north wind, and the Queen had fled to the Synod. Prince Godric had control of the city at last, but the cost…

Our numbers grew each day. Though many condemned us for those lost during our attacks, more had suffered under the magi and Her Majesty's rule in one way or another. I heard countless new recruits say they'd rather fight than wait to die in their homes. In their desperation, the magi began spending themselves in the effort to take out as many of us as they could, plus whoever happened to be in their path of destruction. On a field of three hundred, one magus could focus their power within themselves to a point of combustion, sending out deadly waves of energy, disintegrating all three hundred souls there. I imagined Nicodemus had been the one to develop this new technique.

With our enemy on the run, I, along with Holly, Jones, and Ed, travelled to the capital city to meet with the Prince. We traveled during the day, as the aircraft we used, while quick, was too small for all of us as humans. In fact, it only held two people without supplies, so Jones travelled by horseback and would join us in a few days. The craft could be converted to a zeppelin if necessary, but was far more useful in its aeromobile configuration. As it flew far faster than I could, we'd reach the city before nightfall, so I travelled in a little space between Ed and Holly's seats. Her talent wasn't for illusions, so we could only pray the enemy didn't blast us out of the sky as we passed over their territory.

Thankfully, we soared at such a speed that shooting us would be difficult. Even if one of the few aircraft the Queen had used to escape Godric's coup pursued us in the air, Ed was a skilled pilot, and we carried almost no cargo. Despite these assurances, I couldn't help but hop to one of the small rear windows on the passenger side of the craft and look out as we approached the Synod. Not being able to see out, especially while we passed into such danger, grated against my nerves. If we were going to be attacked, I wanted to see it coming.

The sight of the Eldritch Synod so far below made me think of a spider. One central mass for the body, with wings and extensions to serve as legs. And the web of people and machines moving around it… the sight turned my stomach. I identified the section of the manor where Ducky's old chambers were located. I wanted to turn away, to retreat and cry to myself, but I forced myself to stay put. I stared hard at it, thinking of what had happened to me there, and telling myself I would carve back every piece of dignity Nicodemus had stolen from me.

)(

We touched down in Prism as the golden disk of the sun dipped halfway below the horizon. Holly, who apparently hated flying, stumbled out of the aeromobile, green and shaking. Already, people surrounded us and the craft. Even in my raven form, this many strangers pressing in on us made my heart race. I flew clumsily from the craft, barely getting enough air under my broad wings to take off. I narrowly dodged smacking someone in the face, then shot for an alcove between two buildings. In the dark of the hidden space, I took a deep breath and listened as evening's song began to whisper in my heart. We'd landed in the Agate district, and the walls glowed emerald and rose and plum in the dying light as the enchantment took hold of me. When my human form returned, I peeked back out towards the crowd. I could tell from the sound something had changed while I hid in the alcove.

The throng had parted and become quiet. I saw Ed and Holly bow to someone, a young man. He wore a circlet around his head.

"Weren't there meant to be three of you?" he asked Ed and Holly. "Where's this spy you promised me?"

I suspected Ed had kept one eye on me this entire time, as he didn't even look my way before beckoning me with a hand. Everyone turned in my direction, and the multitude of eyes suddenly trained on me nearly pushed me back into the dark hideaway. Guards, not in uniforms but everyday garb, raised their weapons in alarm, but the Prince waved them down.

"She appears as good as you claim. Come, let us speak in private."

)(

The vast palace was made desolate by how empty it now stood. Prince Godric explained how looters had come through before he and his forces had a chance to fully establish themselves here. It was during this brief tour I discovered Godric was, shockingly, not a magus. I betrayed my surprise with a rather colorful swear I'd picked up from Jones.

"A strange twist of fate," he explained. I couldn't tell from his expression how he felt about it, but he added nonchalantly, "Thankfully, our succession laws don't exclude non-magi… yet. All the more reason to get this business done and dusted."

Despite the skeleton staff, we were offered refreshments as soon as we entered the little conservatory where our meeting was apparently to be held. Ed discussed progress while Holly sat beside him and gazed out the room's broad windows. Still unsettled, I stood and leaned against them, letting the chill touch of the glass cool my heated skin. I could still feel all those eyes on me. How close had they come to seeing me transform?

"And what's your secret then?" I heard. These words rang louder and more direct than the rest of the conversation.

"I beg your pardon?" I asked, forgetting in whose presence, whose palace, I currently stood.

Prince Godric raised an eyebrow at me. Without looking away, he asked, "Edward, do all your spies keep things so close to the vest?"

"Calandra is a special case," Ed replied.

"So let's hear it," Godric pressed.

Both Holly and Ed looked to me, and I scowled at Godric.

"No. I do my job. I do it well. *That* is all you need to know."

"I'm your Prince, and it is a matter of national security."

"I said no. Would you like to call some guards to haul me off to the dungeons, or shall I find a room for myself?"

It was a gamble, I knew. My heart raced as I hoped the cells in the dungeons hadn't changed much since I'd last seen them several hundred years before. Back then, they had not been built for keeping ravens inside. I also had some faith in Ed and Holly's pull with the Prince.

A moment of tense silence passed before Godric chuckled to himself.

"Very well, Calandra. Keep your secrets, but you've set a high bar for yourself indeed."

He turned to Holly as I silently glared. The conversation continued, but I didn't care to hear it. Not until the topic of Nicodemus—Thorne, rather—came up.

"From what we can gather, he's holed up in the heart of the Synod with the Queen," Godric explained. "I prefer to strike at their heart. Kill him, and the rest will scatter and fall."

"I thought we meant to bring him to trial," Ed said. "We cannot sink to their level, remember?"

Godric gave a careless wave of his hand. "Yes, but that's not always possible in these situations. Do you honestly think the Grand Magus will go down peacefully? Our last reports indicated he seemed… unbalanced of late. And his attack in Bone Port suggests that rumor may be true."

Holly took a measured look around the room, her eyes resting on me momentarily. Turning back to the Prince, she argued, "The device may render much of this discussion moot. It will break his power."

I stood completely still. Questions concerning the mysterious device, about which I still knew little, whirled in my head, twisting together with another thought.

Break his power.

I hadn't considered what Nicodemus' death meant. What effect would it have on me? It had always seemed so far away.

~Chapter 14~

In the dead of night, the walls of the palace rumbled, waking all within. The night outside lit up like daylight. We ran to the windows to see the Agate district all the way on the other side of the city alight, belching smoke into the sky. Everyone ran to assist. When I arrived outside the walls of that quarter, I saw even the Prince assisting with the relief efforts.

The very richest inhabited this sector of the Agate district. It was also the home of theatres, galleries, and parks. And every bit burned in flames of orange and green.

"Get up on that wall!" Godric called. "We need to contain this!"

I didn't know who he'd been addressing, but followed the order. Other Lamplighters clambered up to the top of the wall with me. At the top, a fiery lake met our eyes. I had never wished to be able to transform into my other form before that night. We couldn't see more than a few feet ahead. Through the shouts around me, I understood someone was in the middle of the conflagration, maintaining it. The heat was relentless. No one could get close without weapon or craft catching and burning to cinders. Responders called for water to beat back the flames, but it wasn't enough. Magical fire didn't follow the same rules as natural flames. I climbed back down from the wall and tried to draw close, thinking I could withstand the blaze and stop the magus within. Despite all I had endured, my own feet refused to carry me in. A familiar voice yelled from behind me over the din.

"I can shield you."

I turned and found Holly standing there.

"What?" I shouted back, not entirely sure I had heard her right.

"With ice. I can shield you so you make it through."

"It's too much," I objected.

"I'm strong."

I hesitated. Doubt in Holly's abilities wasn't my true objection. On the contrary, I felt perfectly confident about her powers.

No. No. No, my heart beat.

I don't know what showed in my expression just then, but Holly added, "The entire city will burn if we don't do something."

She was right. And I believed she'd already weighed the risks. It was an easy calculation, but I didn't like it. I looked back to the fire and drew in a steadying breath, nodding.

"Do it."

Holly held out her hands and surrounded me in a bubble of magical ice. Even through it, I could feel the heat of the flames. I ran in, forcing myself to keep my eyes open and telling myself Holly *would* protect me. The roar was immense, a physical force pressing in all around me. My head pivoted back and forth, seeking the magus. From what I had heard, he or she should be near where we had landed our craft. I wondered briefly how our arrival related to this attack, for surely it was connected. I recognized the little alcove where I had transformed.

Close.

I should be close.

I had no idea how hard the ice bubble taxed Holly. What would happen to me if her strength gave out? Could my body stand incineration? I didn't fancy finding out, not while Nicodemus still lived. I clamped down on suspicions of betrayal the darkest parts of my memory whispered. I did *not* have time for those. Not now!

I spotted a shadow darker than the flames, a figure that didn't move and dance like everything else. Arms stretched out to its sides, it formed a perfect target. For what? Bloody blazes, I had forgotten to grab a weapon! With no other options, I hurtled towards the figure and drove my fist into its head. The figure stumbled back, and the bulk of the flames dissipated. Countless buildings and their trappings still burned around us, however. The magus, a young woman, panting, doubled over. Her eyes cut to me, and a hateful scowl seared across her soot-smeared face.

"Wretch!" she snarled, lifting her hands back up.

I attacked again, Holly's bubble still surrounding me. Shards of ice sliced at the magus' skin as I came within range. We fought. She had been trained, but not as well as I. In the back of my mind, I thanked Flynn for his merciless lessons. She jumped back and flung her arms out wide.

"Die, underling!" she spat, swinging her palms back towards one another.

I knew what the gesture meant. The magus was combusting herself.

"HOLLY!" I screamed. "SHIELDS!"

I saw the energy wave form and approach as her hands made contact with one another. It trembled in the air, gold and white, rippling out. It passed around me. My bubble flickered but held. I turned to watch it go. I saw people on the walls through the smoke, much diminished now since only natural fires remained. Similar protections shimmered around each of them, every person contained within an orb of safety. More waves followed the first as the energy of the magus' power dissipated. She had been strong. I watched the bubbles hold. From the corner of my eye, I saw the magus simply… crumble. She fell to pieces, which shattered into specks, which then dissolved into the air. This all took seconds, but I remember it in minutes.

After the lethal ripples dispersed, becoming fainter with each pass, our shields faded. The magus' body was nothing more than motes shining in the glow of the fires. I ran back the way I came, exultant and looking for Holly. I was going to hug her. I was actually going to hug a magus! People clustered outside the entrance to what had, until moments ago, been one of the most opulent sections of the Agate quarter, now a charred ruin. I heard Godric's voice shouting orders, calling for a healer. I ran faster and shoved my way through the knot of humanity. Lying on the ground was Holly, pale and unmoving.

)(

The worst was telling Ed. He had been assisting with relief efforts elsewhere. Godric and I sat with him in a small room before a cheerfully crackling fire. The sight of it made me sick. Ed buried his face in his hands and keened. I think both the Prince and I knew nothing could ease his pain, but we tried anyway.

"Holly's sacrifice saved hundreds of lives."

"She was proud to serve and protect."

"She will be honored."

"She was the best of us."

When Jones arrived two days later, I told her myself, not long after she had handed her horse over to the stable master. I held her while she wept.

The war didn't care about our tragedies.

Our operations continued to roll forward. Ed and Jones and all the rest of us carried on in our duties with more fervor, Ed almost frenetic. The next week, our forces moved. We approached by night, and the Synod was lit up like a beacon in the dark. From our camp, beyond firing distance of magic and missiles, we had one more task to complete before beginning the siege. Ed, Jones, and I gathered together in our shared tent.

"This was Holly's greatest creation," Ed explained to me.

I had never been told what the device did exactly, just that it would turn the tide for us. And that it must be used in secret and at the eleventh hour.

"She hated making it," Jones said, her voice low.

"And yet she understood the necessity," Ed said. "Difficult times lie ahead, even now at the eve of our victory."

"What is it?" I asked, not for the first time.

The other two looked to one another and then at the open tent flap. Ed went to close it.

"Calandra," Jones said gently, placing a hand on my arm. "This... you might not survive this. To be honest..." Her voice caught in her throat. "We don't know what it's going to do to you."

"Kill me," I said, almost laughing. "That'd be a pretty good trick."

Jones and Ed exchanged another glance.

Ed's voice was flat as he said, "This machine will destroy the magical resonance permeating our atmosphere. Do you understand? It's going to destroy magic. Completely. Our magi know what's coming."

I tried to wrap my brain around the concept. It was like being told two plus two is seventeen. Failing to understand, I scrunched my features together. "That would be like making the earth disappear beneath our feet."

"Holly found the frequency. From there, she devised a way to create and spread the opposite signal. It's the same thing the magi do when they combust themselves, only in reverse."

I shook my head to straighten out my scattered thoughts. It didn't work, so I tried to talk through them instead. "Assuming this works, you suspect the annihilation of magic might result in my death… because of the enchantment?"

"Yes," they replied together.

"But what about me killing Nicodemus?" I demanded.

"You know we don't have a chance of getting close before we activate the device," Jones said. "Please believe us, we've tried to figure out another way. Truly, but he's too entrenched. We'd lose at least half our people in the fight. This way, as many lives as possible are spared."

"And the Arnavi? What of your promise to them? Your offer to the Allens?"

Ed shook his head. "A necessary deception."

I gawped at them, my face heating. I stared daggers at the infernal contraption, wanting to tear it apart myself, but I stood frozen to the spot.

Lives.

So many human lives.

This price was for all of the Lamplighters waiting for battle around our tent. For those who had already given their lives. For Holly, who had created this… *thing*, knowing it would take away her power and the powers of countless others. And they, our enemies, had no idea.

"This is the solution to save our world," I whispered.

An end to magic. The idea suddenly made my heart spring back to life.

"But Nicodemus…" I said.

I looked up to see tears shining in Jones' eyes.

"We don't know what's going to happen. If you survive, he's all yours."

Anger roiled within me, but I put a damper on it, knowing there was no other way. I nodded. I had lived far longer than I ever should have. If I died here, at least I would find peace with my family.

"Just in case," I began carefully, "if I lose my memory or something..."

"Yes?" Ed asked.

I flicked my eyes to him. "Remind me to never make a deal with you."

Jones nodded and failed at smothering her smile. She reached out, and I took her hand.

Stars, I prayed. *Please let me live to kill Nicodemus.*

Ed nodded and saluted me, a fist pressed to the opposite shoulder. I returned the gesture. Then he turned a wheel on the device. It was about the size of a wine barrel with all manner of levers and dials and a few handles. The dials began to flick to the right under their covers. The machine hummed to life. He turned some of the handles, checked the dials, and pulled a few of the levers. There was a small green section on each dial face. I could tell Ed was trying to make them all hit that range, whatever it was.

"Come on, Holly, help me out," he muttered under his breath, and a tear rolled down his face.

He wasn't sure what he was doing. Blazes. That was when I really began to worry. The device hummed on, squealed for a minute until Ed turned one of the handles back. It began to... moan?

It was a low sound, a resonant bass note, but mournful. The air around us began to waver like the air on a hot day. The dials were all almost in the green. Ed eased one of the levers, and the last dial slipped into place. The noise grew. It sounded like the groaning of a ship and grew faster with each passing moment. The disruption pulsing through the air increased, and Jones drew me more tightly to her. I heard her whispering prayers under her breath, and I squeezed her arm. I didn't close my eyes. I wouldn't. I would face my fate head on.

The waves in the air pressed forward, as if fighting against something. Then, with a great crack, the balloon of dissonance exploded outward, blowing out through our tent flaps, shaking them. The sound carried on, traveling outward, a great rending of the air, receding from us as it spread. I remained where I stood. Nothing felt different. I looked to Jones. She looked like she couldn't believe what she was seeing, like something was wrong.

Cries went up from the camp, a great, collective wail.

"Those are our people," Ed said, looking away from me. "Knowing isn't the same as feeling it happen. Jones, they need us."

Jones looked from him to me.

"I'm fine," I told her, not quite believing it myself.

She nodded and left, not letting go of my hand until the last moment. A few minutes after they left, I walked out of the tent and looked toward the Synod. It sat low against the ground from this distance. I listened for the same cries from there. I knew we were too far away, but I imagined the wind carried howls of despair to me. I wanted to smile, truly, but I felt no warmth from it. Cold satisfaction, yes. This was the first step, but somehow, the victory lacked the joy I'd expected.

)(

Our forces should have attacked that night, but it took longer for us to rally the broken magi than we'd anticipated. Many were ill from the shock of losing their powers. Some said it felt as if their very essence had been ripped from their bodies. Others reported it was like having their hearts carved out with a dull knife. We kept an eye on the horizon for retaliation, but none came. I watched as an aeromobile fell from the sky. Given that magical energy fueled Quarkz stones and Quarkz stones fueled many of our machines, the repercussions began to sink in.

In the hour before dawn, a bright new idea occurred to me. Even though I still lived, perhaps the curse was ended. Yes! That had to be it. Our magi's powers were destroyed, emptied. I had listened to as many as I could throughout the night, each story of pain and despair giving me hope. Do not misunderstand me. I took no pleasure in their grief, but the proof of their loss convinced me the curse must be dead. When I heard the hideous song of sunrise begin to bubble in me, however, I turned to the east and gritted my teeth. Standing beside the tent I shared with Jones and Ed, I told myself this sense was out of habit, a honed skill that would fade with time. I glared at the brightening horizon, denying its power over me. Yet, as soon as that glowing, orange orb crested the horizon, I felt the magic begin to pulse through my veins like a terrible and perfect symphony. The curse invaded me as it always had, twisting me, turning me to its vile will.

Jones found me crying as only a raven can and held me in her arms. She told Ed I couldn't fight.

"Nicodemus' forces are not yet defeated," he said, looking down at me with hard eyes. "Will you really falter so close to our goal?"

"Ed!" Jones scolded.

"The circumstances don't matter," he said. "Only the goal."

No! I protested, squawking and shaking my head. *Circumstances always matter!*

He had finished with me, however, and was already walking away. Jones quickly settled me onto a cot before she too had to leave. I had planned on being a part of the initial strike. Before I knew the device's purpose, my plan had been to wheel overhead and observe enemy troop movements, but now I couldn't bring myself to even lift my wings.

)(

I heard the battle from all the way in our tent and listened closely. The sounds of war are destruction, pain, and chaos. It was stupid, I know, but I kept listening for distinct voices. For Jones and Ed and even Flynn. Despite losing their power, the Synod magi were not alone. The Queen and her men were there too, and they had no doubt trained their magical allies in combat, just as the magus from the Agate quarter had been trained. I thought again of all the lives on the battlefield, of Lamplighter lives that would be lost today. I thought of my friends who might already be lost.

I could help them, spare some of them. I could still move, but my own despair clawed at me, trying to pull me down deeper. It slid along my mind and taunted that my friends were likely already dead. There was no point. I was too late. A failure in every way, as I had always been. Shame wrapped its inky tentacles around me. Flapping my wings in an effort to shake it off, I fluttered out of the tent without meaning to. Outside, I spied smoke in the distance, and my heart quickened. Despair reached for me again, but I took flight, zooming upward. I envisioned myself rising above the dark talons grappling at my heart. They were still there. I could feel them, enticing me to come back and wallow. But I didn't want to wallow. Now that I was in motion, I could keep going. I could outrun despair. The faster it pursued me, the faster I flew.

)(

I scanned the area below. Melee fighters clashed all over the ground, while a handful of our gunfighters had managed to climb up onto the outer walls of the Synod. The Synod's guns and other armaments relied on magic for extra damage, rendering them almost useless now. The Lamplighters had prepared accordingly, though fear of hitting their comrades in the fray below prevented them from taking many shots. Our strategy had been to fight from a distance for as long as possible. The enemy, even deprived of their magic, had not backed down. Seeing their tactical disadvantage, they rushed our army, forcing us to fight at close range. The Lamplighters had breached the outer walls of the manor and were gaining ground, but the building itself was a veritable fortress. My opportunity to prevent surprises had passed, but I could disrupt enemy fighters. I dive-bombed them, flying at their faces with claws outstretched, giving individual Lamplighters a momentary advantage. It wasn't much, I know, but every assist provided a small victory.

Throughout the day, the Lamplighters pushed the enemy back. They barricaded themselves inside. We'd brought heavy siege weaponry, however. Even with our success, the body count was higher than we'd predicted before the Synod members began to surrender. Ed had instructed we take prisoners, and a dedicated team rolled in behind the fighters to facilitate the gargantuan effort. I circled the manse, searching for some small entry point. Sunset approached, and I wanted to find a place within to hide and transform. I wanted to be ready, to find Nicodemus and kill him as soon as possible. Every window, door, and vent was either locked up tight or too small for me to fit through.

Very well then. I'd fight near the main doors where we had nearly broken through. I pecked and cawed and scratched, whirling overhead and diving and zooming back up, always keeping one eye on the manor. The moment we breached it, I'd rush in. Distraction was my downfall.

Night fell.

One of the Queen's men swung a cudgel at me as evening's song sang in my veins. I hadn't been careful enough, hadn't retreated when I should have. The weapon missed, just barely, and I flew up, out of his reach. I had never transformed in midair before. As one might expect, I plummeted to the ground like a sack of potatoes. My leg folded beneath me all wrong as I landed. I swore and cried out in pain. Like wolves on a sickly deer, enemy soldiers homed in on me. Lamplighter gunfire dropped most of them as they broke away to kill me, but one managed to bridge the gap between us. To add insult to injury, he hacked at my broken leg. Thank the stars for armor, but he still managed to get a few decent hits in. I rolled and grabbed an abandoned bayonet, stabbing wildly. It took me a moment to realize what was happening when the man slumped forward, landing on top of me. Blood poured from his stomach, running over my hands as I gripped the bayonet handle, the blade buried hilt-deep in his flesh. More blood gushed from a bullet wound in his neck.

I pushed the body off of me. None of the gunfighters I could see were looking at me. Even if any of them had seen me transform, they had higher priorities than me. Like invading the manor, which we had apparently just broken into. Unable to walk, I dragged myself across bodies and called for help at the top of my lungs. I heard the clang of weapons and the crack of gunfire further in. My cries melded with the groans of the dying. If anyone heard me, they ignored me. So close. I could taste the honey of victory on my tongue. If I could just get up!

Try as I might, I could only crawl painfully towards the sound of battle. Around me, Synod forces backed down, falling to their knees with hands above their head. With each surrender, the atmosphere quieted a little more, save for a dull, regular boom somewhere below.

"Bird brain?"

I turned at the voice. Flynn, bloodied and filthy but standing, approached through the darkness.

"Please, I—" I croaked.

Flynn offered me his shoulder before I'd finished speaking, and I accepted it gratefully. He began to turn us away from the manor.

"No!" I said, perhaps too frantically. "I need to get inside, to Nic—the Grand Magus."

Flynn didn't ask why and turned us toward the manse again.

"Word is he's holed up below," Flynn told me.

"Then that's where we need to go," I rasped, simultaneously trying to hold up a mental wall against the agony ripping through my leg. Blazes, it felt like broken glass churned underneath my skin.

"We can go faster, but—" he began.

"Please! I'll buy you drinks for the rest of your life."

Flynn chuckled and threw me over his shoulder, bracing my legs against his chest. I screamed as pain shot through my leg, but we were moving faster now.

It'll all be worth it, I told myself, clenching my teeth. *Soon.*

More Lamplighters spotted us, called out about getting medical help, but Flynn ignored them and jogged on. As we made our way into the lower levels of the Synod, Flynn told me how the Queen had at last surrendered, but the Grand Magus had barricaded himself in a small room at the base of the building.

Ducky's office.

I knew that had to be it as soon as he said it. When we drew close, Flynn set me down and offered me his shoulder again. The gathered crowd parted for us as we hobbled through, Flynn throwing around his rank. Ed and Jones were there, directing the battering ram team.

"Cali!" Jones cried. "There you are! We sent someone to—"

"Is he in there?" I grated.

She looked around before turning back to me. "We're pretty sure."

I looked around us too. There were too many people here. I'd never get my revenge with all these onlookers. I could see the wheels in Jones' head spinning. She turned back to the crowd.

"Remember," she called to them, "we need him alive. This bastard is heading back with us."

The battering ram made slow but steady progress against the ancient doors. Someone handed me a crutch while we waited. My breath came quicker with each bang of the ram, my heart pounding with it. My palms slicked with sweat, and the pain in my leg faded into the background of my anticipation. With one final heave, the door burst open, and Ducky's original desk screeched against the floor as it reluctantly slid away from the doors back towards the wall.

Looking inside, my eyes landed on a rope hanging from the chandelier and a footstool beneath Nicodemus' feet. On the back wall, scrawled in black and something that was drying to brown, were the words,

Without power, there is nothing.

I forced my gaze up to Nicodemus' face, seizing his eyes in my vision. Emptiness stared back at me. Cold whirlpools of despair.

"Grab him!" Jones shouted next to me.

She, Ed, and a small cadre of furious soldiers hurtled forward.

My mind hadn't put the pieces together. I watched, too far away to do anything now, as Nicodemus rocked back on his stool. My legs moved as my spirit screamed against what my eyes saw happening in slow motion.

No! Not like this! You don't get off that easy!

The stool toppled. Nicodemus' body fell. I skidded to a halt.

"Got him!" Ed cried, grasping Nicodemus around the waist and holding him up.

"No," rasped a broken voice I didn't recognize.

I watched as Nicodemus' pilfered mouth formed the words, but the voice couldn't have been his.

"Grand Magus Thorne," barked Jones, "by order of Prince Godric, you have been declared an enemy of the state. You will be tried for your crimes against the people of Invarnis. Do you understand what I have just said to you?"

"It doesn't matter," croaked Nicodemus. "Nothing matters." He craned his neck up and jerked it back down. The rope barely pulled taut, and Ed hoisted him up further. Nicodemus' eyes swiveled around the room and landed on me. "Kill me. Please."

~Chapter 15~

Several nights later, after we were all back in Prism and Nicodemus had been locked away by himself in a secret location, Jones and Ed escorted me to his cell. It was less a cell and more of a well-fortified closet tucked down in the lowest level of the palace and at the end of a long corridor with no other doors or windows. Ed sent the guards on duty away to a celebration taking place a few floors up.

"You've all been through a lot," Ed said with the barest hint of a smile. "Go. Relax and reward yourselves. You've earned it."

Once the guards were gone, I turned to him, my heart hammering in my chest. "You were so insistent on having a public trial for him? What changed?"

"That's perhaps a fate too good for him," Ed sighed. "Do you really think he deserves the chance to go free?"

"Heavens, no!" I retorted. "Would that… would that really happen?"

"With a fair trial, there's always a chance," Jones explained. "One way or another."

"What does that mean?" I asked, wiping my sweating palms on my trousers.

Jones shot a glance at Ed and said, "I say innocent until proven guilty. This one's been talking about doing it the other way around."

"And what about Godric?" I continued. "What will he do when he finds out?"

"He won't care," Jones said, flapping her hand. "He's too focused on the Queen's trial. It's gonna be a proper spectacle."

"One that you two have to figure out?" I asked.

"Not that we'll get to if we stand here forever," Ed replied, giving me a pointed look.

I nodded and swallowed hard. Jones unsheathed a slender dagger, and the *shhhhik* of it against its leather scabbard sounded far too loud to my ears. I wished I had my lightning rod, but I'd misplaced it somewhere in the chaos of the last week. I told myself it didn't matter, that the thing had probably become a lifeless hunk of metal since we'd set off the device, but a part of me wanted to test it and know for certain. Dismissing these thoughts, I tried to breathe deep, but I couldn't seem to get enough air into my lungs.

"Don't worry," Jones said, offering me the blade. "We're right here. We've got your back."

I looked at it resting in her palm and then back at her. Nodding again, I reached for it. It felt as if my hand moved against a current, pushing me back. I made myself grab the knife, holding it so tightly my knuckles turned white. Ed looked back to me before unlocking the door, and I took a step back when he opened it. I don't know what I expected, but nothing happened in the following moments. Swallowing hard again, I stepped forward, around Ed, and looked into the cell.

Sitting on the floor, bound at his wrists and ankles, sat Nicodemus in his stolen body. His head lolled back as he stared blankly up at the ceiling. His clothes were dirty, the same ones he wore when we arrested him in Ducky's office. Dried saliva and mucus streaked his face. I could tell he had been crying.

I took three more steps, pushing myself past the threshold and into the room.

"I'm going to shut this. Okay, Cali? To… you know, muffle the sound," Jones said gently from behind me. When I didn't respond, she added, "We're right here. Shutting the door now. Going slow."

"No. Please," I said, not looking away from Nicodemus. "I can't. I just… I can't."

I felt the weight of hesitation behind me. Finally, Ed said, "We can't. If—"

"What if I came in there too?" Jones offered, cutting him off. "Would that be okay? Or, if you don't want to—"

"No!" I snapped. "I have to."

"Okay, but we can't have the sound travelling," Jones soothed. "What do you want?"

I stared down at Nicodemus, who continued to gaze at the ceiling. My voice cracked as I said, "Please come in here with me. I'm sorry, I just…"

"No need to be sorry," Jones replied, her voice right behind me now. She put a hand on my arm, adding, "Ed's gonna close the door now. Deep breath."

I heard her breathe with me, and the door clicked gently shut behind us.

"I'm still here. You good?"

I nodded, my eyes still on the husk of a man before me. I took a step forward, breaking away from Jones.

"Look at me," I whispered. Nicodemus didn't move and, surprising myself, I kicked his foot. "I said look at me!"

Nicodemus' head rolled around to face me, but he said nothing.

"Why am I still cursed?" I demanded.

Nicodemus shrugged, and I knelt down. His hands rested clasped on top of his leg. I looked down at them, and fury sizzled in my veins. Like a viper striking, I stabbed the dagger into his hands. The blade pierced flesh and bone, pinning both hands, which had committed so many evils against me and others, to his thigh. Nicodemus cried out, squirming away, but I pressed the blade in deeper, and he stopped moving, groaning to himself.

"Why. Am I. Still. Cursed?" I snarled.

"I don't know," Nicodemus whined. "I don't know anything." I twisted the dagger, and he added, "I never made sense of anything about you. Nothing… in the blood, the bones. No signs of magic anywhere."

I glanced to Jones. She shrugged.

"What does that mean?" I asked. I ripped the knife out of Nicodemus' hand. "Tell me!"

"Magi bodies bear markings non-magical people's don't." His voice almost sounded like a sigh. "They probably don't now. Now that it's all gone…"

I wanted to slap him, but I couldn't make myself raise my hand to touch his face. Instead, I stabbed his hands again.

"You're telling me everything I went through, every one of your sick experiments, was for *nothing*?!" I growled.

Nicodemus yowled. "Yes! I don't know what happened." He gasped to catch his breath. "I told you, you're a fluke."

"I AM NOT A FLUKE!" I cried, pulling the dagger towards me, the blade still buried in Nicodemus' hands and thigh.

Nicodemus shrieked as the dagger found the path of least resistance, slicing through tendon and flesh, gliding along his bones, before flying free in a spurt of blood.

Seeing the grievous injury, all the other things I could do to him flashed through my mind. I could carve off each finger, knuckle by knuckle, more slowly than he had removed mine. I could peel his skin from his bones or carve out his eyes or just start hacking pieces off willy-nilly.

Nicodemus howled, cradling his bloody hands against his chest. I sat and watched, twisting my face in disgust as the subject of my nightmares blubbered and moaned. Still sobbing, he turned his eyes back to me. The imposter I had known for so long stared out at me from those glassy orbs, but all hope had left him.

"What does it feel like?" he asked. "To still touch the power of the Dritch?"

He rolled towards me, bleeding hands reaching, and I shot to my feet.

"Hey!" Jones snapped, delivering a swift kick to his side.

Nicodemus curled into a ball like a snail into its shell. Jones looked at me, her mouth an apologetic 'o'.

Sorry, she breathed.

I gave her a nod.

Nicodemus peeked back up at me, wet-faced and blood-smeared. His voice was mournful as he whispered, "Be grateful you still have such a gift."

Before I knew what I was doing, I stooped beside him and spat, "It isn't a gift!"

And I sank the dagger into his neck, burying it to the hilt. He jerked and gurgled on his own blood, coughing it onto the floor beneath him. Eyes wide, he twitched like a fish on a line for a few moments, blood pooling underneath his neck and head. Jones motioned for me to step back, and I obeyed, never even blinking as I watched the light leave Nicodemus' eyes.

When he'd stopped moving, she reached down, carefully avoiding the blood, and slid the knife back out of his throat. I continued to stare, not quite believing what I'd done. Jones cleaned her weapon before re-sheathing it and stepped around the body to stand next to me. She said nothing.

The scene from Ducky's office just a few days ago replayed before my eyes.

"He wanted to die, Jones," I whispered. "And I gave him what he wanted."

Part 3

The Dawn Age: Rebuilding

~Chapter 16~

The first time I laid eyes on the so-called Halls of Justice, I wasn't sure whether to laugh or cry. Located in a grand building in the Ivory district of Springhaven—formerly Prism—it served as the Enforcers' base of operations and had been constructed relatively recently. I'd heard it was magic-proof to keep all the former Synod magi within contained, though how could anyone tell if the precautions worked? The interior rivaled the palace, with cream walls and white marble floors streaked with black and grey. Unlike the palace, however, every inch of the place reeked of misery and despair. This was the permanent home for all criminals.

"Quite a setup you have here," I said, slamming open the door to First Ed's office. First Edward to his men.

The First reigned as head Enforcer. Jones held the title as well, down in Bone Port. Under the First were Seconds, under them Thirds, and so on, all the way down to the Sixths, who were new recruits. Jones never was good with naming things.

Ed jumped to his feet, but relaxed when he saw me. His eyes scanned me in his usual manner.

"You look terrible," he said. "I thought you'd been with Jones this whole time."

"I have been," I replied, swaying as I strode in.

"Stars, have you been drinking, Calandra?" he asked.

"Just a little, but it hits hard when you're a wee birdie," I grinned. "I was bored and wanted to see what would happen."

To be honest, this was not my finest moment. Not only does alcohol make flying difficult, resulting in a less-than-graceful entrance into the Halls of Justice, but I'm not sure I would have gone to see Ed that day if it hadn't been for the ill-conceived experiment.

Ed made a noise of disgust in his throat, and I curled my lip at him. "It's not like I have anything better to do."

"Still a bitter shrew, I see," he sighed, looking back to his desk.

"Still a dour prat, I see."

"Is there a reason you're here?"

"Yes. I have a file to complaint." I stopped, thought, and shrugged. "Your Enforcer… force, they're pretty ruthless, aren't they?"

"They're effective," he said, raising an eyebrow at me.

"Effective isn't the word I would use. Automatic life sentence for *all* crimes? Plus brutal treatment and living conditions for inmates. I'd describe that as… Nicodemus-y."

Ed glowered at me. "How dare you?"

"I'm just calling it like I see it." I bared my teeth at him in a cold facsimile of a smile. "Your new society is as bad as theirs. Have you seen what Jones has done? Perhaps you should take a leaf out of her book."

"People only understand consequences. Seeing what happens to lawbreakers will deter others from following in their footsteps. The only way to prevent people from being hurt is to keep people from committing crimes in the first place. Think of the war—"

"I'd rather not."

"—If the magi had been scared enough of us, think of all the lives that would have been spared. We waited too long, Calandra, made some bad choices, but we can, we *are* doing better this time."

"If only you and Godric could meet in the middle," I said, rolling my eyes. "To be honest, I don't think Holly would agree with you. She believed in the strength of kindness, the power of choice. She—"

"Don't you *dare* talk to me about Holly!" Ed snarled, standing up and leaning over his desk. "You always hated her. You—"

"I was wrong!" I shot back. "I've admitted that, so don't go throwing it in my face!"

We stared each other down across the desk. Ed relented first, taking the high road. I did not follow.

Plucking a pen from a cup sitting between us, I said, "I'm taking this. You going to lock me up? It could be interesting. What will your men say when they find a raven in the cell instead? You think they'll be so convinced that magic is gone?"

Ed closed his eyes and took a deep breath. "Calandra, I'm sorry. I'm sorry for your curse and Nicodemus and... for how everything has played out. I truly am. The rest of us have moved on. I think it's time you did too."

"Move on?" I barked out a laugh. "Move onto where? How?"

I laughed some more, and he shook his head at me.

"I can't help you, Calandra."

My laughter subsided, and my voice grew harsh. "No. You can't even help your city."

I'd flown in as a raven, but walked out through the front door. When questioned by passing Enforcers, I told the truth.

"I was visiting an old friend. Ed and I saved the world together."

)(

My argument with Ed refused to stop playing in my head. *They're effective*, he'd said of his gang of thugs. The memory burned me up inside. An idea began to form and, a few days later, I walked to a shady bar I frequented. The owner was a gent called Indigo, and I knew him to be a small-time criminal. Nothing serious. More than anything, he provided a place for other people to make felonious deals, but he had his fingers in a few other pies. His establishment squatted inside one of the few, original Old World buildings left in the city, which was half the reason I liked it. I sat down in my usual spot at the bar—a dark corner at the end—and Indigo slid over to me.

"Always so nice to see your pretty face, Raven," he said. Using code names was standard practice in places like this. Indigo's grizzled stubble smiled at me as much as his mouth did.

I dropped a few coppers onto the counter. "Let's start with this. And stop pretending it's my face you're happy to see."

"Not your best day, eh?" he asked, grabbing me a glass.

"Oh, there's more," I said, giving him a lazy smile. Stealing as a raven is easy. Transporting the goods is the hard part, which makes jewelry and gems the best targets. "I need to talk to you."

He raised a dark eyebrow at me. "Why don't you come into the back. No chance of this rabble hearin' us."

I followed him back. Some mismatched leather armchairs sat arranged around a fireplace. The chairs were worn and comfortable, and I settled into one, drink firmly in hand.

"What'cha got for me then?" Indigo asked.

He resembled an armoire in the dim light. Broad shoulders and dark skin. If I had to guess, I'd bet his parents were both Arnavi, but we never exchanged questions like that. That was one of the reasons I liked him.

"I want to work for you," I said, before taking a long sip of my drink.

"Work, eh? What kind of work?"

I shrugged. "Information is what I do best. Purely on a contractor basis."

"You mean a mercenary informant," he said, scratching his stubble.

"More or less."

"Why?"

I smiled. "To annoy someone."

That's how our partnership started, how all my partnerships started. Indigo wasn't terribly ambitious. In fact, he was fairly lazy when it came to business. He smuggled goods illegally because he couldn't be bothered with all the tariff paperwork and permits. More money for less work. He was one of the better folks I worked for, which meant I wasn't surprised when he got squeezed out by another chap, Cabernet, a few years later. Cab had all the ambition Indigo lacked, twice the charm, and none of the goodness. I slipped him information when it suited me, but I preferred working for people who weren't so… prickish. Besides, he did fine on his own. All the more reason for me to take my talents elsewhere. I never liked anyone having too much power.

That was my life for a long time. It became a game of sorts, keeping balance between the various crime syndicates as they rose and fell. It got me "killed" a few times, especially when certain people liked to believe they owned those around them. Seeing their faces when I sauntered back in the next day or so was priceless, doubly so when I used the lock-picking skills Flynn had taught me to get past their security measures. I was beheaded once by an especially unpleasant fellow. I actually laughed as the axe came down. Don't ask me how it happened. I just woke up the next day, late afternoon, as a raven. I had mixed feelings about that, to be honest. Now I was well and truly certain nothing could kill me, but certainty offered no comfort. I sold him out after visiting him one last time.

)(

The end of the war, now commonly referred to as the War of Light, would have been the perfect time to start a new age, which they did, but not in the old way. Instead of entering the Sixth Age, the high council—the intermediary body charged with forming this brave new world of ours—even rebuilt our calendar system. Every age would be one hundred years now, instead of waiting for an appropriately momentous event. Prince Godric dubbed this shining new era the Dawn Age.

The business of creating a new country had been a complicated one. As promised, Bone Port and the Southern Plains were made a single, new, independent region. The same went for Duskwood and the Bladed Mountains and Valley. As promised, Prince Godric abdicated the throne of Prism and instituted a new hereditary Parliament. Seats were given to families based on their service in the war. His own family, the Pendragons, received the most seats. One was granted to the Allen family, though it wouldn't be filled until one of their daughters claimed it. Meanwhile, the Allens were granted authority to rebuild Bone Port's governance from the ground up. They decided the people would elect their own representatives.

The Allens' plans for better relations with the Arnavi went up in flames. Our friends from across the sea were furious about Ed's deception and the destruction of magic. Prince Godric, Ciara and Luis, and others tried to parley with the Arnavi by offering gifts and new trade deals written ludicrously in the Arnavi's favor, but members of and representatives for the Arnavi Nish were too incensed to accept any of these. The Arnavi are a proud people, even prouder than we Bone Portis. They cared nothing for our reasons of security and secrecy. We had betrayed them, a sure sign they could no longer trust us. They didn't declare war on us, thankfully, but what they did was almost as damaging. The Arnavi withdrew, cut off trade, and left our shores entirely. Our new world's economy was crippled from the get-go, but our leaders pressed on.

There was the issue of public safety, of course. Those were some heated debates. Because magic had suffused every facet of life, much could no longer function without it. Electricity, for instance, which had depended on magi, was no longer available. And Quarkz stones were now nothing but pretty rocks. Some of the advances made possible by but independent of magic were now considered too dangerous to exist, which raised questions about all non-magical technology. For instance, black powder was a force almost as powerful as magic. Our new leaders decided to destroy the knowledge of how to create it.

"This is madness!" I shouted to the high council. "If we forget our mistakes, we are doomed to repeat them! Keep the information so future generations might know of the danger. Pass legislation regulating black powder's use if you want, but destroying knowledge will only lead to more problems."

"People determined to make and use it will do so no matter what laws we pass," Godric said calmly.

"So good to know you have zero faith in the power of law," I spat. "Why have laws at all if that's the case?"

"Cali," Jones said gently. "I know you're upset, but this can't be how we handle one another."

I dismissed her. Of course I was bloody upset. I wanted to feel passionate about making something of this world I had hoped for, but I couldn't find it in myself to care.

"If this is how you're going to conduct yourself, you will no longer be welcome in these meetings," Godric warned.

"What does it matter?" I muttered, glaring at all of them.

"Magic has tainted everything, Calandra," Ed said. His eyes were hard and sharp as he spoke. "You know this better than anyone. We must wipe clean all that we can bear."

"It's not our place to make this choice for all of Invarnis," I shot back. "Let the people decide."

"Now isn't the time," Godric argued. "Our foundation is too new and therefore fragile."

"Well, that is a grand way to start things off, isn't it?" I jabbed before storming out.

That night, I secreted a few books to my room. I couldn't risk taking too many, lest the others notice and suspect me. I had planned to steal more later, to start my own forbidden library, but the offending volumes went under lock and key the very next morning. The locks were complex, well beyond my capabilities, so I went to Flynn.

"You want me to defy direct orders just so you can keep your bedtime stories?" he scoffed, spitting into a porcelain teacup. I pitied the palace dishwashers.

"It's a mistake," I told him.

Flynn shook his head. "No can do, bird brain. I chose the locks myself. Ed said to make sure they kept you out."

I balled my fists at my side, my face heating with anger. At least I'd had the good sense not to mention the books I'd already squirreled away. I left him without another word. We rarely spoke again after that.

Jones and Ed were given the task of establishing new security forces, Jones in Bone Port and Ed in Prism.

"We're calling ourselves Enforcers," Jones explained to me one night. I did say she was always terrible at naming things.

"That's a bit severe," I snorted.

"Enforcers of the law," she said. "It's self-explanatory."

"Have fun with that," I said.

There was a long pause.

"Come with me, Cali," Jones said at last. "Being back home will do you good."

"I don't really have a home anymore," I replied, "but I suppose I could join you for a while."

After the war, people celebrated like thousands upon thousands of souls hadn't lost their lives in the battle against tyranny. I spat on the celebratory bonfires that destroyed our history and culture. When I returned to Bone Port, I brought my illegal tomes with me. There, I stored them away in a cave, one which was difficult to find amongst the pitch-black pathways lining the inside of the Giant's Maw. Wrapped in oilcloth, I tucked the books in a sheltered place. I've never gone back for them, as I don't yet know what purpose they might serve.

I stayed with Jones and saw her work with the Allens. Together, they established a new form of government. Every three years, the people elected members to a ruling council they called Admirals. The head of this body was called the Harbormaster. The people also elected their own judges and other civil servants. Voting was compulsory. Ciara and Luis stepped down from their positions as Count and Countess—Ciara was elected Harbormaster the first year and Luis the second, but they both retired after their first terms. Together, the people of Bone Port and the Southern Plains built a beautiful new city-state, which took joy in its culture and celebrated life, hard work, and cooperation. Despite layers of sickening censorship, the people remembered much through oral traditions. And to this day, they encourage learning and discovery.

To be surrounded by joy and hope when all you can feel is anger and impotent hatred is a special form of torment. I stayed in Bone Port a few years before getting fed up. Jones tried to convince me to stay, but too many memories, reminders of everything I had lost, all for naught, hovered around me there. I returned to Prism, now called Springhaven as part of this renewal scheme. What I found there matched my mood better, but it was not better. It wasn't long after my arrival there that I had my blowup with Ed.

)(

Ed eventually passed away. A heart attack took him thirty or so years into the Dawn Age. I wasn't terribly surprised. The stress combined with this new world's appalling lack of medical knowledge made something like this bound to happen. And, as I've learned, the universe has a twisted sense of humor. Jones came for the funeral, an evening service. She said some lovely words. I remained silent throughout. Afterwards, we went out for dinner.

"You look very good," I told her.

She really did. Her tanned skin practically glowed with health, and she looked as fit as I had ever seen her.

"Living in Bone Port will do that," she said, giving me a wry look.

"I credit coffee," I replied. "Tea's fine and all, but it doesn't kick you in the teeth."

"Are you looking for a kick in the teeth?" she asked. "Because I can oblige."

I raised an eyebrow at her, smirking. "What's that for?"

"Ed and I were pen pals," she said. "He knew about you, what you've been up to all these years."

"Oh, I see." I rolled my eyes. "Someone had to keep him and his little army in check."

"Actually, he appreciated what you've been doing. He just wished you had joined his side."

"Female Enforcers aren't so much the done thing here." I crossed my arms smugly.

"Heavens, I know!" Jones groaned. "Damn Godric and his absurd propaganda about women being *delicate*." She flapped her hands in the air and mocked, "We have to protect and shelter them." She followed this up with a disgusted noise in her throat.

"A fair few of those who fought were women. Proof positive they're the weaker sex, right?" I joked back.

"Proof positive of something. I think the death toll shook Godric, and protecting the ones who can bear children is the only way he knows to deal with it." She paused before speaking again. "Ed would have taken you on, you know? No questions asked. He always hoped you might cross over. That's why he protected you."

"And he knew an arrest wouldn't stick."

"That too." Jones lifted her drink to me. "Even so, you need to watch yourself now."

"Thanks for the concern," I said, tapping my glass against hers. "Tell me about life in Bone Port then."

"Why don't you come back and see for yourself?"

"Because I don't want to. If I did, I would have."

Jones sighed and set down her drink. "I wish you would. I don't have a lot of time left myself."

"What does that mean?" I asked, leveling my gaze at her.

She reached across the table, and I drew my hands back.

"Cali, I've got cancer," she said quietly.

I swore loud enough to make several people stare. Shaking my head, I growled.

"That's bloody perfect. Let me guess, it's curable, or would be if we hadn't torched the cure."

"Cali," she said, "those same cures unlocked terrible weapons. In another form, it's poison."

"I don't care," I murmured. "I just don't care. Everything comes at a price."

"Like magic? Healers could have fixed me right up too."

"It's not the same, and you know it. You can't regulate people."

"Isn't that like what Godric said to you?" Jones asked.

I gripped my head in both hands, swearing again. Jones kept her hands on the table, extended towards me.

"Come back with me," she urged, almost pleading.

"Why?" I croaked, not looking at her. "So I can watch yet another one of my friends die? Why would you ask this of me?"

"The time we have together is what counts," she said. "I miss you, Cali. Please."

"No. I can't do it, Jones. I'm sorry."

)(

Though I didn't like it, I'd realized a long time ago I needed some kind of semi-permanent residence. I rented a room in a cheap boarding house. It's called Madame Sincerity's Boarding House for Ladies now, a high-end establishment from what I've gathered. Back then it offered pretty much the same sort of services, only it wasn't just ladies. The woman running it rented the room to me—it was more an attic than a proper room—because it was too small for her other tenants', ahem, professional activities. A few days later, I found a letter waiting for me in my room. I recognized Jones' handwriting immediately.

Likely asking me to reconsider, I thought, tossing the letter onto a crate, which served as my bedside table.

I didn't even have a bed, just a pile of blankets. It was cramped at night, and the sounds floating up through my floor weren't terribly pleasant, but during the day, it was downright cozy.

I didn't attempt to contact Jones again. We'd fallen out of touch before anyway. Why start up a correspondence now? Several months later, I received another letter. A message scrawled across the back read:

Notice of Passage

Inside wasn't much more informative.

It is with a heavy heart that Bone Port bids farewell to one of its most beloved citizens. Agatha Jones, former Lamplighter Troop Commander, has passed away. She left no heirs and has chosen to pass her belongings on to the city of Bone Port. She will always be remembered as a hero of Invarnis and a leader within her community.

I threw the letter away as if it had bitten me. At a loss for words, a ball of heat built in my chest. Tears prickled behind my eyes. Fists clenched, I ground them against my traitorous eyeballs, urging the tears back. Inexplicably, Ed came to my mind. Then Holly and even Flynn. And so many more. I couldn't contain the wail that escaped my chest. My knees buckled beneath me, and I fell hard onto my bare, wooden floor. I laid there and wept, sobbing until my taut muscles hurt and my throat cracked.

I stayed there all night and the day after. When evening came again, I opened the letter Jones had sent to me during her visit months back.

I'm not going to ask you to reconsider.

The beginning set me weeping again. It was a while before I could continue.

I'm not going to ask you to reconsider. I just wanted to tell you, since I don't think we'll meet again, how much you mean to me. You are precious, Calandra. You are an important piece of this universe...

I never deserved Jones. This world didn't deserve her. The rest of the letter was more of the same, along with some things I'm not willing to share. The next few days were a fugue of misery and pain.

~Chapter 17~

I eventually lifted myself off the ground. Hunger-turned-to-pain drove me. When I left to buy food, I watched the city around me. It still reeled from the loss of magic, even thirty-some years later. Some of the magi had adjusted, but others… it really was as if a piece of their souls had been ripped away. They stared hollow-eyed, always searching and never finding. I felt for them, which did something to my soul I'm not sure I can describe. I wandered the dark streets and eventually found myself in the old Agate district, now known as Char. Nothing could wipe away the black streaks. Plenty had tried, and more would vainly try in the future.

I walked for decades like that, wandering, conducting my own search. I considered going back to Bone Port. My heart ached for the sight of my old home, but I knew nothing except more pain awaited me there. What was I to see? The graves of my family and friends, all gone now? I abandoned my room in the boarding house and took up a sort of residence in the Char quarter. It suited me. I never felt closer to my lost compatriots as when I leaned against those blackened walls. I know I frightened many a soul as I cawed throughout the day, camouflaged by the permanent devastation, my mournful cry echoing off the broken walls and down the ruined, crooked avenues. I saw others start as they glimpsed me drifting along the roads by night. I'm sure in my neglected dress, dark hair, and dusky skin I looked like a specter. I let them be.

I took to feeding only in my raven form and stopped working entirely. Being abandoned, the Char district became a hotbed for criminal activity, and I quickly learned the areas to avoid. I rarely spoke to other human beings during those years. Though it was by my own choice, I can't say it made me happy.

)(

One night, as I ghosted about, a strange noise caught my attention. Turning a corner, I happened upon a boy. He looked to be no older than ten, though his various disfigurements made it difficult to tell.

His arm was mangled like a twisted tree limb. He wore a simple cloth mask over one side of his face, but through the small eyehole I could see there was something very wrong with the orb within. It was milky and bulging. He was missing a leg and had replaced it with a crude collection of scrap metal, wood, and rope. One of his gnarled digits was caught in the joint of his leg which, from what I could tell, was jammed. The boy cried as he sat on the littered ground, trying to free himself from his own contraption.

"May I help you?" I asked.

I don't know if lack of use or a desire not to scare the lad softened my voice. Either way, he jumped and then cried out in pain as the joint closed more tightly around his finger. I knelt down, still several yards from him.

"I won't hurt you," I promised.

He reminded me of war victims I had seen. Both magic and our weapons left terrible scars and injuries in their wake. He was far too young for that, though. I didn't know what year it was anymore, but I had a sense it had been a long, long time since Jones' death.

He didn't answer me, and I asked, "What can I do?"

He finally found his voice and called, "Felly!"

His voice was perfectly normal, which increased my curiosity about his deformities. From the shadows limped a girl, moving quickly despite whatever ailed her. She must have been somewhat far away given the time it took for her to arrive. The girl—Felly, I presumed—appeared about the same age as the boy and had remarkably similar features. They both shared regal noses, strong jaws, and thick, wavy hair, though his was rather lighter than hers. She was heavier set than he, and they were both clearly in need of a good meal. The main difference between them was their expressions. His was frightened and open, hers sharp and hard.

"We don't want no trouble," Felly growled at me.

She knelt next to her brother. He spoke to her quietly, telling her what had happened, and she gently helped him extricate himself. It was easier with three good hands than one, but she always kept an eye on me. I didn't move. Once the boy's hand was free again, he stood and sucked on the injury, which oozed blood down his hand and onto his tattered shirt. His gait looked painfully uneven with his shoddy replacement leg, but he made it work. The children said nothing more to me, nor I to them.

After they'd left, I followed as far as I could, having let them out of my sight. I marked the area in my memory, now being as familiar with the Char district as I had once been with Ducky's manse or Bone Port, and returned the next day as a raven. For good measure, I had spent the rest of the night checking the most dangerous sections of Char and just beyond to ensure the children had not stumbled into them. I breathed a sigh of relief each time I found no trace of them.

At midday, searching from above, I found the two sleeping in the corner of an old courtyard. The original house, once a grand place, had long since fallen, but the courtyard had been paved with marble and surrounded by short walls of the same, plus an iron railing. The plants were long dead—nothing grew in Char then, just as nothing grows there now—but they had created a little nook for themselves between a fallen column and crumbling wall. They shared a threadbare blanket, and snuggled together in the shade of the wall, Felly's arm draped over her brother. I flew away and did what had become second nature to me. Several hours later, I had built up a small mound of tiny treasures at their feet. It wasn't much, but it would be enough for a few days' worth of food.

They awoke before sunset and spotted the pile instantly.

"It's a gift!" the boy exclaimed, tumbling forward.

His sister grabbed him and pulled him back. She held out a hand, shielding him as she crept forward, brandishing his false leg in the other. He'd removed it to sleep, along with his mask. His lid had covered the bulbous, milky-filmed eye, making it look somehow even more wrong.

As Felly slunk forward, I spied through her torn dress a large, poorly healed wound along her leg. It was angry and red, the skin broken in a spider web of tiny cracks, blood and pus dried in places. It appeared as if a beast had taken a chunk from her, leaving venom behind. I cawed, and both children looked towards me. Felly's expression turned puzzled, followed by the boy's. They looked back to the money, to me, and to the money again. Felly poked it with the false leg. When it fell over, as normal stacks of coins are wont to do when you poke them, she relaxed. Scooping up the prize, she looked to me again, still uncertain.

"Lowell, get your cloak," she said. "We're goin' into the city."

In the following days, I gathered what little bits and bobs I could for the two. I left them before evening fell, and I was glad to see their ribs fill in. Felly's leg grew no worse, nor did it improve. One afternoon, as Felly and Lowell talked softly to one another, discussing their plans for the evening, I stretched my wings to take flight.

"Calandra, no," Felly said.

I jumped, stumbled, and fell off the fallen column on which I roosted. Lowell looked alarmed as I struggled to right myself on the ground, an undignified spasm of feathers and wings and upturned feet. Felly's face was impassive.

"Don't leave," was all she said.

Finally on my feet again, I looked at her, cocking my head to the side. I cawed once, unable to stop myself despite knowing she couldn't understand me.

"I wanna see," she answered.

See what? I thought. A picture of myself in my human form appeared in my mind as evening's song whispered to me.

"Yes," Felly replied.

"But, Felly," Lowell whispered, looking to his sister. "Magic is dead."

"Not here," she said, turning towards him.

They exchanged a look I had seen before but had yet to understand. Felly looked to be in deep concentration, her eyes closed, while Lowell studied her intensely, almost looking past her face. His brow wrinkled.

"I don't understand," he told her.

"Just watch. Calandra, stay."

I bristled my feathers. Felly sounded like a master telling a dog to sit. She made a face at me, and I cawed indignantly.

The song of approaching night rose in my blood, sang through my veins, and surrounded me in its symphony. I watched as Lowell and even Felly's eyes widened with awe as the bedraggled raven before them grew and transformed into a human.

Lowell's eyes moved from my face to my dress. He reached out and stroked the fabric.

"She's real." He looked back to my face. "Are you a cursed princess?"

I grimaced. "Close enough."

Felly raised an eyebrow at me.

"And you, little miss," I scolded, turning to her. "Explain yourself."

"I don't need to explain nothing to you," she spat.

"Felly—" I began.

"Felicia," she snapped. She explained as if I were simple, "My name's Fel-i-cia."

I took a deep breath and told myself these were apparently not normal children. I was not a normal adult. Nothing about this situation was normal.

"Very well, Felicia," I said. "You wanted to see. You've seen. What now?"

"I remember you," Lowell cut in. "A few weeks back. You offered to help me."

"We don't need her help," Felicia growled.

"Funny. My help was good enough for you when I was a raven," I said.

Felicia said nothing to that, and Lowell tugged on her arm. "Oh, let's keep her, Felly. Please?"

The word struck a chord in me, shaking my insides. Despite being a human again, despite them being mere children, I took a step back. My eyes snapped to Felicia, suddenly hard like obsidian. She looked surprised. Lowell looked between us. His eyes were soft when he spoke to me.

"Miss, erm, Calandra…" He pronounced my name hesitantly, looking to Felicia again for a moment. "We wouldn't hurt you. You've been good to us."

Felicia said nothing and smiled unkindly at me.

"Felly, stop!" Lowell scolded, swatting her hand. "She's been so kind."

"She wants somethin'," Felicia replied so quickly it surprised me.

"Oh, yeah?" Lowell challenged. "What? What does she want?"

Felicia shook him off her. "I dunno yet! But she does. Why else would she help us?"

"Because you needed it," I said harshly.

Silence fell. Lowell looked to his sister, his eyes glistening, both the good one and the bad.

"I'm scared, Felly. Please don't drive her away. I don't think she wants to hurt us."

"I don't," I replied, my voice barely above a whisper.

"We can't trust no one," Felicia hissed.

Anyone, I thought automatically.

She stuck her tongue out at me before turning back to her brother.

"But she took care of us," Lowell argued, his voice cracking. Tears slipped from his eyes, the deformed one turning pink. "Please, Felly. I think we can trust her. And if we can't, we'll know. Yeah?"

"I can take care of us!" Felicia snarled.

Lowell cried harder. I sat motionless on the column.

"I believe you," I told her softly, "but I want to help."

"Why?" Felicia shot the word like a dart.

I had no words to explain. I only knew I'd found purpose these last few weeks and now saw it ready to evaporate like steam. My chest caved in on itself as I thought of returning to wander that grey plain of listless nothingness. A long silence passed before anyone spoke again.

"Just keep your distance," Felicia grumbled at last.

)(

I went back to work, so to speak, slipping back into the criminal underworld of Springhaven. It proved more frustrating than I expected. The hardest part was figuring out where to place myself, with whom I should work. The Dawn Age was about a decade from ending by then. I had lost more time than I realized, and all the players had changed. It took time I didn't have to observe and test and get positioned. With two new charges to care for, I felt an urgency I hadn't known in years. They had needs I'd long forgotten about.

Felicia's leg was one of my biggest concerns. It looked ready to accept infection any second, and the cost of physician services had risen sharply since I'd last connected with the rest of society.

For a raven, secrets are easier to collect than money, and I blackmailed the doctor into seeing her. That backfired slightly, as he stuck us with an apprentice for most of the examination, a young woman who smiled warmly but spoke with words made of iron. Curiously, she did not question how such an odd injury had occurred, as I had dreaded she would do. Felicia refused to tell me, and I hadn't been able to think up a probable lie beyond a sudden, unexplained ailment. The apprentice prescribed a salve and told us to keep the affected area clean.

"The skin also requires conditioning to stop the cracking. The Oran Apothecary can provide what you need," she said, handing me a slip of paper. She turned her smile onto Felicia. "Tell them I sent you, and they might even give you a spice cake as a treat."

Felicia smiled back at her, and I couldn't tell whether it was fake or real. She was, it turned out, quite the little actress. Felicia's leg began to improve within days, and her limp subsided with the recovery.

I eventually procured a place for us to live in the Agate quarter. It was a desperate, one-room situation, but it had a roof, running water, and a working kitchen. Felicia and I worked out a communication system for us during the day, using whatever strange talent she possessed. If Lowell was within range of his sister, so to speak, he too received the information. It was an effective arrangement, save for when Lowell was out of range at the time of my directive and Felicia was being petulant. Lowell quickly learned how to tell from my squawks and body language when his sister was hiding something, and he'd demand to know what I'd said. From what I gathered, as long as she didn't recall my message to the front of her mind, she was able to keep it a secret. Sometimes, when she was being especially difficult, she'd keep everything she could to herself until evening and blurt it all out as I changed back. During one of these arguments, wherein Felicia tried to pull some kind of self-appointed rank and Lowell refused to have any of it, he indirectly informed me he and Felicia were twins.

Cooking, it turned out, wasn't a problem. Almost immediately, both Felicia and Lowell took command of the kitchen. Lowell often tried to have dinner ready for me each evening, and I was rarely disappointed by his meals. I noticed he took this responsibility upon himself after enduring a few abysmal dishes I had managed to scrape together.

"The ingredients here are different," I tried to explain after one particularly soggy, unpalatable meal of beans on toast.

"Different from where?" Felicia asked, quick as lightning.

La la la la la la la, none of your business, went my brain, singing the tune over and over.

Felicia smirked at me.

"Not to worry," Lowell said, forcing another forkful into his mouth. "You've given me an idea."

Unsurprisingly, Lowell's rendition of my meal was much better, complete with flavor!

Neither of the twins was well educated, and I took it upon myself to teach them what I could. Lowell was voracious for knowledge, and took to reading like a fish to water. When he was older, or when he could convince Felicia to go with him, he'd dress in a disguise and go to the museum, though neither she nor I liked these excursions. Other children bullied him terribly, even with a mask and proper clothing covering his leg and arm. I came home to more than one story about how Felicia had mocked the offenders into tears.

I became endlessly grateful for everything my parents dealt with. Felicia's will combined with her ability—which she has never fully explained to me, but I have come to understand better from experience—made her almost impossible to parent if she didn't want to do something. I had to devise ways to make things appealing to her, like learning. She had no interest in improving herself until she gleaned what I did for a living. After that, she realized how she could use her abilities in similar ways and how it could profit her.

She began to focus on how to appear as a grand young lady, and Lowell followed in her footsteps. He loved the theatricality of the affectations dapper young men put on and melted into this new path. Felicia was quieter about her growth and training, as she called it, always thinking carefully before she spoke. She used words to wrangle people into position to get what she wanted. While Lowell and I developed a sweet relationship, fed by his craving for love and security, Felicia and I had never connected. She was always wary of me, always ready for the other shoe to drop. I knew she'd be involved with the same people I was as soon as she thought she could manage it.

"Above all, I want you to be safe," I told her. "There are people out there who can physically overpower you, and everything you know about them won't help if there's no one else around to use as leverage. And killing you isn't the worst thing some of them will do."

"I know you won't abandon me," Felicia replied smoothly. "And Lowell has plenty of toys to help me."

Lowell, fascinated by engineering, was forever tweaking his false leg, creating add-ons and improvements for his bad arm, and building all manner of other contraptions. He was at that very moment attaching what he called a wrist rocket to himself.

"Yes, but neither of you are invincible," I replied. "Lowell might be at risk depending on who you decide to associate with."

"So what does that say about you?" Felicia fired back.

I had no response. I had gone to lengths to keep my job as a caretaker separate from the deeds keeping a roof over our head. After that conversation, I wrestled with myself. I considered going back to pickpocketing and stealing, but selling secrets was more lucrative. Then again, my lock-picking skills would allow me to steal more valuable items, but that path held more risk too. Recalling how rusty I'd gotten made me imagine what Flynn would have to say on the subject, so I abandoned that train of thought before old wounds had a chance to reopen. I'd stored up a nice little nest egg for us over the last few years and had planned on buying a house in the Limestone district. I began to wonder if there was a better use for the money.

)(

The Cobalt quarter is an area I avoided in those days. The smell of the ocean, the sounds of the harbor, and the constant bustle of people reminded me too much of home. It was the best place to gather information, but knowing where to go posed a problem. One was spoiled for choice among so many people doing all manner of business—legal, not, and everywhere in between. Nevertheless, I flew there after losing that last argument with Felicia. I needed to think, and none of my old haunts were helping. The scent of the sea hit me like a punch to the gut. I descended and perched atop a pergola stretching over a restaurant's patio.

Grief I thought buried washed over me. Having been busy with Lowell and Felicia these last few years, I hadn't had time to reflect on the past. I had lost so much and then forced myself to forget the ones who'd meant something to me. I thought of them all that afternoon. I'd lose Lowell and Felicia one day too. I wondered what I would have to show for it. I was already losing Felicia, and Lowell would follow his sister to the ends of the earth. When evening came, I flew through the window of an abandoned building. I didn't want to see other people just yet. I wasn't ready to leave my solitude, and so wandered through the building and continued to think.

The property was taller and thinner than most of those within Springhaven. Squashed between one of Cobalt's twisting alleyways and one of the broader avenues of the Sand quarter, sitting right on the line separating the two districts, it rose above all the other buildings around it. The top floor where I had entered was mostly open with a few small bedrooms, one bathroom, and a kitchenette. Below stretched an entirely empty space. A staircase wound its way around the curved walls of the building all the way up to the flat-topped roof.

The unique construction of the place distracted me from my melancholy. Its bones, dark stone and equally dark wood, had a heaviness to them modern and updated buildings in Springhaven lacked. No plaster coverings; everything was exposed. There were even gargoyles attached to the walls outside. This was an Old World building, and it spoke to me.

I reached back into my memory for what this might have been during my court days. I couldn't recall, though it might have been built after my captivity began. Nevertheless, I began to make inquiries about it. I expected it would be difficult to complete the purchase given my situation, but the city was so eager to unload the place, they bent over backwards to make it happen. In truth, I got it for a song. I didn't yet know what I was going to do with it, but I knew it would serve as a business establishment in some way.

"What do you think?" I asked my young charges when I first brought them to see our new home.

"It's grand!" Lowell said, tromping around on his false leg.

This one was far better than the sad thing he'd had when I'd found him, but it still couldn't keep up with his enthusiasm.

"It's like a castle, isn't it, Cali?" he continued. "This shall be our tower! We shall reign over the city as kings and queens."

I chuckled and turned to Felicia. She looked around with that appraising eye of hers.

"It's awfully big, isn't it?" she prodded.

"I'm going to run a business out of here," I explained. "We'll live upstairs."

"What kind of business?" Lowell asked, returning to me.

I brushed my hand over his hair as he hugged me around the middle.

"I don't know yet," I replied. "We need to figure out what makes good money. Suggestions?"

"Food," Lowell said.

I smiled. "And you'll create our menu, I suppose, my little chef?"

"Of course!"

"And drinks. Drinks more than food." Felicia fixed me with a challenging stare.

By the numbers, serving alcohol was a good business plan. The more customers imbibed, the more they wanted. Was that truly the kind of establishment I wanted to run with children just above, however? What would I be teaching them?

"People make their own choices," Felicia told me. "You wouldn't be doing anything evil."

No. I knew that all too well. The picture of evil floated before my mind's eye. Felicia looked away, darkness clouding her eyes. I had never spoken to her or Lowell about what had happened to me. They had never asked, though I knew they must have had an inkling.

"We don't need to decide now. First, we need to get this place tidied up. We've got quite a job ahead of us."

Lowell hopped into the air and began babbling about all the tools he'd need and all the things he wanted to try. Felicia only shrugged.

~Chapter 18~

We created our new home first. Lengths of richly colored fabric served as walls and room markers where necessary. Lowell rigged a clever system of rollers that allowed us to pull them back when we wished, and Felicia took on many of the aesthetic decisions. I let them do what they liked—within reason—to make the place feel like theirs. I expected Felicia to eschew the work, but she happily fell into the details of making everything look just so. Her tastes gravitated towards the opulent, which we couldn't afford even with the money I had saved, so she adapted her ideas to bits of colored glass and paint instead of jewels and embroidery. With such tall ceilings directly beneath the roof here, my daytime ability to fly came in quite handy.

"I wish I could turn into a bird," Lowell gushed as he watched me carry a length of rope to the apex of the room.

I was pleased this face could not betray my feelings when he said that, though I had to ignore the pointed look from Felicia as I hooked the rope around a rafter. One night soon after, when Lowell was asleep and Felicia was determined to finish a project even if by petrolsene light, she spoke to me on the subject.

"Why don't *you* ever talk about it?" The way she said it hinted to me she had her own reasons for never talking about her and Lowell's past.

We sat together at a rickety little secondhand table. Felicia had spread her supplies around her like a rainbow. I, meanwhile, worked on updating our household accounts.

"Because it's painful," I replied softly, looking up from my work. I wondered to myself where this conversation was headed.

Felicia nodded as she moved her brush carefully along the fabric. It was a tiny thing, no more than a few hairs. How she had the patience to paint such intricate designs was beyond me. Her dark hair, once tangled and rough, fell in glossy waves now, and I couldn't help but be proud of how much both her and Lowell's health had improved since coming to live with me. Not that Felicia would ever mention it.

"You have the advantage of hundreds of years. I imagine memories can't last much beyond that," she said.

"It's not an advantage, and they don't fade as easily as you think," I snapped. I don't know whether it was having my private thoughts invaded or the pain of my history that made me react so harshly, but I immediately apologized.

"Don't." Felicia set her brush aside and looked at me. "You've earned the right to treat people however you like."

The way she spoke, it was sometimes hard to believe she was barely an adolescent.

"I can't say I agree with you," I said. "In any case, I choose to treat people well."

Felicia scrunched up her face at me like I'd just suggested she dunk her head into a bucket of enraged lobsters. "Why?"

"Because there's already too much pain in the world." As I said the words, I recalled my parents' voices saying them to me so long ago, picturing their faces in my mind's eye. "It is within my power, just as it is within yours, to make the world brighter."

Felicia's face flattened into a series of unimpressed lines.

I turned her own question back onto her. "Why don't *you* ever talk about it?"

Felicia sighed and looked away. We sat like that a long time. I expected her to get up and walk off, as she had so many times before, but she remained seated and spoke again instead.

"People don't understand, and they fear what they don't understand."

"And frightened people turn cruel?" I suggested.

"No, people are already cruel all on their own. Frightened people turn violent."

"You think all people are cruel?"

She huffed. "Enough of them are."

"I'm sorry."

"I said—"

"I know what you said. I make my own choices, Felicia. And I *am* sorry for what you and your brother have been through. Whatever it is." I hesitated. My heart struggled against itself, a deep war fed by experience and pain and something else. I let the something else win. "I love you, Felicia. I love both you and Lowell."

"Thanks," was her only response.

)(

When the time finally came to make a decision about my new profession, I realized only being able to work at night—as a human anyway—severely limited my options. In the end, I decided, yes, I would serve alcohol, in addition to small plates of food. As mistress of my own establishment, I reserved the right to cut off patrons as I saw fit. My determination to exercise this authority eased my conscience about raising children in what would essentially be a public house environment. I had Felicia and Lowell help me choose and create games that would do well for large game nights, which was one of the main ways we initially built up our customer base. At Felicia's suggestion, we served only higher-quality drinks, nothing bottom shelf, which would serve several purposes. And, as promised, Lowell created a menu for us.

Raven's Tower was born.

I needed to hire an assistant. Someone who could work independently during the day and didn't mind that I was unavailable until sundown. I published a rather detailed ad in the Springhaven newssheets and, with Lowell and Felicia's assistance, scheduled interviews, all over evening drinks in establishments similar to what mine would be, during which Felicia played the innocent daughter, busy with drawing. It was her idea.

"You're trusting them with an awful lot," she argued. "Better to vet each candidate now than find out what they're *really* like later."

I didn't like it, but we reached an understanding on the matter. She would join me and only tell me whether she believed each candidate was a good fit. If I asked other questions, she answered them. If not, she told me nothing else. In the end, I hired an eager fellow by the name of Hector, who was more than happy to be out of his parents' house and doing anything besides attending luncheons and soirées. He was exactly the type of dapper young man Lowell wished to be, and he trailed Hector endlessly. Felicia kept a discreet eye on both of them. Like her, I feared for Lowell's feelings, but my respective warnings to both children went ignored. I shudder to think what might have happened had Hector mistreated Lowell, but he was a consummate professional. If he ever thought ill of his young fan, I never heard about it.

The staff was small at first to save on costs. It still is, but bigger than the three we had back then. Our cook, a stern but kind older woman by the name of Laura, worked in the back, and Felicia baked bread. Lowell did not come down into the main room when patrons were in.

I hadn't taught Felicia how to bake. Like cooking, I had never taken to it much myself. Nor did I ever see her learn or practice in our home, not that there had been much space for it in our matchbox-sized kitchen. It must have been something she'd carried from her former life, and she was shockingly good at it.

The first loaf she ever made for us, while not perfect and certainly not very pretty, was warm and soft and so slightly sweet I would have missed it if I hadn't been paying attention. It had baked up chestnut brown and crusty, and it smelled like pure comfort when sliced.

"Careful, young miss," Laura said to Felicia. "You serve that once, and you'll have to make it every night after."

In response, Felicia beamed. "Good."

)(

It was during the small hours of the night when the first hiccup in our quiet, new life occurred. The Tower had been closed for an hour or so, and I'd sent Felicia and Lowell off to bed a few hours before that. I often closed up by myself. It gave me time to recharge after a busy evening of managing, chatting, and generally being "on" for my patrons. It's strange the tendencies that never change despite what happens to us over the years. I was busy in the kitchen that night cleaning and organizing for the next day when a rattling of bottles startled me. I spun, grabbing the closest weapons at hand: a broom and an empty pint glass. The twins sleeping upstairs surged to the forefront of my mind as I prowled forward. A shadow moved between the liquor crates in the darkest corner of the room. It rose, and I threw my pint glass. The figure caught it faster than my eyes could comprehend. I spun the broom handle around and raised it to strike.

"Please don't stake me!"

The voice rolled low and smooth despite its supplication. Something about it tapped at an old memory, but I couldn't recall it just then. The figure slowly raised its free hand while the other put down the glass. That hand joined its mate in the surrender. Like the sea with the first rays of morning, the inky shape gained definition and color. The black eyes and elongated teeth drew my eyes first.

I struck out with the broom handle, my muscles recalling lessons from Jones and even longer before then, from the back of my memory. Instead of fighting back, the Vampyre shielded himself with his hands.

"Please! Stop!" he begged. "I'm not going to hurt you! I thought…"

I whirled the broom back around and hit him in the face with the straw end of it. He spat and made a face. His expression changed back to one of fear when I broke the broom over my knee and pointed the new, jagged stake at his chest.

"Get out! You don't want me!"

"I thought you were like me!" he blurted. I drew back, aghast, and he seized his chance. "Aren't you?"

"I?" I gawped. "I? Like you? Do I look like a Vampyre to you?!"

He looked away sheepishly. "I… I don't know."

I placed a hand against my head, unable to believe what I was hearing. "You don't know? How is that possible?"

What was I asking? How was it possible he was even here? Vampyres had been eradicated in Nicodemus' day. Or, if not, the machine which had destroyed magic should have killed the rest off.

"I've never seen one," he explained. "Only myself, and I thought perhaps… maybe they don't all look like me."

I hooked a finger under my lip and pulled it up. "No fangs. Shee?"

He looked at me and spread his hands before him.

"Oh heavens…" I motioned towards the crate with my stake. "Sit."

He obeyed. I looked him over more closely and realized how young he seemed. He looked no older than me, though appearances mean nothing where curses and vampyrism are concerned. Messy hair swept along his shoulders, cut in a fairly current style, and his face still held some visage of youth, though regret and worry buried it.

"I'm not a Vampyre," I said. "They all have eyes and teeth like yours. When did you last feed?"

His eyes darted around the room.

"Don't lie to me," I warned. "I can tell it's been a while."

"A week ago," he muttered. More insistently, he added, "It was a cow, not a person."

"Animal blood can supplement, but you'd be better with a bear. The more willful the creature, the better."

"Oh," he said, looking away.

I sighed heavily, cursing myself for the thoughts running through my head.

"Look, I'll let you feed from me, but you have to leave after that. I can't hide you."

His eyes grew wide, mouth falling open. "You'd… you'd let me…" He didn't seem able to finish, his expression folding in on itself.

"Yes, though I don't think you'll like it."

"I don't mind! I mean, I'm sure it's fine. Thank you."

I wiggled the broken broom handle at him. "Don't try anything."

He shook his head so hard I thought it might fall off, and I extended my wrist towards him. As if handling a baby bird, he took it in his hands. Then, drawing it close to his lips, he wrinkled his nose.

"I told you," I said.

"No! No! I'm sorry. It's fine."

I could tell he was fighting back another face as he bit into my skin. I let him drink as much as he liked, which I noted was less than Thomas ever had. Afterwards, obviously unsure of what to do next, he awkwardly dragged his lips across my skin, smearing the leftovers.

"Clean up after yourself," I told him. He looked utterly baffled, so I added, "Clean your plate."

I wasn't aware Vampyres could blush, but his cheeks turned red as the blood still eking from my wrist. He stuck out his tongue and pointedly avoided my eyes as he licked my wrist clean. Then he handed my own arm back to me.

"Thank you," he said quietly.

"Did I hurt you?" I asked. "When I hit you?"

"Not really."

I nodded, and silence fell between us. The Vampyre stood and swung his arms like he was walking, but his feet didn't follow.

"Um," he said after a moment, "so, if you're not… like me, what are you? You're not norm—a regular human."

"Cursed," I replied.

"Ah." He continued to stand there, fidgeting his hands.

"Yes?"

"How do you know so much about… uh—"

"Vampyres. You should work on getting used to the word."

"Yes. Those."

"I knew one once. He taught me."

"Oh. Is he, erm, around?"

"He's dead." The Vampyre's face fell, and I added more gently, "He died a long time ago. I wish he hadn't." I paused. "What's your name?"

"Kieran." He twiddled his fingers together, not meeting my eyes again. "I… don't really know what I'm doing."

I rolled my lips under my teeth to hold back a comment. Once I'd successfully sent it back behind my internal filter, I repeated, "I can't hide you here."

"I wouldn't ask you to, but… may I… come back? When it's quiet? I… think I need help."

I sighed and shook my head, thinking of the twins upstairs whose blood didn't taste like metal and smoke. "I can't. I'm sorry."

Kieran started to object, but I held up the stake again. He quieted and dissolved into the shadows. I hurried up to Lowell and Felicia's rooms and found them safe in their beds.

)(

Kieran was more persistent than I would have liked. He appeared again a few days later. I spied him peeking around the corner as I swept the main room with a new broom.

"Don't make me destroy another one," I said, pointing it at him.

He said nothing, but remained where he was.

"Why are you here?" I asked.

He slunk out from his hiding place, looking at the ground, and asked, "Do you know how often I have to feed? By the numbers, I mean?"

"By the numbers?" I repeated.

He finally raised his eyes to mine. "The average human body contains about a gallon and a half of blood—"

"And how would you know that?" I demanded, cutting him off. I advanced with my broom.

"B-b-because I'm a doctor," he babbled, backing against the wall. "Rather, I was in training to be one."

I stopped. "Beg pardon?"

"I was only… turned a few years ago. Before that, I was attending medical school. I'm trying to figure out how many people I need to feed from to… stay. Safely, mind you. I don't want to… to…"

Kieran looked away. I backed off but still held my broom before me.

"Have you ever killed anyone?" I asked gently.

He nodded, and his throat bobbed. "I didn't mean to. He was old, and… I didn't realize…"

I raised my hand to stop him. "I understand."

"I almost killed my best friend… that night. The night I was turned. He offered, and I didn't know how to stop."

"So how did he survive?"

"He asked me to let him go, told me it was too much. If he hadn't, I—"

"But you didn't. We must assume he's fine now."

"Oh, I know he is. I've just come from seeing him," Kieran said, looking back to me at last.

"You went back to see him?" I gaped. "Do you have any idea how dangerous that is?"

Kieran shrugged, "They're the only people I have left. What else am I supposed to do?"

If I hadn't been so flabbergasted, I might have been hurt. Instead, I just exclaimed, "*They*?"

He nodded again, and a small smile crept up his face.

I shook myself and managed a marginally calmer tone. "And what do they think of your new form?"

"My… the woman I used to court threw things at me at first—"

"I like her already."

"—but we're fine now. We're all fine. They're willing to let me feed from them. I got the idea from you actually, but I don't want to take from them if it's going to come to nothing. I was hoping you could help me with the calculations."

"I wish I could," I said, holding up my hands. "I haven't the foggiest, however. I think you're just going to have to figure out your needs yourself."

"But—"

"Look, it's your friends' choice if they want to volunteer. And I don't suspect you're going to get anywhere without trying."

I returned to my sweeping. Kieran wandered behind the bar. From the corner of my eye, I watched as he idly picked up and replaced glasses and bottles.

"You want a drink?" I asked.

Kieran knitted his brows at me. I smirked, and he smiled back. A sheepish but sincere smile, the tips of his fangs peeking out from under his lip. Setting my broom aside, I walked over and picked up a glass and a knife.

"What are you…" Kieran began.

He hissed as I drew the knife across my hand and pawed at the air just beyond me. I eyed him curiously, noticing the way he never actually touched me. Meanwhile, I allowed the blood to run into the glass.

His eyes were wide with concern as he asked, "Wh-why did you do that?"

"It'll heal," I replied calmly.

"You need stitches. May I examine it, please?"

"Why?" I chuckled. "Are you going to sew me up?"

In response, Kieran pulled a small pouch from his pocket. A set of initials had been embossed onto it. His thumb covered all but the first letter, a P in delicate scrollwork. Within sat a needle, waxed thread, carefully wrapped gauze, and a small bottle, all neatly arranged. I raised an eyebrow at him, and he shrugged, cheeks going rosy.

"I told you, I wanted to be a doctor," was all he said.

I had him hand me a clean towel from under the bar and pressed it to the wound, insisting I would be fine. Then I poured an equal amount of scotch over the blood.

"Try this," I said, lifting the glass to him. He looked dubious, so I added, "It's to cover the taste."

He nodded slowly and took the drink. His expression said it all, though he apparently still felt the need to comment.

"It's still terrible."

I laughed. "Sorry."

)(

Keeping Felicia and Lowell in the dark about Kieran was difficult, though I had learned some techniques over the years to block my thoughts. By then, Felicia was used to me singing to myself. I don't know if I was entirely successful, but I never heard about Kieran from either of them.

As much as Felicia had wheedled from me about my past, there was so much I didn't know about them. Lowell was cagey, though nothing like his sister, but he did occasionally share nuggets of their past with me. More often than not, it was unintentional, a drop of new information in a bucket of conversation.

Over the past five years, I'd learned they came to Springhaven from Duskwood, though I got the impression it had not been a direct trip. I gathered they'd travelled for a while with some people who were not their family, and I guessed those were at least some of the folks who had mistreated them. Whatever the case, the twins had ended up alone, which they'd come to prefer by the time I found them. I didn't even know their surname until I overheard Lowell teasing Felicia in the other room.

The colorful curtain-walls allowed for conversation to flow easily between the common areas. Only the bedrooms were properly enclosed. I could tell the two were working on some project of their own while I preened my feathers. I had flown in through a window not too long ago and, having learned Felicia's talent had a limited range, I stayed on the other side of our flat to avoid her notice.

"That looks lovely, oh sister mine," Lowell gushed. "Cali's going to love it. Does she know you know her birthday?"

"She will now," Felicia replied. I puffed out my feathers proudly as I heard genuine excitement in her voice.

"Is this her old home?" Felicia made a noise of acknowledgement, and Lowell went on, "It's a strange place for a countess to live. Shouldn't it be a little castle or something?"

"It's accurate. And she's not a countess. Well, not exactly."

I quite enjoyed listening to these exchanges on the sly. It gave me more insight into my secretive, young charges.

"Imagine if we were nobles," Lowell said dreamily. "I'd sleep on silken sheets and have a workshop of my own."

"We were noble. Once," Felicia replied flatly. "At least, our forebears were."

"Oh, you know what I mean. If we were rich."

"Maybe one day." I didn't like the tone in Felicia's voice just then. I could practically see the smug, calculating smile creeping up her rosy cheeks. "Then we'll both have everything we want."

I heard the clink of our simple drinkware as Lowell exclaimed, "To the future, Lady Thorne."

I froze. My already fast heartbeat became a solid buzz in my ears. An idea crawled inside my brain and attached itself with black, barbed tethers. I left the way I came.

~Chapter 19~

I avoided Lowell and Felicia that night and arrived back barely in time to open the bar. Hector was already there, of course, as was my head bartender and bouncer, Gabriel. I spoke to them no more than necessary and buried myself in my duties. I was thankful it was a game night, as it provided plenty of distractions for my spinning mind, from circling the room and ensuring my patrons were happy, to running the games, and even arbitrating the occasional disagreement. When Felicia came down to get dinner from Laura, I went downstairs under the pretense of restocking some of the liquor shelves. I watched from the curving stairway, using the long mirror along the back wall to get a better view, waiting for her to leave.

Lowell and Felicia were fifteen now, almost sixteen. Nearly of age and having long been independent, they didn't need me to check in on them, though I did nearly every evening before things got too busy downstairs. They were usually asleep when I returned from closing the Tower and later transformed, so our evening time had become precious to me. We spent time together during the day, certainly, but it wasn't the same. I knew from my daily excursions into the city what the twins got up to—mostly running errands for me and indulging their interests. I never told them I sometimes followed them, and I kept enough distance between us to avoid Felicia's—and therefore Lowell's when they were together—detection. At least, I don't think they ever suspected. It's impossible to truly know what Felicia gathers and keeps to herself. I didn't do it often, wishing to keep faith in the fragile trust we had established.

I followed Lowell more than his sister. Given his personality and impairments, I worried for his safety. He was as savvy as she, to be sure, but he gave all people the benefit of the doubt, something both Felicia and I had tried to discourage without success. I didn't worry about Felicia in the same way.

As I hid and watched Felicia thank Laura, I imagined I saw Nicodemus' Thorne-nose in her, the shape of his mouth in her face as she smiled. I shook my head.

No, you don't know that, I scolded myself.

But the thought had speared its tentacles deeper into my mind. I left the next morning before they awoke. I knew I'd have to face them that evening. Lowell and Felicia would know something was wrong if I was absent two days in a row. I made plans to busy myself, devised excuses to offer, and flew in just as the sun dipped below the city skyline.

"There you are!" Lowell cheered as I alighted on a chair.

He bounced up and down, the false leg bending smoothly beneath him. He had come so far in their designs. I should have been impressed, but I forced myself to look away.

"We've made you a cake!" he carried on. "Better to wait until you're human again, of course."

"Lowell," came Felicia's playful admonishment. "You're spoiling the surprise."

"How?" he asked, his enthusiasm undiminished. "She's here now, and she's surprised. Aren't you, Cali?"

I braved a peek back at them. They stood side by side, waiting for me to change. Their broad smiles shone painfully bright, and a vision of the other one who had smiled at me like that blossomed in my mind. They waited for an answer, and I managed to bob my head. A faltering tune ran through my brain. It became difficult to keep up as I considered what was unfolding before me. I tried to force myself to be cheerful, flapping my wings and standing up straighter, but I failed to make a convincing show.

"Are you quite alright, Cali?" Lowell asked, coming over. "You don't have your usual bounce today."

He reached for me as he had done countless times before, and I couldn't stop myself as I shied away.

Don't touch me! cried my subconscious, bursting through the tune.

Felicia stiffened, and Lowell followed a moment later. He looked back to her. Felicia's eyes focused on me, turning hard the way they always did when she was determined to have her way. I tried starting up the tune again, but memories of what Nicodemus did to me played in my mind. I turned away, shaking my head, trying to make it stop. The transformation came, and the scenes played on. Human again, I gasped and collapsed to the floor. I saw Lowell and Felicia and Nicodemus all in my mind as my heart raced. Invisible spiders crawled up the back of my neck, and I shook as if I was deathly cold, unable to make myself stop. I felt their eyes on me, knew they saw everything, first one and then the other.

"Oh, Cali," I heard Lowell say, his voice cracking.

I can only assume he reached out towards me because Felicia said in an icy voice, "No, don't." She paused before adding, "Come on."

Their footsteps, Felicia's smooth and even now, Lowell's still clomping but so much better than when we'd first met, receded from the room. I don't know how long I knelt there, grasping at anything to bear me up from that place of panic and helplessness. I closed my eyes and focused on my breathing, the same way I used to in the Lamplighters' compound: deep through the nose and slowly through the mouth. I did that until the tremors subsided and my heart rate returned to something like normal. Once I'd pulled myself together enough again, I escaped. Down past the barroom, beyond the stockroom below, and into my private office. Locking the door behind me, I'm ashamed to say I hid there most of the night.

My neck and cheeks burned even as tears streamed down them. I didn't know how I was going to face Felicia and Lowell after this. My stomach churned as I found myself grateful for the impending change back into a raven. It was easier for me to hide my thoughts within that head, and it would give me time to figure… what? What could I ever say to them? That I believed they were the spawn of Nicodemus and must carry the same evil within them? Hector checked on me once, followed by Gabriel three times after the former had left. It was unusual for me to be away from the main room for so long. I made pathetic excuses, not caring how transparent my lies must have been.

"I'm shutting down," Gabriel called through my office door. It sounded as if a solid wall spoke to me. The interval between went on so long I would have thought he'd left, except his footfalls are like dropped cinderblocks. "You need me to stay?"

"No," I called wearily back. "Thank you."

Another pause, "Have the twins come get me at home if you need anything."

My voice caught in my throat as I replied, "Will do."

Finally, he left. As dawn began to whisper at me, no more than the lightest of breezes against my mind, I stood. I needed to do something. My heart rent in two as I reached for the handle. My precious little ones, I couldn't abandon them. Even with... everything. I needed to know they knew I didn't hate them. I wasn't sure if that was actually true, but I needed them to hear it. Climbing the spiral stairs made me gulp for breath. My footsteps echoed so loud in the silence. The twins were sleeping, no doubt. I crept to Felicia's bedroom first.

The material which created a short corridor to her room, rich purple and painted with intricate gold lines, had already been drawn open. This was strange. Felicia preferred for her space to be as closed off from everyone else as possible, though I'd drawn the line at locks. The door to her room also hung wide, and I quickened my pace.

The room was not only bereft of Felicia, but most of her things were gone as well. The paints, the gems, fabric, blank journals, and writing utensils, all gone.

"Felicia?" I called to the empty room. I turned. "Lowell?"

I ran to his room. He liked everything bright and open, so I couldn't guess whether he was there until I sped through his doorway, skidding as I hung onto the frame.

The same sight met my eyes.

His three best false legs were gone, along with his tools and bag of materials. I called their names again and again, rushing through the flat, shoving fabric out of my way and sending it rolling back on its tracks. I entered the sitting room and found a cake sitting on the table. The once-glossy icing had gone soft, sliding down the sides. An envelope laid next to it, as well as a parcel wrapped in glittering turquoise paper.

I snatched up the envelope and ripped it open. My eyes scanned the words three times before my brain realized they weren't what I wanted to see.

Happy birthday, Calandra! To brighter days and happier years.

I could tell Felicia had painted the picture on the card. She had undoubtedly pulled the scene from my memories. Teal waves foamed onto a golden beach as seabirds wheeled above. A painstakingly detailed crab scuttled along the bottom of the image, and in the background rose a cliff of countless slate grey monoliths, like stony fingers reaching for the sky.

I placed a hand over my mouth as tears filled my eyes.

"Felicia. Lowell," I called again, my voice tripping and breaking over every syllable.

I turned our little home upside down as quickly as I could, searching for any sign of where they might have gone.

Stars, they must feel so betrayed. For years, Felicia had been waiting for something like this.

Dawn's cold melody wrapped around me.

"No, no!" I cried. "Not today. Don't! I have…"

My voice trailed off as the curse melted my voice box and reshaped it. It pulled my lips into a beak, and my words became indignant, rasping cackles. Very well, I resolved. I would turn the wretched thing to my own purposes.

I took flight, only to realize something I had missed during my manic search.

Every window had been shut up.

NO! I screamed inside my head.

I flapped against the shutters and pulled desperately at the latches. They held fast, and not even my nimble feet and beak had the ability to unfasten them. I had closed the door to our flat when I came in. I tried all day but remained trapped until night returned.

)(

As soon as I was human again, I rushed for the stairs, spiraling so quickly down them I grew dizzy.

"Miss Calandra," Hector called when he saw me. I assume he had questions for me, as he held a sheaf of papers in his hand.

"Have you seen the children?" I accosted him, grabbing him by the arm.

"You mean Miss Feli—" he began.

I shook his arm. "Of course Felicia and Lowell! Have you seen them? Last night? Today?"

"No, ma'am," Hector replied, freezing up like a deer on alert. "Not since the day before yesterday."

I swore and released him, running back towards the stairs.

"What shall I do if I do see them?" he asked.

"Make them stay put!"

I changed course and headed back up towards the barroom. Unfortunately, neither Gabriel nor any of my other staff had seen them since the night before.

"We've got things covered here," Gabriel told me.

With that, I was gone. I searched every alley and lane, popping into restaurants, bakeries, fishmonger stalls, everywhere that was still open. I asked everyone I could, eschewing fears of drawing attention to my young charges. One baker had seen a young woman matching Felicia's description, and the lad with her had seemed "a bit gimpy" to him, though he couldn't actually see a false leg due to a combination of trousers and counter height.

"Where did they go?" I demanded.

He waved vaguely in the direction away from the harbor. "Thata'way. Bought a dozen sausage rolls."

"Show me your paper," I said.

Thankfully, he'd stamped the name of his shop on the beige bakery wrapping. I can't remember if I thanked him as I ran out, my eyes peeled for new clues. I found a crumpled wrapper with the baker's seal on it. Springhaven provides bins to encourage clean streets, and I discovered that one hint of Felicia and Lowell's possible direction after pawing my way past a foot of other refuse. I combed the Cobalt district before heading into Agate and Char.

Not being of age yet, they shouldn't be able to procure lodgings for themselves. Felicia was the wiliest person I had ever met, however. She could doubtless convince almost any landlord to overlook the few months left until their birthday. And a great many abandoned manors sat and crumbled in Char and Agate, not to mention the warehouses, which had once housed grand businesses and shopping centers. The list of places they could hide grew with each new realization.

I cursed my human feet and eyes. As my insides twisted around into tighter knots, I suddenly realized how limited I was in this form.

I searched all night, simultaneously urging morning to come and choking on every passing minute. I ducked into an alley scarcely long enough to transform before bursting out of it on wings of renewed purpose. I soared over the city, flew under awnings, and zoomed across verandas. I hadn't searched for anything with such zeal since the war. I broadcast my thoughts, hoping Felicia would hear them and maybe, just maybe, find it in her heart to forgive me and come forward.

I'm sorry. I'm so sorry. Please, I need to find you. I love you. Lowell. Felicia.

The day went worse than the night had. Not a single token of their passage showed itself. It was as if they had vanished into thin air. I cursed how much energy flying required and how often I needed to eat, though the darkest parts of my heart jeered that it didn't make any difference. They were gone.

)(

Having spent the following evening and half the night continuing my fruitless search, I returned to the Tower before closing. Frustration, fear, shame, and desperation tore at me as I trudged up the stairs. In a distant part of my mind, I was surprised to see Hector still there. He approached me as I passed through the stockroom.

"Any luck?" he asked.

I shook my head, though I suspected he could already tell from the expression on my face.

"Do you know what happened?" he pursued. "When they went missing?"

I opened my mouth to speak, but no words came out. I had no idea what to say. There was so much I couldn't tell him, so I made a clueless gesture with my hand instead.

"Try not to worry." I felt he was trying too hard to be helpful as he added, "Worrying will use up energy you need to put forth elsewhere."

I ignored him, trying to figure out what to do next. I was exhausted, not having slept in more hours than my brain could calculate just then. My stomach gurgled, though I barely noticed it.

"You need to eat," Hector said. "Why don't you sit down? I'll ask Laura to fix you a plate."

I allowed him to guide me to a little table we kept there in the stockroom. I don't think I noticed he had left until he returned with the promised meal. I ate without thinking or tasting. About halfway through, the fog in my brain cleared enough for me to start putting pieces together.

"Why are you still here?" I asked. "Your shift ended hours ago."

He bobbed his head. "I wanted to offer my assistance."

"I'll pay you for the overtime," I said.

"That's not necessary. I didn't request prior approval after all."

I smiled and wondered how I could smile at a time like this. "I'm going to."

"Rules are rules," he insisted.

"And I'm the one who makes the rules," I replied, raising an eyebrow at him. "It's my prerogative to change them as I wish."

Hector smiled back and nodded. "Thank you, Miss Calandra."

He sat silently with me while I finished my meal. I considered him from the corner of my eye. Hector had never been more than my assistant. He came in, did his job, and left. I paid him well and rewarded him when he'd gone above and beyond. That was the extent of our relationship. I assumed Felicia must have worked her charms on him without me being aware of it.

"I suppose I should check in with Gabriel," I sighed, picking up my bowl.

Only then did I realize dinner had been lamb stew, one of my favorites and a rare treat for the establishment.

Hector took my dishes from my unresisting hands and said, "He has things covered at the bar. A fight broke out earlier, but he stopped it. Didn't even have to pull them apart. He just bellowed, and everyone stopped. I'll tell him you're back. You should rest."

I smiled again and thanked him.

"Of course, Miss Calandra. Let us know whatever you need."

The words struck me oddly, and I mulled them over as I made my way up to my flat. My hand felt heavy pressed against my front door, and I imagined a vindictive wind rustling the draping walls as I crossed the threshold. The cake was still there in the sitting room. It was too cold for bugs, thankfully, but this realization made me worry more. A part of me didn't want to get rid of the thoughtful creation, but the frosting had begun to turn. After dropping it into our little bin, I returned to the table and picked up Felicia's beautiful card. I tucked it into my pocket without thinking and turned to the package.

I hadn't opened it, and my heart tightened in my chest as I slowly untied the shimmering bow. A noise stopped me, and I spun towards it.

"Felicia? Lowell?" I said, barely daring to hope.

No response. I placed the gift back on the table and stepped towards the sound. Part of the fabric-wall, shrouded in shadows, moved as if breathing slowly. The material was sheer and russet orange in color, and nothing but more darkness waited beyond. When I was no more than an arm's length away, the darkness took shape. I recognized the gaunt figure hunched against the solid wall of the flat, obscured behind the material.

A new, horrifying thought entered my mind.

"What have you done?!" I snarled.

I ripped the wall away, tearing the first two hooks from their rollers above. I shoved Kieran back, and his eyes grew wide.

"I haven't done anything!" he insisted, circling away from me.

"Then why are you here? What makes you think you can come into my private home an-and…"

I didn't know where I was going with that thought. As my words left me, so did my energy. I leaned back against the wall and rubbed a hand over my face.

"I sensed you were alone," Kieran whispered, as if addressing a wild animal he didn't want to spook. "I overheard you and some of the others downstairs. Your children, they've gone missing?"

"Yes," I mumbled from behind my hands. "In a sense."

"What happened?" he asked.

I tried to speak, but my voice caught in my throat. Everything from the last few days came back to me in one horrific tempest, washing over me, crushing me beneath its force. I slid down the wall and drew my knees against my forehead, hiding from the pain. I began to weep, and words poured out of me unbidden.

I told Kieran everything, every sordid detail of what Nicodemus had done to me. I scooped grief from my heart and laid it between us with every sentence. I named each person I had lost, what they had been to me. The pile of invisible misfortune grew, soil over a grave of lives lost, my own included. Kieran drew closer to me as I laid my tale before him. When I at last explained what had happened to drive Lowell and Felicia away, I choked on my sobs, nearly collapsing. Through the blur of tears, I saw Kieran's hands extended, offered in comfort, but only if I chose to take them. I did, and his hands wrapped around mine, offering warm strength where mine failed. Even after my words left me, my weeping continued, and Kieran remained. Dawn came before I was ready.

"I must sleep," he told me, his eyes shining and sad. "It doesn't matter where, but…"

I gestured in the direction of my room. "The windows are shuttered."

He nodded and said, "We'll find them."

Then, giving my hands one last squeeze, he stood and retreated with silent footsteps. While I still could, I rose and unfastened the windows on the side of the flat farthest from Kieran. I had forgotten to in my haste before, and I refused to be trapped again. I pulled out food for myself and prepared it, but waited until I transformed before having any. Once again, I was thankful for this strange facet of the curse and ate my fill far more quickly than I would have been able to as a human.

~Chapter 20~

I visited all my old informant haunts, keeping my ears open for any newcomers to the criminal underworld. People like Felicia and Lowell couldn't go unnoticed for long. Stars, would Felicia really pull her brother into something so dangerous? I didn't think so, but Lowell was almost as stubborn as she. I had been out of the game for so long, I didn't recognize many of the code names I heard: Spades, Bonnie, Marlowe, Fetch, and Snook.

Blazes!

I swore to keep an ear to the underworld ground from now on, if for no other reason than to stay in the know. I'd brush up on all my old skills too… just in case. Springhaven was an enormous city. The twins could be anywhere, and I could do little as a raven besides seek and observe. I searched all day, but in the back of my mind, I made plans for the evening.

I'd put the word out, track down a few of my old contacts, grease a few palms, make a few deals. Someone somewhere had to know something. I ate again when I returned home. Dusk couldn't fall fast enough. As I waited, I checked on Kieran, though I don't know what I was concerned about. As long as sunlight didn't touch him, he would be fine.

I didn't see him when I first alighted to my wardrobe. I'd expected him to collapse onto my bed, but I hadn't considered the propriety issues with that idea until just then. I often had trouble adjusting my mindset to the rather stringent ideas of the day. The New Age was nearly upon us, yet I often felt like we had regressed millennia in certain ideological areas. In Bone Port, we made do with what we had. The idea of giving up my bed for someone who was, for all intents and purposes, a guest—Vampyre or no—was nothing to me. Something about it obviously didn't line up with Kieran's way of thinking because I eventually found him curled up on the floor between the vanity and the wall. I know Vampyres enjoy material comforts as much as the rest of us, though something about sleeping in coffins, or at least boxes, and a bit of soil appeals to them. Seeing he was fine, I left. Doing nothing ruffled my feathers, metaphorically speaking, and I didn't want to make him uncomfortable by being there when he awoke.

When the sun finally set and I stood upon human feet again, I hurried into my bedroom so quickly I didn't see the inky shape standing there amongst the shrouds of darkness blanketing the room. I ran smack into Kieran's solid form. He stopped me from falling over but released me as soon as I steadied myself. I barely noticed.

"I have work to do. Are you fed enough to stay here without being too badly tempted?" I spoke so quickly I wasn't sure I was intelligible.

Kieran nodded. "Yes, but I thought I could help you."

I had already turned away, having only half heard him, and stopped.

"Is there something you can do?" I asked.

"I can try to track them," he replied, folding his hands before him.

I paused. "Is it safe for you to do that?"

"While it is proper dark, yes."

"Why?" I asked, stepping closer. "Why would you help me?"

"Because you need help." He said it as if it was the most obvious thing in the world.

An icy splinter, pulsing red and angry in my heart, melted away with those words. Pain, even if only a little, subsided, and I found myself nodding, smiling, and hugging him.

"Thank you," I said. "What do you need?"

"Their scent."

I watched as Kieran investigated Lowell and Felicia's rooms, sniffing the furniture, their bedclothes, and the air within like a wolf on the hunt.

"I'll return as soon as I can," he told me. Then he walked to the open window and became one with the shadows.

I had opened my mouth to stop him so we could make a plan together, but he disappeared too quickly. I penned and left a short note for him to let him know I too would be back as soon as I could. I furrowed my brow as I scribbled the words.

"What does he think? That I'm just going to sit here?" I asked myself. I resisted the urge to write that too, wanting to get out the door as quickly as possible.

Someone, I didn't know who, had opened the Tower while I'd been upstairs. I stopped behind the bar to speak to Gabriel.

"I'm going out again," I told him, putting on my most intimidating face. I don't think Gabriel is capable of being intimidated, but I wanted him to know how serious I was. "If—"

"Don't worry, boss. We got your back," he interrupted, juggling three different orders at once.

I opened and closed my mouth a few times before finding my voice again. "I'll pay you for taking on the extra responsibilities."

"Thanks." I changed tack and began to apologize, to explain this wasn't how I liked to conduct business, but he cut me off again. "It's fine. Stuff happens. You'd do the same for any of us."

I was baffled again, but decided to investigate this curious generosity another time. I thanked Gabriel and left, heading back into the Char district. I knew someone there who had their fingers in many pies. I just hoped he hadn't been killed while I had been away.

)(

"Hello, Toad," I said, sauntering into his ramshackle, little office.

Toad was a small-time loan shark, smuggler, and informant. He advertised himself as an "odd job man," but I saw him as someone who didn't know how to focus and build. Delegation, however, was his forte. He hired on more people than I suspected he could count.

Toad's lair, as I liked to call it, squatted in one of the abandoned warehouses of the Char district. Nothing more than a set of rickety tables and chairs adorned the walled-off space hanging a story above the rest of the empty warehouse. If memory served, this used to be a large, high-end clothing store. Now a thick blanket of time's grime covered everything. Climbing the stairs to the office proved an adventure, as many of the steps had rusted almost to the point of crumbling.

I stood with a broad grin on my face, keeping an ear out for any bodyguards behind me that might decide I posed a threat. I couldn't be bothered to deal with time-wasters tonight, though I didn't really expect trouble anyway. Toad didn't play high stakes.

His small eyes flicked to me and back down to the cards in his hand. Several others, all men, were gathered around the table with him, and I spied money spread out between them.

"You decide to come crawling back, Raven?" he asked flatly.

"Information for information," I replied. "Same deal as always."

"I'm busy." Toad jerked a fat thumb over his shoulder and shifted his cigar from one side of his broad, squashed face to the other. "Give the brat your request. I'll try to get to it…" His voice trailed off as he moved his cards around. With even less interest, he finished, "At some point."

I looked as a boy, dressed in little more than rags, scurried from his spot in the corner. He grabbed a notepad and pen from the table and brought it to me. Scribblings from various hands covered the pad, and several pages had been folded over, presumably previous requests and messages Toad had yet to attend to. Looking back to the lad, I didn't fail to notice the knife hanging from his belt. He looked a few years younger than Lowell and Felicia. With a mental snarl at myself, I banished the tears springing to my eyes. I took the notepad from him and watched as he very seriously waited for me to complete my task. I looked back to Toad. He was already making another play in his card game.

"No," I said.

I offered the pen and notepad back to the boy, but he took a step away from me, keeping his hands too casually by his side.

"Sorry, what's your name?" I asked him.

He narrowed his eyes at me as his mouth flattened into a defiant line.

I turned back to his boss. "Toad, if you don't help me, you know I'll go to one of your competitors."

"Leave a message. Don't leave a message. I don't bloody care," he grumbled.

I cocked an eyebrow at him and scrawled a quick message across the page. When I handed it back to the boy, a smirk like a drawn dagger curled up his face. I started to leave, but a touch on the back of my hand stopped me. I turned back and found the boy tapping me with the pen. I resisted the urge to stoop down and draw level with him.

He winked at me, and the page I had written on had disappeared, while a bit of white stuck out from the boy's hand. He turned on his heel and returned the pad and pen to their proper place. I left pleased with one result and annoyed with the other.

)(

I hadn't been lying to Toad. I peddled what snatches of secrets I could to three other contacts that night. It wasn't my best work, but it didn't matter. No one had seen or heard anything about a young lady or gent matching Felicia and Lowell's descriptions, though I left my accounts vague enough to protect my young charges' identities. I had flipped back on that issue, knowing Felicia would be cross if I outed her. The last thing I needed right now was to give her more reason to hate me. It seemed odd not even my queries about Felicia pinged any hits. Granted, not many women were involved with Springhaven's criminal underground, but *nothing*? A new idea entered my head, and I vacillated between anger and melancholy.

)(

"I think she's working against me," I told Kieran as soon as he appeared later that night.

I had been back at the flat for a little under an hour and had spent the majority of the time pacing across the floor. Kieran began to speak, but I cut him off.

"Stubborn, willful child!" I jabbed a finger at Kieran. "I taught her everything she knows about that world. Well, not taught. Blazes, why do they have to be so clever?"

"Calandra," Kieran began gently.

"Do *not* tell me I'm being paranoid! I know her!"

"I picked up their trail."

With my hand raised in the air, striding as if in preparation for battle, I froze. "You what?" I asked, not quite believing what I had heard.

"I picked up their trail," he repeated, his eyes searching me.

"H-how? In this whole city, how did you find them?"

Kieran shrugged. "Vampyre nose."

An enormous, beaming smile split across my face. I threw myself at him and hugged him. He remained stiff at first as I held him, probably surprised by the sudden gesture, but he recovered as I broke away.

"Oh, Kieran. Thank you! Show me! Let's go!"

I barely spared a thought for how soon dawn would be here and how slowly I moved across the vast city compared to a shadow-walker like him. I did, however, think to grab the still unopened gift from the table. Perhaps it could serve as some kind of a peace offering. I just hoped dawn didn't come while I still had to carry it.

Kieran didn't complain, only smiled. He told me to meet him at a popular cross street in the Rose district.

)(

The cross street sat near the edge of the Rose quarter, abutting the Sand district. Thankfully, the petrolsene lights had burned themselves out by this unholy hour, leaving the waning moon one of the few sources of light. A screen of clouds ghosting over that pearly slice of luminescence assisted my efforts at remaining hidden. Even though I was officially dead several times over, I had no desire to be caught out by an Enforcer. It didn't matter who you were or how you looked, being out at this time of night was bound to arouse suspicion.

The wind nipped bitter cold at every piece of my exposed skin. I had forgotten to grab a coat in my haste, and I wondered if Lowell and Felicia were keeping warm. I stood shivering and rubbing my arms as I pressed back into the shadows and against the wall of a café.

I smiled ruefully at the name, trying to distract myself from my growing concern at Kieran's lack of appearance. Café came from coffee, which I missed rather acutely just then, but it hadn't been imported to Springhaven in so long, most people weren't familiar with it. I wondered if I should perhaps add it to the menu at the Tower, but excitable people didn't part with their money as easily as tipsy people did. Maybe I—

"Calandra..." whispered the wind, brushing past my neck and sending a brand new chill up my spine.

I spun, almost yelping in fear, but a hand covered my mouth. I would have gone into fight mode except I recognized my silencer in the next moment. I relaxed, and he removed his hand.

"Kieran!" I gasped. "What the blazes was that? It felt like the dark..."

Despite my distaste for the current obsession with propriety, I didn't want to finish describing what it had felt like. It had been almost intimate. Kieran flushed. He must have realized what I meant.

"Apologies. It's sometimes difficult to wrangle these abilities."

"Hardest in the dark?" I guessed.

He nodded, and a flash of unease crossed his expression. I wanted to move on, but his vulnerability lay exposed before me just then.

"Keep fighting," I told him. "You'll get better at it." He didn't look convinced, and I laid cold fingertips on his surprisingly warm hand. "If you want, I'll help you figure out a way to practice. *Safely*."

He smiled awkwardly and nodded. Selfishly, I was already past the moment. Together, we slipped along the streets, Kieran leading the way. He could see, hear, and smell better than I could, so he made sure we avoided all other human beings. As the sky was lightening from diamond-studded coal to shrouded indigo, we arrived in a neighborhood of tidy lanes and well-kept houses. Well, I say houses. They were more like miniature manors. I looked to Kieran, who kept glancing at the sky. The way dawn was distantly calling, I knew he must have been worried.

"Tell me where to go," I said, releasing his hand.

"Down this road and on the right. Apricot door and mint green shutters," he said, before pressing a hand to his head and squeezing his eyes shut.

I hadn't realized how bad even the pre-dawn light was for him. "Go," I told him. "Thank you."

He barely nodded before retreating back into the dark. I prayed he would reach safety, especially after all he had done for me. I trotted down the lane, looking for a house matching Kieran's description. It wasn't difficult to pick out once I actually laid eyes on it.

Tall, thick hedges and a wrought iron fence edged the perimeter of the grounds, blocking my view of the house until I reached the entry gate. The paint on the shutters and door was bright and fresh. The rest appeared neglected. The grass was overgrown, and the rest of the building's exterior needed an update. The hedges too looked a bit wild.

The gate whined agonizingly loud in the silence as I entered. Now that I was here, I grew nervous. I didn't doubt Kieran's abilities. If he said he had sniffed them out here, I believed him. I just didn't know what kind of reception awaited me. Who else might be here? And why hadn't the house been better tended to? I wanted to wait, to observe, and get a better idea of what I was dealing with, but dawn's song whispered in my ear now, and I didn't want to put resolution off another day. I quickened my pace, trotting up to the door, and with a continuous motion, lifted the door knocker. It was new as well and in the shape of a catamount's head. Again, the sound echoed through the still air, making me clench my teeth.

No answer. I took a deep breath and risked another knock.

"Please answer," I whispered, willing the occupants within to hear me.

After the third knock, I heard movement inside the house. Without realizing it, I tensed. I don't know why, but I stood ready to run. The door opened no more than a few inches, and I recognized the bit of face which appeared in the gap. Despite the sharp, angry angle of the eyebrow, I breathed a sigh of relief.

"Felicia. Thank the stars!"

The eyebrow smoothed into a vaguely disinterested inspection of the bags under my eyes, my wild hair and bare arms.

"I'm sorry," I blurted. "I'm so sorry. It… I can't… there's no…"

I had no words. Nothing I said could explain the despicable comparison I had made between the children I had cared for and the monster I had known.

"Please, forgive me," I said. "I know I've broken your trust. I fouled up, and I'm sorry."

Felicia, still gazing at me with cold detachment, opened the door wider. I saw now she was wrapped in her thick but tatty, old dressing gown. I must have woken her up. That would explain the initial death glare.

"Why don't you come in?" she said with a voice I had never heard her use and immediately disliked. It was smug and promised nothing good. "I'll put on tea, and we can have a chat."

~Chapter 21~

The inside of the house matched the outside. A few bits and pieces looked like they had been recently updated, but every other corner, wall, and surface reflected neglect. Carpets and wallpaper needed to be replaced, plenty of rooms needed dusting, and several fixtures needed repairing. The newer features—a few pieces of furniture, a fresh coat of paint in one room, and tidying up in another—told me whoever had made the changes had done them not in the last few days, but rather in the last few weeks.

Lowell joined us within minutes. He was a heavier sleeper than his sister, but I didn't think he could have missed the repeated rappings, as I quickly learned how loudly sound echoed in the mostly empty house.

"It's not much yet," Lowell told me as he and Felicia settled into the familiar routine of making tea. "We've got a lot of work ahead of us, but I think it's going to look rather spiffing when all is said and done."

We were gathered in their little kitchen now. It was a sharp contrast to the rest of the house. Orderly, warm, and already arranged with all manner of cooking and baking implements. I sat on a rickety chair with a thin, threadbare cushion to stay out of the way.

I made myself smile. I knew it trembled, but I held it up anyway. "I think so too."

A smile barely twitched on his face before dying out like a spark without kindling. He turned away, and I felt distance settle between us as cold as the air outside. Both he and Felicia had their backs to me as they went about their work. I glanced out the window and saw the indigo sky had brightened to lilac. Dawn was practically at the doorstep.

"I really am sorry," I tried again. Neither twin responded. "Please, say *something*. Shout at me. Tell me how angry you are because I did what you always feared I would."

Lowell turned from where he was preparing food for the tray, and his eyes glimmered with reluctant tears. He opened his mouth to speak when Felicia broke in.

"It sounds like you have it all figured out, Calandra." She said my name like a snake might, biting out each syllable.

"I don't want to play games, Felicia. Please, I *am* sorry. Can we—oh, blazes. Not now! I—"

Felicia turned fully towards me and watched, leaning back against the counter. Despite my protestations, the change still came, as it always did. I flapped angrily in my chair, cawing and cackling. The gift I had tucked in my pocket sat behind me now.

Felicia laughed. "Such language! Goodness, what's ruffled your feathers so badly?"

I suddenly realized what Felicia had done, putting me off until dawn. She'd never intended to reconcile with me in my human form. True, it was harder for her to read my thoughts in this form when I resisted her, but when I didn't, everything was laid bare. No filters or edits or polish to sift through when every thought came directly from my mind. Each one shone bright and immediate, raw and potentially incendiary.

I want to solve this, I thought. *I've killed myself trying to find you—*

"Not literally," Felicia put in, a cruel smile painted across her face.

Dammit, Felicia! I am sorrier than you can imagine! You and Lowell are all I have in this world, and—

The facade dropped from Felicia's face. Lowell turned. He wasn't wearing his mask, and every emotion showed. His eyes were mostly on his sister, but his gazed flicked to me now and again, pained and confused.

"You have the Tower!" she snarled. "Don't cry about—"

Sod the Tower! Who cares about money or business when I don't have my family?!

Felicia threw an arm out as if physically flinging her anger at me and shouted, "You didn't think we were family when you discovered our ancestry! As soon as the possibility of our relation to that… that devil or whatever he was presented itself, you turned from us. You rejected us like offal, despite the lunacy of the idea!"

He was a man, a magus, I corrected. I realized my mental image of Nicodemus must have made him seem like an otherworldly creature of nightmare and darkness. *He was real. He kept me captive and tortured me. He stole people's lives, including that of one of your ancestors.*

I allowed Felicia to see Nicodemus as I initially had, relived our first meeting, which I hadn't recalled in ages. She saw the battle against the Rukk and our wedding, the betrayal and those horrible moments wherein I lost Uncle Ducky, my life, and my freedom all at once. This was different from sharing with Kieran. With him, I had chosen what to reveal and what to hold back. Now, without barriers, *everything* showed through. I wanted to shield her from the worst of the tortures, but a floodgate had opened in my mind. I feared I would drown in the memories, that my mind might break beneath the deluge of misery, but its walls of resilience had built up over the years.

With each torment I had endured and come out the other side, the strength of those walls had grown, little by little, and they held strong now. I didn't crumble beneath the weight of my past. Instead, I grew livid. I told the pain *no*, holding onto the flecks of light that had pulled me through each horror. Like a luminescent bouquet, I gathered them and held the great, shining mass close as I revealed the truth in full to Felicia.

Unfortunately, this meant Lowell saw it all too. His eyes widened, and his knees began to buckle.

"Lowell, go," Felicia said.

Not all of my history had played for them yet. It didn't come as one orderly stream, but in clutches of experiences. The overarching history came first before drilling down, boring into the most vivid memories. Even from that point, with far more left to go than had already passed, the atrocities were beyond measure.

When he didn't move, she said more sternly, "Get out."

Lowell either ignored her or couldn't bring himself to move. He turned to face me. Tears streaked down his face, and he trembled.

"Cali, I…" He turned back to his sister. "Felly, are we…"

No.

"No."

Felicia and I spoke simultaneously, though I don't know if Lowell received my message. I had learned Felicia processed mental speech differently than she did pictures. Words didn't duplicate in her mind the same way visuals did, from what I understood.

"No, no, no," she emphasized.

Meanwhile, I hummed to myself to try and stop the flow of memories. They became disjointed against the tune, but they would not stop. Felicia shook her head and squeezed her eyes shut. I had seen this before. It had often been when she was younger and we were in a large crowd. I deduced it was a sign there was too much going on for her to process. Lowell's brow furrowed as the intermittent stream of images continued. I flew from the room.

)(

I caught snatches of Lowell and Felicia's conversation. I didn't want to lose track of them, lest they escape again, but I wanted to stay out of range, so I settled on a stained and moth-eaten sofa in the next room. Exhausted as I was, memories still burbled up from the spring of my mind, though the flood had mercifully tapered off into a slow trickle.

"If we're descended from that…"

"Stop. Even if we are, people make their own choices, Lowell. *We* carve our path."

"Should we be doing this job? Is it evil?"

"Would Calandra have done it if it was?" In contrast to Lowell's tremulous voice, Felicia's was steady, shot through with warmth and comfort.

There was a pause. "No, but she left that life."

"Yes, and that was *her* choice."

"But she did it for us."

Felicia sighed heavily. "Yes, she did. For our protection, not because it was evil. Alright?"

I heard Lowell mumble something. It sounded like assent. If they discussed it further, I didn't hear it. I fell asleep without meaning to in my little corner of the sofa.

I awoke with a start, immediately thinking I had lost Felicia and Lowell again, that I either had dreamed the entire experience or that they had left me while I slept. Another second later, my heart slowed when I spotted the two sitting on either side of me, Lowell on the couch with me and Felicia in a chair across. The promised tea was laid on a shabby, splintered pine table between us.

"Apologies," Lowell said. "We didn't want to disturb you, but we thought you might be hungry."

My stomach grumbled in response.

Thank you, I said, nodding to them.

Lowell filled a plate for me. He always insisted on good manners, which didn't include human-turned-ravens eating straight from the platter. As he did, I looked from him to Felicia. Instead of thoughts, my head was filled with awkward uncertainty. I didn't know what to say or do after an experience like what had happened this morning. By the position of the sun outside—the windows needed a good clean—I could tell it was midmorning, leaning towards noon. So I hadn't been sleeping for more than a few hours. The twins must have either put off our tea from before or this was their second helping.

A part of me wanted to be angry with them for leaving instead of talking, but the thought had barely reared its head before the boot of knowledge crushed it. I knew these two had been on their own from a young age. If their parents had abandoned them, perhaps out of fear, I could understand why…

"Our parents didn't abandon us," Felicia said softly.

I looked up, cocking my head to the side. She shook hers. Lowell set the plate of food before me, along with a cup of tea, which I likely wouldn't touch. Drinking from a teacup as a raven is tricky, to say the least, and I couldn't taste it properly anyway.

"They were wonderful," he said with a sad smile, preparing the next plate for serving. "They loved us dearly."

Felicia added, "They gave up what little wealth they had for us, for our welfare. Lowell and I were born conjoined. They had to cut us out of our mother's belly."

"It should have killed her, but Mama was strong." Lowell exchanged a smiling glance with his sister. "She recovered which, sadly, made some people in our little village angry."

"They were frightened. It was a miracle she survived. As I'm sure you can imagine, our situation didn't improve the public opinion of our family. Our parents wanted to give us independence. They sold everything they could, saving for an operation to separate us. It was…"

Felicia drew in a breath. I saw anger brimming in her eyes, but she was clearly trying to tamp it down.

Lowell finished for her, handing her the plate and a fresh cup of tea. "It was unpleasant, to say the least."

"More for you than for me," Felicia said gently.

"You didn't escape unscathed," he replied. "Besides, the heavens knew what they were doing when they gave me my talents, sister dear."

Felicia smiled at him, and I did my best to do the same. Both their faces grew dark as they sipped their tea. I thought they had told all they would tell when Felicia picked up the thread again.

"After we recovered, the people in our village began to say things. We probably shouldn't have survived our operation either. We didn't know that back then. I'm not sure our parents did either, but survive we did." She paused, and her tone grew soft and low. "Words can be like a spark. People feed the flames, going round and round in their own little circles, stoking one another's fear and anger. Not everyone is like the people here in the city, content in the certainty that magic is gone. They built their fires so high, the heat drove them to violence. Our parents died to give us a chance to get away."

Lowell had begun crying again, fat tears rolling slowly off his nose and down his chin. Felicia's eyes shimmered, but her jaw was firmly set. I hopped over to him first, and he picked me up, stroking my feathers as he held me against him. I wished I had arms instead of wings so I could return the embrace. Instead, I rubbed my head against him. It was the best I could do.

Thoughts and questions whirled in my head as I processed what I had just learned.

"Yes, I'm doing what you used to," Felicia said, latching onto a mental puzzle piece as I put it into place. "I know, I know. I need to be careful. And I *am*. I've made sure not to leave myself defenseless. Lowell's helped with that. Nothing I'm doing is technically illegal, unless I'm guilty by association, but there's no proof of what I do. Even our overzealous civil defenders need at least some evidence. And I've built securities around myself, given people a taste of what will happen should anyone try to harm me. And they pay me for silence."

How long have you been at this?

Felicia exchanged a look with her brother. At least, I assume he returned the loaded glance. I couldn't see since he still held me against him.

"Longer than I think you'd like to know," she said at last, incapable of suppressing a smug smile.

I huffed and shook. Lowell released me, and I stood on his good knee, ruffling my feathers again.

I've already decided to keep an ear to the ground from now on, I told her. *You should know I went back to several of my old contacts in search of you, so some of them might connect us. That is, unless you warned them I might be coming and convinced them to lie for you.*

Felicia blinked at me and shook her head. "No. To be honest, I didn't expect you to come after us."

Her words cut me deep. An unhappy coo escaped me, and I looked away. When Felicia spoke again, her voice was quiet and hard.

"I'm sorry for what he did to you. I didn't realize. Sometimes it's difficult to interpret things through personal filters. I… I understand why you reacted as you did. I suppose we should apologize for running off like we did."

"Pish tosh! Suppose nothing," Lowell scolded. "We *do* apologize, Cali. Please say you'll forgive us."

I looked back up and caught Felicia mid-eye roll. I was already bobbing my head, though.

"Jolly good!" Lowell said. "There. Now we can be one happy family again."

Felicia glared at him with half-lidded eyes, but a smile played at her lips. I hopped back to face her.

Would you mind telling me your code name? I can find out on my own, but this way saves time.

A smile like a cat's slid up Felicia's face. "Fetch."

)(

Felicia and Lowell had indeed been working for far longer than I realized, though Lowell's part in their scheme turned out to be much smaller. He occasionally disguised himself as a beggar and hung around the Agate and Char districts to pick up tidbits—people disregard beggars almost as much as they do ravens—which he brought back to Felicia. His responsibilities currently focused on the house more than anything else.

"We bought it!" Lowell crowed over a proper dinner together that evening. They'd been good enough to time their supper so I could join them in my human form. "You know how charming Felly can be, so she got a good price and convinced the estate agent to overlook our age."

I cut my eyes to Felicia, who waved a shamelessly proud hand at her brother while she sipped her wine. I noticed the practiced way she enjoyed it, despite my insistence they wait until they came of age to drink alcohol. I began to think I should have respected her privacy a little less.

"We're not but a few months away," she grinned. "A minor technicality."

I decided to leave my admonishments inside my head, shielding them. "So you bought this house… as a permanent residence?"

Even Felicia looked sheepish as she and her brother exchanged glances. Their eyes told me each was waiting for the other to provide an explanation. Lowell capitulated first, turning back to me. He pulled a small box from his pocket and set it between us. It was my gift, the one I had brought with me and left in the kitchen that morning.

"This isn't how we planned for all of this to go," he explained, tapping the parcel towards me with a gnarled fingertip on his bad hand. "We meant to tell you at your surprise party. We understand if you want to keep the flat at the Tower. Not a bad commute to work, after all, but we wanted you to know you're always welcome here."

I picked up the gift, unsuccessfully trying to keep my hands from shaking. The shimmering paper fell away to reveal a small box. I lifted the lid and found a key nestled atop a bed of shredded gold paper, which looked rather like sand against the turquoise wrapping. I looked to one and then the other, uncertain what to say. My heart throbbed with an all too familiar ache, though I noticed it wasn't as sharp as I expected.

"You two are… you're moving out," I said. "Rather, you already have."

"Again, this wasn't how we meant for things to go," Lowell said softly, placing his hand on mine.

Unconsciously, I stroked the rough skin of his hand with my thumb, gently curling my fingers around his twisted ones.

"We wanted to have this old place fixed up better before we made the change," he added. "It's a bit dour at the moment, you know."

I nodded and swallowed hard. I considered offering up the idea that they could come back to the Tower and stay a while, to follow through on their original plan. I didn't look to Felicia, as I wasn't making an effort to block my thoughts from her now. I didn't want to see whatever reaction—or lack thereof—she might have to that thought. Instead, I nodded and forced myself to smile.

"What an exciting adventure for you both. Of course, your furniture is yours to take if you want it. Or we can sell it and put the funds towards your new home."

I did allow myself to look at Lowell. He smiled at me.

"That's quite generous," he said, his voice cracking. "Goodness, look at me. So unseemly for a nice dinner like this."

It was a rather nice meal considering the mean furnishings. Felicia had baked bread while Lowell put together a hearty stew for us. A fire crackled cheerfully in the grate, driving away the cold seeping through the rest of the house. I gazed at it, giving us all time to collect ourselves.

"We used to have systems that heated our houses all the way through," I said. "Well, not in Bone Port, but they were built underneath the houses here in Springhaven, and in Duskwood too.

Networks of pipes ran under the floors. Hot water was pumped into them, which heated the house, and you could shut or open the valves to control the temperature from room to room.

"Fascinating!" Lowell said. "I'm certain there's a way to do the same here."

"Without ripping up the entire floor?" Felicia asked, raising an eyebrow at him.

Lowell pressed his spoon to his lips, thinking hard. He never gave a direct answer to the question, and we chatted on. Lowell and Felicia offered for me to stay the night even as they confessed they didn't have a place for me.

"You're more than welcome to sleep on the sofa," Felicia said.

We both looked at the battered, old thing and returned to each other's sight with rueful smiles.

"That's very kind, but I think I'll pass," I said.

"You're welcome any time," she said with a chuckle.

"As are you."

I fretted a bit more before I left, asking if they had enough blankets and if they needed a top up on their pantry.

"I know a place that does pretty good food," I smirked. "I can probably convince the woman in charge to let me take from her."

"But you'd risk Laura's wrath. Eek!" Lowell replied, and he raised his fists to his mouth and made a frightened face.

They made sure I had my key and watched me go until I had disappeared around the hedges, waving one last time before I did.

~Chapter 22~

When I arrived back at the Tower, I slid into my work, picking up where Hector had left off and sending him home with a paid day off the next day. All the staff would receive the same over the next few weeks.

"Is all well again?" Hector asked as he donned his hat.

"Well enough," I replied with a tired smile. "We're all… okay."

He nodded and left. Gabriel asked me the same later, and he accepted the nod I gave without further question. Kieran appeared after I had sent everyone home and closed up.

"Are you alright?" he asked, his voice slinking like shadows across the barroom to me.

"Yes," I said, but my face fell. "No?" I sighed and shrugged. "I will be. They've left the nest."

"I see," he replied, walking over and sitting down on a barstool.

He said nothing else, and a long but comfortable silence passed between us.

"I'm not surprised," I said at last. "Even Lowell was only ever half settled here. I think they were on their own for too long to do anything else."

I didn't say what my heart had been weeping since dinner: *I wasn't good enough to make them want to stay.*

"Forgive me for being insensitive, but might I have a snack?" Kieran asked. "I'm rather famished, and I've fed on my friends too recently."

I raised an eyebrow at him.

"I know," he grimaced. "My timing is terrible. I hope you know me well enough to know I wouldn't have asked unless it was serious."

I extended my arm without a word, and the corner of my mouth ticked up in the barest hint of a smile when his nose twitched unhappily. I said nothing until he was mid-drink.

"Just because you can taste emotions doesn't mean you can discern thoughts."

Kieran coughed and sputtered, releasing my arm and spraying blood from his mouth.

"Ugh!" I said, making a face at him. I hadn't expected a reaction like that. "People eat here, you know? I am supposed to be complying with health codes."

Kieran wiped his mouth and looked at me like a child who'd gotten his hand caught in the cookie jar. I offered my arm back to him.

"Clean up."

He curled his lip at me but obeyed.

"I wasn't trying to deceive you," he said afterward, helping me wipe up the rest of his dinner. It wasn't a big mess, but I wanted to erase the evidence before it stained. "Truly. I just thought… maybe if I knew more, I could help."

My voice softened as I replied. "I know. You have noble intentions."

"Your Vampyre friend taught you quite a lot," he said.

"We were trapped together a long time." I sighed, allowing myself to slump. "Next time, just ask me."

He nodded and said, "I'm sorry. What else troubles you?"

I told him. Without hesitation this time, tired of having no one to share with.

"I don't blame them. I don't blame myself either. What kind of a mother figure can I be when I spend half my life as a blasted bird?"

"It's far better than them being alone," Kieran replied. "From what I've seen, they were deeply grateful for you."

"From what you've seen?" I asked, peering hard at him as I leaned back against the bar.

He looked away, rubbing the back of his neck. Even in his discomfort, a challenge thrummed underneath his tone. "How do you think I know when you're alone? I wait."

I smiled at him, and he turned back to me with the hint of one tugging at his lips.

"You're extremely patient then, but a terrible liar." I paused. "Two excellent traits for a doctor, I think."

His smile appeared in full, fangs and all, but it was laced with remorse.

"You've got a place to stay now if you need one, but you'll have to disappear when Lowell and Felicia come to visit," I said gently.

"We did just establish I'm extremely patient. It shouldn't be a problem."

I waggled my wrist at him. "Did you get your fill? Don't you want to finish drinking?"

"Stars, no," he replied, making a face.

"And a discerning palate to boot," I laughed.

)(

I saw Felicia and Lowell quite a bit over the following week, as we sorted their furniture and other belongings. The largest task finally came about early one evening, about two weeks after their disappearance. I was glad we were the moving company's last job of the day. I wanted to be present to ensure everything went smoothly. Lowell had stayed home to cross a few tasks off their seemingly endless to-do list. I had to wonder if he was perhaps avoiding some kind of emotional turmoil this final event caused him. Though he hadn't objected when I'd first offered to assist their transition, Lowell later showed hesitation about accepting such generosity.

"It seems terribly boorish after the way we left," he at last confessed after we had gone back and forth several times about the issue.

I assured both him and Felicia I was more than happy to help. Though Lowell abandoned his verbal protests, uncertainty still swam in his eyes when we discussed logistics. Felicia didn't seem to have any such reservations. This didn't surprise me in the least, but something else did.

As we watched the movers haul away the beds, dressers, and other large items by the light of petrolsene streetlamps, Felicia leaned into me and linked her arm with mine. A tune started up in my head, an automatic defense mechanism by now.

"I don't like that one much," she said. "Can you sing another one, please?"

A blank appeared in my mind as I tried to think of a different song.

Felicia laughed and said, "Even better."

"It's harder to maintain, though," I said, smiling at her.

"I'll bring you a harmonoloq next time. Having something playing in the background should help."

"How do you know?" I asked.

She grinned, looking up at me. "You. Your songs provided a distraction, something for me to focus on." She looked away again. "It gets terribly noisy at the Tower with all those people."

"Oh, Felicia," I cooed, placing my other hand on her arm. How had I never conceived what things must have been like for her in such a crowded room? I had always assumed she could turn her ability on and off as she liked, preferring to glean as much as possible. "I'm so sorry. I..."

She waved my next words away. "It's been good practice. And I could always head back upstairs if I needed to, though Lowell was always there. Even though I can't hear his mind, he does so love to talk. I took refuge in your room most of the time. I hope you don't mind."

I shook my head, and new wonderings, unintentionally unprotected, began to drift through my mind. Felicia stiffened, a sign I took to mean she was listening.

"Don't think I won't come back here as often as possible," she said a moment later, distracting me from my own thoughts. "I need to keep sharpening my skills, but it'll be nice to have a quiet retreat with space to roam." She paused. Her voice was still light when she added, "Honestly, I'm not sure I would have left if it weren't for the noise. Or left as soon anyway. And don't forget, you always have a room at my house."

I made a noise of acknowledgement, trying to suppress the smile lifting in my cheeks. I leaned into Felicia and whispered, "Don't flinch. Some have eyes sharp enough to catch even just that."

I expected her to pull away. Instead, she looked at me again, smiled, and nodded.

)(

Two years later, Invarnis celebrated the closing of the Dawn Age and rang in the New Age with all the imaginable pomp and fanfare. I knew I should have been counting down and cheering with my patrons at the Tower, and I did during other New Year Celebration nights, but not that one. I joined Lowell and Felicia in their now-grand dining room as they served up a succulent feast of roasted goose, mince pies, figgy puddings, and mulled wine.

The house looked magnificent! The twins had combined forces to create the palace they'd dreamed of. It was far from done, as projects like hand painting wallpaper and fixing up all the floors took time, but it was coming along. They'd even made accommodations to the room reserved solely for me when I stayed over.

"There's a little door here," Lowell explained when he and Felicia showed me the finished product. "It's spring-loaded, so all you have to do is pull this little lever and presto! You're out. And see, there's a wee ledge outside for easy takeoffs. Don't worry about shutting it up after yourself. I'd like to meet the person who manages to break in through there. I imagine he or she would be jolly interesting to speak with."

"It's very clever," I told Lowell, giving him a kiss on his head.

"It rather is, if I do say so myself," he beamed.

As planned, I dipped my toe into Springhaven's criminal underbelly now and again and trained to sharpen my other skills. I was pleased the name *Fetch* became synonymous with *not-to-be-trifled-with*. I'll confess, though, a certain harrowing event almost drove me to beg Felicia to reconsider her career path, even if the incident did increase her reputation.

One evening when Felicia didn't come home, Lowell came to me to see if she'd changed her plans without telling him—something we both knew wasn't likely, but not entirely out of the realm of possibility. Between us, we quickly figured out she must be in trouble and, also between us, assisted her in getting out of it, simultaneously ruining the miscreant who had caused it in the first place. As I employed my lock-picking skills that evening to rescue Felicia, I sent up a silent prayer of thanks to Flynn.

Lowell was beside himself after the fact. Even with the gadgets he'd created for his twin, they hadn't been enough to protect her. I couldn't bring up my misgivings in front of him, and by the time we'd calmed him down, I'd half talked myself out of most of them.

All I said to Felicia in private later was, "I almost lost my daughter today. I know it'll happen eventually, but you do everything in your power to make sure it's not because of your job."

Felicia nodded seriously to my directive.

)(

Kieran visited intermittently. With only two "good" sources of blood, he was never able to stay long in Springhaven. I gathered he acquired another source some years later, though I never asked who or how. Despite my many offers and a few other failed experiments, like the blood-whiskey concoction we tried during our second meeting, he rarely fed from me, even though my blood would have allowed him to remain in the city longer.

"It turns my stomach," he told me once. "Besides, my friends would be suspicious."

"I think your friends would understand," I said, eyeing him.

"Hm," he said, turning to gaze at a new painting on the wall as he leaned against the bar. "That elevates the decor of this place."

"I know. I have commissions out for several more."

During those first few years, whenever Kieran visited the city, he stayed in my flat during the day. Later, after his friends married, he didn't come around as much, save for during their honeymoon. He lived with me for a solid week then.

"I'm surprised you've remained in the city," I said, sipping my tea. "You could head north and find some bears. They'll all be fattening up for the winter. Or south to feed on panthers. What a hunt that would be."

Kieran didn't respond. He traced the tabletop with his index finger. He had been like this for several weeks now, growing gloomier each day. I set my cup down and reached my hand across to his, stopping the idle movement.

"The bride, she's the woman you were courting, isn't she? Back before you were turned."

Kieran nodded and replied, "I couldn't have wished a better man for her."

"Except you."

He didn't reply. I continued to hold his hand in the silence. After a while, he pulled away and poured himself a cup of tea. Lifting it, he injected cheer into his voice as he spoke.

"To Mina and Neal."

I followed and repeated the sentiment.

"May the happy couple find a lifetime of bliss and adventure," he added. "Three cheers for the Allens."

I dropped my cup. The delicate porcelain shattered on the table, and Kieran's eyes snapped to me, searching.

"Your best friend is an Allen?!" I gaped.

"Ye-es," he said carefully. "Why is that significant?"

My hands fluttered as if chasing the right words through the air. "Allen is *my* surname! He's my… well… I don't know how we're related, but we are." I had stopped keeping track of my clan members long ago.

Kieran's face changed, an odd mixture of wry humor and pained compassion. "What are the odds?"

I pressed my lips together, considering the question. "You'd be surprised. The universe has quite the sense of humor."

"It really does," he said, nodding, and I wondered what else he might be thinking of that made him agree so heartily. "Why didn't you ever tell me?"

I shrugged. "How many people do you know who flaunt their surnames around like a banner?"

"The Pendragons."

"Besides them! I never needed to give you my full name." I paused as new ideas queued up for attention. "Goodness, I can't believe this. You have to get him to come here. I want to meet him."

"Truly?" Kieran asked, raising his eyebrows at me.

I nodded. "It would be nice to see what's become of my line."

He gave me a broad, fanged smile and agreed. I smiled back, making mental notes about other ways I might ease his melancholy.

Kieran had to leave again before his friends returned from their honeymoon, and he decided at last to give panther hunting a try. When he returned a few weeks later, he renewed our former conversation.

"I can still mention this place to Neal," he said. "Would you like me to?"

I told him I did, giving him a grateful smile, and he was even able to forewarn me as to the night. I confess, I was nervous that evening. I don't know why, but I feared Neal would somehow know me, which would create a very awkward situation indeed.

Kieran didn't dare come down from my flat to point out his friend and instead described Neal to me as I prepared myself for the encounter in the safety of my sitting room.

"I know I'm being ridiculous," I said, forcing myself to take slow gulps of air, "but stranger things have happened."

Kieran offered his hand, which I took, and gave me a comforting squeeze. "I know. And you don't have to do this. It's fine if you don't."

"I know, but…" I took another deep breath. "Kieran, I *want* to do this."

"All right. I'm cheering you on from up here. Quietly, of course."

He gave me a smirk, and I managed a weak smile in response. I forced myself to keep walking down the stairs and into the barroom. I scanned the room, schooling my features and heading behind the bar. It was another refuge, which gave me strength. I spotted Neal; he matched Kieran's description perfectly.

Just go greet him, I told myself. *You are the mistress of the Raven's Tower, for goodness' sake!*

Donning the armor of my professional pride, I fixed my smile in place and strode forward.

"Good evening," I said, rounding Neal's table. I waited for him to look up at me. "Welcome to Raven's Tower. I'm Calandra, owner and operator. Everything going well tonight?"

I had given the greeting so many times, I could do it in my sleep, which gave me a moment to study my descendent. It's strange how distinct characteristics, such as the shape of a nose or the texture of one's hair, come back around throughout the generations. I saw a strong resemblance in Neal to his ancestor, Ciara Allen. His skin was lighter than hers had been, but no one could mistake his Arnavi heritage.

"Do I know you?"

My heart stopped at those words, and I looked to the other side of the table. A familiar woman, the one who had asked the question, sat leaning forward and studying me. I had been so focused on Neal, I hadn't noticed her. I returned her curious gaze, and the answer came to me a moment later.

"You're the one who treated my daughter's leg," I said, reclaiming my handle on the situation. "She's doing very well now, thank you. What was your name again?"

"Doctor Philomena Allen," she replied, extending her hand. I shook it, and she continued, "This is my husband, Gwenael." She said the word *husband* with a particular affection.

"Neal will do just fine," he said, also shaking my hand.

"Please, call me Mina," she added. "You said your daughter is doing well?"

I nodded, not wanting to remind Mina of our long-ago visit any more than necessary. I didn't know if she actually remembered the event or had just recognized me, but the less she recalled the better.

"Is this your first time to the Tower?"

They both replied it was, and we chatted idly for a few moments as I did with all my new patrons. I wanted to stay, to find out more about Neal and even Mina. I wanted to ask them about Kieran. I wanted so much from them in that moment, but my senses told me it was time to move on. I closed up the conversation, wishing them a good evening, and told them to let me know if they needed anything. I usually phrased that part as,

"Let me or my staff know," but I made an exception in this case. I checked in with a few more customers for appearances and headed back up the stairs to my flat. Kieran's voice floated through the fabric walls as I stood leaning against the door with my eyes closed.

"How did it go?"

My heart was already beating as fast as it did when I was in my raven form. I willed it to slow down, not knowing how it might affect him.

I took a deep breath and replied, "I did it."

"I can smell them on you."

I opened my eyes and searched for Kieran. He stood at the other end of the hall. "That is an impressive nose you have there."

He chuckled, which made me smile and helped to calm me.

Neal became a regular visitor to the Tower, and I'm not ashamed to say he's one of my favorite customers. Yes, I know I'm probably biased. Mina, I learned later, didn't enjoy my establishment as much, but that didn't offend me. Everyone has their own tastes.

Not long after this meeting, Kieran explained to me his feelings for Mina. Certain desires, it seems, don't transfer over when a human is turned into a Vampyre, but their hearts remain capable of just as much love and care as before. The revelation surprised me only because I had not asked. We had been discussing the wine I was currently drinking.

"If you don't mind my asking, what brought this on?" I ventured softly.

Kieran turned fully towards me from his place on the sofa we shared. We were comfortably settled for the night in my sitting room. His fathomless, onyx eyes glittered at me as he spoke.

"Forgive me if I'm overstepping my bounds. I don't want to cause you more pain."

I gave him a gentle smile. "Whatever you need to say is fine."

I waited, not pressing him and wanting to be careful with his feelings. In the short time we'd known each other, we'd become familiar with the subjects that caused the other heartache. Several moments passed before he responded, his throat bobbing.

"I'm… afraid… of what else I'm going to lose. I know it's terrible of me to bemoan these problems to you after everything you've been through, but..." His voice trailed off as I shook my head at him.

"My suffering doesn't invalidate yours."

I extended my hands, and he took them, gripping them tightly. "My parents died soon after I was turned, and I wasn't there for my sister, Annabelle. I was still wandering the wilderness when it happened, and I haven't had the heart to face her. She's... run into some trouble since I left. If I had been there..."

Kieran's tone told me he was trying to detach himself from his emotions, with limited success.

"It's not your fault," I said. The strength of my voice surprised me. "Do you hear me, Kieran? It is *not* your fault."

He took a deep breath through his nose and set his jaw, but his voice fell to a whisper as he replied, "Had I been here. Had I made different choices, I... I might have..."

I stroked the back of his hands with my thumbs and matched my tone to his. "You couldn't have known, and you are not to blame for that. You were in pain. You'd just had your life ripped from you, and your circumstances matter."

He finally softened. I imagined the hardness I had just seen in him would have served him well when fighting for a patient's life, but he seemed unable to sustain it for himself. "What am I going to do, Calandra? How will I ever bear losing them all? What if I never speak to Annabelle again?"

I held back enough of my tears to keep myself collected and allowed the rest to flow freely. Old wounds opened and bled in my heart, familiar pain that would never truly heal, but I had grown stronger in bearing it.

"Only you can decide if and when to reveal yourself to your sister," I told him. "Just don't give up because you blame yourself. And whatever you decide, reach for happiness, because you are worthy of it. As for the rest, cherish what time you have with them."

Kieran nodded, taking another steadying breath. I recognized the tactic and wondered how often he had borne his grief alone. I scooted closer to him on the sofa.

"Thank you for sharing with me," I said, giving him a watery smile. "And you should know I'll be here to support you through all of it. I'm not that easy to get rid of."

Kieran returned my smile and squeezed my hands in his. "Thank you, Calandra Allen, for making my life brighter."

~*~

Read on for more from the Broken Gears universe.

~*An Excerpt from* Out of the Shadows~

She wasn't going down without a fight. Maybe by some miracle she'd catch a break and get free again. Lenore drove both elbows back as hard as she could, which may have just worked if it weren't for the fact that she and her captor were already falling backwards. She landed on something soft in complete darkness and was on her feet again in less than a second. There was that complete darkness thing, though. When she had been running a moment ago, her path had been lit by the soft glow of petrolsene lights and the moon. Where was she now? Lenore backed up until she hit a wall and remained ready to fight. She began inching her way to the side, thinking there might be a door somewhere. The sound of heavy boots running approached and then faded, followed a few moments later by a single match light. The match light became an oil lamp, and the area all around Lenore was suddenly bathed in a warm, yellow glow. She saw the man first, gingerly holding his arm across his abdomen. She was about to cry out, "You!" but a delicate hand clamped itself over her mouth with a determination that belied its delicacy.

"Shhhh!" a female voice hissed in her ear. "Do you want to get us all caught?"

Lenore did not try to speak, but shook her head earnestly. Of course she didn't, but what did her would-be accusers have to worry about?

"I'm going to let go of you now, but you must stay silent. Understand?" the woman said firmly.

Lenore nodded this time and was released. The woman joined the man and began to poke and prod him in a way that looked more like a medical examination than anything else. The man made no move to stop her, and Lenore watched them both warily. Finally, when the woman seemed satisfied, she kissed the man on the cheek and turned her attention back to Lenore. She glanced at what Lenore could now see as a cellar door and motioned for her to follow. Lenore had no desire to do any such thing, but couldn't think of a better idea. There were Enforcers outside looking for her, but these two could just be planning to turn her in later. That logic didn't really make sense, though. If they had any kind of sense, they wouldn't waste time that the Enforcers could use to accuse them of helping Lenore. Besides, there were no Enforcers inside…as far as Lenore knew, anyway. That being the case, she followed, but at a distance that kept her safe from the couple's reaching arms in case they tried to grab her again.

The three walked up a narrow staircase and up into a large kitchen replete with a potbelly stove large enough to cook an entire lamb in. From the kitchen they walked through a butler's closet—*closet my eye,* Lenore thought—and into a grand dining room. The woman motioned for Lenore to sit, which she refused to do with a defiant glare.

"Suit yourself," said the woman with a very unladylike shrug.

She then sat while the man stood behind her and put his hands on her shoulders.

"First of all," the man said kindly, "let me apologize. I am deeply, deeply sorry for drawing attention to you. We did not mean for you to be discovered."

Lenore was very confused and intrigued by this, but still said nothing.

"Allow me to make the introductions," the man continued. "I am Sir Gwenael Allen and this is my lovely wife, Philomena."

"Mina will do just fine," the woman interjected suddenly, giving her husband's hand a squeeze.

He smiled and added, "You may call me Neal."

Lenore didn't call either of them anything. She simply remained silent, wondering whether or not she could make it out the cellar without being caught.

"We're not going to turn you in," Mina said after several moments.

"Why not?" were the first words Lenore said to the couple.

The two shared a smile that seemed to hold a great meaning for them and then turned back to Lenore.

"We do not…agree with the severity with which criminal punishment is exacted," Neal explained.

"Don't think that means we condone criminal behavior either, however," Mina added firmly, giving Lenore a hard glare.

"Well, I appreciate you hiding me and all. Trust me, I really do," Lenore said defensively, "but, seeing as how my criminal behavior is going to continue, I'll just be on my way."

Lenore turned to leave, but Mina spoke again with such force that Lenore stopped in her tracks.

"And just what is so important for you to get back to?"

Lenore narrowed her eyes at the woman there who was now standing tall and ramrod straight. She didn't like the woman. Who was this stuck up peacock to think she had any business asking Lenore such personal questions?

"Thank you both again," Lenore snipped. "Good night." With that she turned on her heel and left the way she came.

)(

Bitsy was waiting for Lenore back at the attic when she arrived just before dawn. It wasn't really an attic so much as dead space between the attics of her parent's old house and the one attached next door. It grew almost unbearably hot in the summer and bone achingly cold in the winter, as simple wooden walls were all that separated Lenore from the outside. She'd discovered the space when she was little, having accidentally found the hidden latch to the small door and crawling through. She'd found a similar entrance on the neighbor's side and jammed the handle with some scrap metal. Thankfully, no one on the other side seemed to know about the space. At least, Lenore had never heard anyone try to get in. If they did, she didn't know what she'd do or where she would go.

Lenore had to move in her cramped little space carefully, always being as silent and stealthy as fog creeping over the earth, lest the neighbors or new occupants of her parent's old house heard her. She only ever came and went when it was properly dark outside, sneaking out via a window in the attic and the large tree growing just outside.

As for Bitsy, Lenore never worried about her little companion; it was easy for him to disappear when necessary. He was sitting on a rafter when she came in and leapt down to greet her ecstatically. The little creature nuzzled her neck and wrapped his long bushy tail around it as he chattered happily.

"I'm glad to see you too," Lenore sighed. "That was a close one tonight. Glad I caught a break for once…"

Lenore's mind drifted back to the couple that had saved her from certain torture. They were certainly different, odd maybe, but they had been kind, and Lenore had not experienced real kindness in a long time. Oh well, it was done now. Lenore took just enough time to fill her stomach with some stale bread and dodgy-looking cheese before falling asleep to the sounds of a waking city.

)(

Ninth Year of the New Age, Second Day of the Earth
Official report submitted by Fifths Campbell and Ellis:

We were alerted and gave chase to a thief this evening. The thief was preying on citizens visiting the gardens. Cries from the latest victims—a Mister Malachite Nichols and Miss Temperance Hester—alerted us to the trouble just after a quarter past twelve as we patrolled our usual route. Mister Nichols reported a prized piece of Old World Jade as stolen. See the end of this report for a record of the eyewitnesses' descriptions of the thief. As we began pursuit, the perpetrator made for the Rose quarter of the city. Visual contact was difficult to maintain through the alleys she took between the manors. She disappeared completely somewhere between the Chicory Lane and Anemone Green. We recommend working with local shopkeepers and residents to put up barriers and fences to block these types of escape paths.*

Eyewitness Description Report: Female, small, probably about fourteen years of age. Most likely a vagrant, judging by the clothing, which was black, made for a boy, and very shabby. Very dark eyes and long, dark hair. Light skin.

**We understand there were two other eyewitnesses, but they disappeared before we arrived, and neither Mister Nichols nor Miss Hester could name them or remember anything about them.*

~Acknowledgements~

When I sit down with my list of people to thank, I'm overwhelmed by the evidence of how fortunate and loved I am.

Firstly, thank you to God for the talents and passions he's given me. I truly believe he gives us these gifts for a reason, and I hope the world can be made a little brighter through me.

Mark, you are an *amazing* editor!!! Your input and expertise have been invaluable. I'll never look at a chapter the same way again. ☺ This book is so much improved thanks to you. Editors are the unsung heroes of the book world, but I am singing your praises!

Mike, my incredible husband. The list of all the ways you support me is endless. Thank you so much for all the dinners, show help, emotional support, and so much more. I'm so thankful to have you as my teammate. Many thanks to Bruin and Badger too, my little wolves, for all the cuddles and kisses.

Heather, thank you so much for the chapter heading designs. I know I am exacting and demanding, and you turned my words into gorgeous reality. I still don't think we agree on what the word "distressed" means, though. ☺ To the rest of my family, thank you for always supporting me in so many ways—rent-free book show lodgings, listening to me whinge, and always encouraging me. Dad, extra thanks to you for being, as Stephen King would call it, my Constant Reader.

To all my sweet friends in the Bookstagram community, thank you, thank you, thank you x a million! I never imagined I'd have such an amazing community before I joined, and now I can't imagine being without you. Thank you all so much for your kindness, encouragement, bookish excitement (*flail!*), group wailing about #AuthorLife, and support. And to my writing group, it's so good to have people to sit around a table with who understand! Thank you all for your support and commiseration.

And so, so many thanks to you, my wonderful ARC readers! You all are such an amazing squad, and I am so fortunate to have you! Chandra (@wherethereadergrows); Faith (@faith_therivens); Catheryn (@thebooklioness); Beverly (@theconstantvoice); Sarina (@sarinalangerwriter); KJ (@k.j.chapman); Alex (@paperbackpiano); James (@jamesfahyauthor); DJ Gray (@graydeej); Jenn; and Mary.

To Sally, Chris, Hannah, Becca, Brynn, and all the rest of you wonderful people who have walked through this process with me, listened to me, reminded me to breathe… thank you all for being so wonderful!

And finally, oodles of thanks to you, dear reader. Thank you for picking up this book and taking the time to get to know Cali, Ducky, Jones, and all the rest! I sincerely hope it's added something to your life. I love you even if I haven't met you yet. Double and triple thank you if you took the time to leave a review on Amazon, Goodreads, etc. You have literally helped put food on my table, you hero you!

~About the Author~

Dana Fraedrich is an independent author, dog lover, and self-professed geek. Even from a young age, she enjoyed writing down the stories that she imagined in her mind. Born and raised in Virginia, she earned her BFA from Roanoke College and is now carving out her own happily ever after in Nashville, TN with her husband and two dogs. Dana is always writing; more books are on the way!

If you enjoyed reading this book, please leave a review. Even it's just one line to say you liked it, that really helps independent authors like Dana continue to create kick-awesome things for you!

Find Dana online at www.wordsbydana.com
Facebook: https://www.facebook.com/wordsbydana/
@danafraedrich on Instagram, Twitter, and Tumblr
Follow Dana on Goodreads or her Amazon Author page

Made in the USA
Columbia, SC
06 May 2018